THE SHAPE OF MURDER

Where was Arthur Banning, the Croydon rent-collector whose car had crashed on a Sussex road? Why had he told his wife he was going North on a 'business trip'? Who were the figures seen to scramble from the wrecked vehicle and run off into the night? One of Inspector Kane's questions was answered when Banning's injured body was found on a nearby common. But who had attacked him, and why? When Banning died in hospital, fear and suspicion suddenly obscured a case over which began to loom the shape of murder . . .

J. F. STRAKER

THE SHAPE OF MURDER

Complete and Unabridged

LINFORD
Leicester

First published in Great Britain in 1964

First Linford Edition
published 2004

British Library CIP Data

Straker, J. F. (John Foster)
   The shape of murder.—Large print ed.—
Linford mystery library
   1. Detective and mystery stories
   2. Large type books
   I. Title
   823.9'14 [F]

ISBN 1–84395–126–6

Published by
F. A. Thorpe (Publishing)
Anstey, Leicestershire

Set by Words & Graphics Ltd.
Anstey, Leicestershire
Printed and bound in Great Britain by
T. J. International Ltd., Padstow, Cornwall

This book is printed on acid-free paper

1

Arthur Banning hummed nervously to himself as he trotted down the steps of the office block in which the Croydon branch of London and Provincial Properties Limited was housed. At street-level he paused to look back. The sun was a dull red ball in a darkening sky, and the wide entrance to the building lay in shadow. In the years that he had worked for LAPP he had been up and down those steps many thousands of times, but he could not recall ever before having experienced any emotion other than boredom in the process. Now it was different. Now he was full of emotions; fear at what he had done, exhilaration at what he was about to do, doubt of his ability to do it. At forty-eight, and steeped in the routine of job and home, a man does not take easily to adventure.

Dismissing the doubt and the fear, he cocked an undignified snook at the building and strutted away to the car park.

He was still humming as he drove through the town in the firm's Morris. But his thoughts were shifting from the future to the immediate present, and as he turned into the street in which he lived he fell silent. Stopping the car outside No. 27, he sat frowning at the semi-detached villa that was his home, his eyes on the grey brick and the blistered paintwork and the rusted railings, but his thoughts inside with his wife. How would Ruth react to the news he had to tell her? If she were in one of her happier moods she might accept it without comment; there would be a few perfunctory questions, and he fancied he could cope with those. But cheerfulness was not characteristic of No. 27. More likely there would be a row. Not a violent, implement-throwing row of roused passions and angry words, but a sullen, nagging row that had no zenith and no nadir and never knew when to stop. Well, he could cope with that too. But it would be unpleasant, it would leave a nasty taste in the mouth. It would be a poor beginning to adventure.

As he pushed the gate open it squealed on its hinges, and he looked with distaste at the wilting shrubs in the small rectangle that separated the railings from the house. Both Ruth and he disliked gardening; they had planted the shrubs from a lazy sense of duty and had then forgotten them. They would give a touch of green to the front of the house, Ruth had said, make it less stark. But the shrubs were no longer green. Dust and dirt had turned them to a sullen grey.

Ruth was in the hall when he let himself in. She put up a cheek to be kissed, and then turned away as his lips brushed it obediently.

'You're early.' There was neither pleasure nor reproof in her voice, it was a plain statement of fact. 'Supper isn't ready. I still have the potatoes to do.'

He looked at her, seeing her afresh in the light of this particular day. She was taller than himself but equally plump, with a large shapeless bust and a round face and a mere button of a nose, her cheeks mottled with red and brown patches and untouched by powder. Ruth seldom used cosmetics. As a girl her hair had been a mass of warm gold; now it had coarsened to a dull yellow, and stood out bushily from her head like a sweep's brush. She had nice legs and narrow feet, although the feet were made to look broader by the flat woollen slippers she invariably wore indoors.

Banning sighed. Ruth had never been beautiful, but at one time he had found her attractive. It was only recently that he had realized how quickly that attraction had faded. Strange, he thought, how proximity and familiarity can blind a man to change in a woman. And depressing when he is suddenly jerked into awareness of it.

'It doesn't matter,' he said cheerfully. 'I have to pack. Westwood wants me to go up north on business. I'll be away for two or three days, I expect. It depends on how things pan out.'

She gaped at that, as she did at anything unusual. Her teeth were surprisingly white and even, and all her own.

'What sort of business?'

'They have traced one of our former tenants who decamped in August owing several months' rent. Westwood wants me to have a shot at collecting it. Is Philip home?'

She shook her head, frowning.

'Why you? I thought they had proper debt collectors for that sort of thing?'

He shrugged. 'Search me! But he was on my round, so maybe Westwood thinks the chap will cough up more readily to some one he knows. Anyway, I'm going. Be off as soon as I've packed and had a bite to eat.'

He could hear her muttering as he went upstairs and she to the kitchen. She had taken it more calmly than he had expected, and as he started to pack he found himself humming again. Then, recognizing the tune, he grinned and stopped. *So Nice to Come Home to* was inappropriate. Ruth and Philip were all he had to come home to, and although he still retained some slight affection for Ruth, he had none for Philip. And even Ruth . . .

He tried to remember when he had last

made love to her. But it was too long ago, and he abandoned the mental effort. He had more exciting thoughts to occupy his mind.

Ruth continued to mutter as she stood peeling the potatoes over the sink. Her lips moved continuously, although only half the words were spoken aloud.

'It just doesn't make sense. Twelve years you've worked for them, and never once been farther than head office. And they've got branches up north, haven't they? Why can't they deal with it?' She jabbed the point of the peeler into a potato, twisting it to gouge out an eye. 'I just hope you manage to make something on the expenses, that's all. But it won't amount to much. Not with Mister Skinflint Westwood keeping his eye on the till.'

It did not occur to her seriously to doubt her husband. She would make some show of it, perhaps, but that was merely for form's sake. The faults she found in him were petty ones; he had never exhibited an inclination for intemperance or loose living. It was the same with their not infrequent quarrels; mostly these originated in trifles, since neither felt deeply about the other. Only Philip could rouse them. Or perhaps their married life had been too drab for passion. It had been lived on the surface.

She put the potatoes into a saucepan, added water and salt, and placed the pan on the stove. She had had a presentiment only that morning, she remembered, that something unpleasant was about to happen. But then Arthur's forthcoming departure couldn't be described as unpleasant. It would be nice to have Philip to herself for a few days.

'You had better leave me the house-keeping, seeing as you may not be here Friday,' she said aloud, fumbling in her apron pocket for matches. 'And Philip's grey flannels are through at the knees. He'll need a new pair, and he can't afford to buy them himself. I'll need extra for that.'

The gas lit with a loud *plop*.

They had married fifteen years ago, when Ruth was thirty-six and Arthur three years younger. She had not been in love with him; but he had had a small business of his own and seemed the steady type, and to a widow with a two-year-old son to rear and educate his proposal had seemed heaven-sent. Even had she known that within three years the business would fail, and that they would have to exist on a rent-collector's salary, she would still have married him. There had been no other offers. And life with Arthur had not been entirely bad. It bore no comparison with the five wonderful years she had had with Dick before that dreadful train accident had ended their marriage so abruptly; but it had given her a home, and security of a sort, and Arthur himself had not been unkind. To Philip, yes; but not to her. Just dull and unpractical and largely indifferent.

She was straining the potatoes when her son sauntered into the kitchen. Philip Underset was a short, stocky youth, brown-haired and fresh-complexioned, plump like his mother, and with the same rather discontented expression. He gave her a slap on her broad behind and turned to inspect the stew she had taken from the oven.

'I see the old man's home. The car's outside.' He dipped a finger in the stew and sucked it. 'I suppose he wouldn't let me take it round the block? I don't often get a chance to drive.'

'You know he can't, dear. It's the firm's car. It would be different if it were his.'

He snorted. 'Would it hell! Supper ready?'

'Yes, dear.' She knew his youthful passion for cars, and since she adored him it hurt her that she could not give him the things he wanted. It hurt her too that Arthur did not share her affection for her son. For Philip was right. Arthur would not have let him drive the car, no matter whose the ownership. 'Dad's going up north on business as soon as we've eaten. He's packing now.' She ladled the stew on to plates. 'It'll make a change for him.'

'Make a change for us too. Is he taking the car?'

'I think so.'

'And he's going to-night? That's daft.

Why doesn't he wait until morning?'

'I don't know, dear. You'd better ask him.'

Later she was to regret that suggestion.

Philip was newly employed by a local printer, and as they ate their meal she would have liked to hear how the day had gone with him. But he did not volunteer the information, and she did not ask. Nothing Philip did or said was right with his stepfather; and although Ruth was accustomed to bickering, even welcoming it at times as a break in monotony, she was anxious not to involve her son. Neither Philip nor Arthur aided her in this, but she did her best to keep the friction between them at low heat.

Philip finished his stew and pushed the plate away. The action was deliberate; he knew that it irritated his stepfather. But Arthur did not rise to the bait. Normally a slow eater, he had been the first to finish. He sat staring dreamily at the empty plate, a faint smile on his lips.

Philip said, 'Mum tells me you're going up north on business. Where?'

'Eh?' Arthur came out of his dream. 'Oh, Leeds.'

'LAPP have an office in Leeds. It says so on their notepaper. What's the job?'

Arthur repeated what he had told Ruth. Philip snorted derisively. He said, 'And they're sending you all that way when there's a chap on the spot who could probably do the job a darned sight better? They must be barmy.'

It was the sort of remark that could be guaranteed to needle his stepfather into instant wrath. But, preoccupied as he now was, the sharpness in Banning's voice was more mechanical than intentional as he retorted, 'They don't need a young pup like you to teach them their business.'

Ruth recognized the signs, and hastily proffered second helpings. Both men declined. They watched in silence as she cleared away the dishes and put the sweet on the table. Neither offered to help.

The calm was short-lived. His mouth full of apple pudding, Philip said, 'Why go to-night? Why not wait till morning? It's not that urgent, is it?'

Banning sat with his back to the

window, facing the heavy mahogany sideboard that practically filled one wall of the small dining-room. He had eaten in front of that sideboard for as long as he could remember (it had been in his parents' home before his), and he could trace every intricate piece of carving with his eyes shut, he knew it better than he knew his wife's face.

'Because I prefer to go now.' His father had loved that sideboard. Built to last, he used to say, running his gnarled, arthritic fingers along its shining surface. But it was poverty, not sentiment, that had prompted Arthur to transfer it to his own home. New furniture was expensive. 'Any objections?'

'Not me.' Annoyed that he had succeeded in provoking only a mild reproof instead of the expected outburst, Philip dared further. 'If you want to act daft that's your worry.'

Banning's hands came up and gripped the table edge. Reaction was no longer mechanical. Glaring across at Philip's round face, his dreamy anticipation of the future was suddenly swamped by remembrance of all the vexations his stepson had caused him in the past. He was a little man, balding and corpulent, unstable in health and not given to violence. But there was violence in his heart as he slowly got to his feet, pulling the tablecloth towards him.

Ruth stood up too, the lines in her forehead deepening. She said quickly, 'You've no right to speak like that, Philip. Just you apologize to your father at once.'

Dismay rather than anger made her tone sharp. Always at the back of her mind was the dread that one day Philip might go too far and that Arthur would forbid him the house.

Was this, and not Arthur's trip, the cause of her presentiment?

'He's not my father.' Philip's tone was sullen. But a reproof from his mother indicated that he had overstepped the mark beyond which he could no longer count on her support, and he said weakly, 'Why all the fuss? Can't either of you take a joke?'

Banning's grip on the table relaxed. It was not an apology, and he knew it. But he had taken a hold on his anger. This was no time to indulge in a sordid family squabble. He would deal with Philip later.

He said flatly, 'One of these days, young man, some one is going to give you a lesson in manners. It could be painful. You might think about that while I'm away.'

He strutted from the room, leaving the apple pudding untouched, and hopeful that the warning had sounded sufficiently ominous to cause them both uneasiness. He was not entirely sure what he had meant by it, or if he had meant anything at all; but its very vagueness seemed to allow for more than one dire implication.

He hoped his stepson would consider them all.

As the door closed Philip said, 'What was all that in aid of?'

'Nothing, dear. He's upset, naturally, but it will be forgotten by the time he gets back.' Although her son was a constant source of anxiety to her, Ruth seldom let him see it. She stored it up and added it to the sharpness of her tongue when next she came in conflict with her husband.

'All the same, Philip, you shouldn't have said it. Not even in fun. You know how touchy he is.'

'Well, it's true, isn't it?' He pushed his plate towards her for a second helping. 'He *must* be daft to set off for Leeds at this hour.'

Ruth helped him liberally. She knew that too much starch and sugar were bad for him; but she had not the heart to refuse, she could indulge so few of his youthful desires. Watching her, a grin spread slowly over her son's round face, and he said, 'I hope he remembers to pack his shorts.'

Ruth gaped at him. Arthur had never been the athletic, outdoor type, and since that bout of pneumonia five years ago it had seemed to Ruth that he was always ailing. Certainly he was not a fit man. It was unthinkable that he should strut around in shorts.

'What on earth are you talking about, Philip? Arthur never wears shorts.'

'Doesn't he?' He started on the pudding. 'Sorry. My mistake.'

She continued to gape at him. Then her

15

eyes caught sight of the clock, and perplexity was pushed aside.

'Hurry up, dear, do. You'll be late for the Tech.'

Philip scowled. He was ambitious for success, but reluctant to work for it. Evening classes at the Tech. had been his mother's idea, not his, and they had provided him with yet another grudge against his stepfather. Arthur Banning had been to a minor public school, had been given capital by his father to start in business; had he done the same by his stepson, reasoned Philip, instead of fobbing him off with a secondary education and no start at all, there would have been no need for evening classes. That the salary of a rent-collector would not run to public-school fees only aggravated the youth's bitterness. He despised his stepfather for being a failure.

He had left the house by the time Arthur Banning came downstairs. Banning had a large suitcase in one hand and a sheaf of green notes in the other. He had decided that after what had happened at supper an air of resentment would not only be fitting, it would check any reproaches his wife might be considering. But the anxiety on her face, the hurt look in her blue eyes, made him forget his decision. He even experienced a feeling of remorse. Yet — why remorse? he wondered. Nothing he was about to do would harm her. If anything she would benefit from it.

'That should see you through until I get back.' He thrust the notes at her and lifted hat and raincoat from the elderly hall stand. That too was a relic from his childhood. 'If I look like being delayed I'll let you know.'

'Why should you be delayed?'

'One never knows. Things can crop up.'

As he picked up his suitcase she was reminded of Philip's remark at supper. Shorts. Such an odd thing for the boy to say. And yet . . .

'Well, I'm off,' he said briskly. 'I've given you an extra three quid for Philip's trousers. That enough?'

She would have disagreed had she not been so surprised. She had mentioned the trousers at supper, but she had not expected Arthur to remember. Usually she had to nag the money from him. Especially if it were for Philip.

He did not give her time in which to recover. He pecked her briefly on the cheek and hurried out to the car.

Ruth did not stand at the door to watch him go; their leave-takings were never prolonged. But after she had washed the dishes and tidied the kitchen she felt restless. It was unusual to have the house to herself of an evening, and she did not switch on the television-set but went upstairs to tidy the bedroom. Arthur was an untidy person, and as always he had not bothered to put away his discarded clothing. She picked shirt and under-clothes from the floor and deposited them in the dirty-linen basket, and draped his suit on a hanger before hooking it to the wardrobe rail. Her husband's lack of care for his clothes was a constant source of friction between them. It distressed Ruth that a man who could afford so little should be so neglectful of what he had.

Smoothing the creases from the tie, she crossed to the chest and tugged at the top drawer. It did not budge. She tugged again, thinking it had stuck; but when she rattled it up and down it moved freely within its confines, and she released the handle and stepped back, gaping at it in perplexity. In all her fifteen years of marriage she had never known a drawer or a cupboard in the house to be locked. But this one undoubtedly was. Why? She had not even known it possessed a key.

She was testing the other drawers when the telephone rang in the hall. She did not recognize the caller's voice, and he gave no name. He wanted, he said, to speak to her husband.

'I'm afraid he's out,' she told him.

'Oh!' There was a pause. 'Well, perhaps you would ask him to ring me when he returns.' He told her his telephone number. He had a smooth, purring voice, yet she sensed agitation in it. 'The matter happens to be urgent, or I wouldn't bother you now. I believe you're off to-night for a short holiday. Your husband mentioned it. I hope the weather holds. It looked rather threatening a while back.'

And then, when she did not answer, 'Hello! Are you there?'

'Yes,' she said dully. 'I'm sorry, but my husband has already left. About twenty minutes ago.'

'Alone? You mean you're not going with him?'

'No. It's a business trip, not a holiday.'

'But he said — ' It was his turn to be confused. 'I'm sorry. I must have misunderstood.'

'Yes.' she said. 'You must have misunderstood.'

She had replaced the receiver before the last sentence was complete. She knew instinctively that the caller had not misunderstood. It was all part of her presentiment; Arthur had told him one thing, herself another. But why?

Thinking back, she realized how uncharacteristically her husband had behaved that evening. His dreamy, detached air at supper, his tardy reaction to Philip's gibes and the speed with which his eventual wrath had evaporated, his unusual liberality with money; none of that was typical of Arthur. And there was the locked drawer in the bedroom. She remembered now that she had opened it only that morning, when she had put away his clean handkerchiefs after the laundry man had called. Arthur must have locked it while packing. Why? What did he wish to conceal from her?

She shivered. It was unlike Arthur to lie. His truthfulness was a form of laziness rather than honesty, but it was real. Yet he had lied to her that evening. Again — why?

Standing by the telephone, wriggling her toes in the warm slippers, she tried to conjure up further evidence of her husband's apparent deceit. Was it her imagination, or had he really been more detached these last few days? They had so little to say to one another that it was difficult to be sure. He had been late home the previous evening, and very late the evening before that. But lateness was not unusual in itself. Often he had to call back of an evening to collect rent from a tenant who had been out during the day.

There was nothing else. Or if there was

she had not noticed it.

Confused and troubled, she shuffled into the sitting-room and lowered her body into an armchair, to gaze unhappily at the blank television-screen.

2

The Morris was going like a bat out of hell, and it took what driving skill George Wilson possessed to keep its tail-lights in sight. The Anglia was past its best and due for replacement in the spring; the steering was sloppy, and he sat erect, cap almost touching the roof, hands clasped firmly on the wheel. He could not understand why the man in front should be driving so recklessly — veering wildly from side to side of the road, never dipping his headlamps to oncoming vehicles and missing them only by inches — but he meant to find out. Perspiration beading on his lean face, he hung on grimly and waited for disaster.

It was not long in coming. They raced northward through Offham, and as the Morris careened out of the last bend Wilson saw the lights of an approaching car. They were dim lights; they could not compete with those of the Morris, undipped and swinging. Wilson was too concerned for his own safety to watch closely what happened in the next few seconds, but it seemed to him that the oncoming driver was mesmerized rather than dazzled by the lights rushing towards him. Like a rabbit. Only at the last moment did the man appear to recognize his peril and veer sharply to the left; and by then it was too late. The Morris had drifted over the crown of the road and kept on drifting, apparently out of control. Wilson imagined rather than witnessed the actual crash. Braking hard, feeling the Anglia shiver and rock, he saw the newcomer swing across the road and hit the bank, to bounce back into his path. Wheels locked, tyres screaming, Wilson fought desperately to avoid the inevitable; pedals flat on the floorboard, the steering wrenched hard over. The Anglia was reluctant to respond. She skidded gently into the rear of the car ahead, to stop with a loud splintering of glass and a jarring crash.

For a few moments Wilson stayed in his seat, dazed more by the mental shock than by the force of the impact. His head had hit the roof as he was jerked forward, although the felt cap had cushioned the blow. There was a pain in his chest, and when he moved his right leg the knee felt sore. One of the Anglia's headlamps had gone; by the light of the other he saw that the car he had rammed was an old Vauxhall, and that the driver struggling to get out was a woman. He knew that he ought to help her. But as his brain cleared he remembered the Morris, and he burst open the offside door and slid out on to the road.

The Morris lay on its side in the ditch about a hundred yards ahead, its lights beamed at the sky. The woman was still struggling with the door of the Vauxhall, and as he started to limp down the road she shouted at him. Wilson ignored her. From the noise she was making she could not be seriously hurt. He had to discover what had happened to the occupants of the Morris; they were more important than the woman. The woman must wait.

He was still some fifty yards away when two figures emerged from the darkness of the ditch and stumbled on to the road, their forms silhouetted vaguely against the rampant beams. But they did not pause. As Wilson shouted at them they ran into the darkness on the other side of the road, and by the time he had drawn level with the Morris they had disappeared.

He stood for a while peering intently in the direction he thought they had taken, listening for some sound of their progress. All he heard was shouting from the vicinity of the Vauxhall, where already other cars had stopped. Their headlamps had been switched off, giving him no help in his search.

To pursue the fugitives would entail climbing the hedge and wandering aimlessly in the dark fields. Wilson did not attempt it. The pains in chest and knee were worse, and reluctantly he turned away and limped back to the Anglia.

★   ★   ★

Miss Oliphant was an imposing figure of a woman. She wore a brown tweed suit which emphasized her bulk, the long skirt tight at the hips, the jacket flaring out from the waist as though escaping from an impossible constriction. Her face was red and full, adorned now by strips of plaster implanted there at the hospital to which she and Wilson had been taken; and she had a real shiner of a black eye. But it was her chin that fascinated Wilson; it was large and square, the most aggressive chin he had ever seen on a woman, and he envied her it. His own chin was lost in a straight line from lip to neck, a nascent handicap of which he was highly sensitive and from which he had never recovered. He had tried to hide it with moustache and beard; but the hair had grown limp and straggling, so that instead of disguising his lack of chin it had seemed to emphasize it. He had shaved off the beard. The moustache, however, remained. It was at least a symbol of masculinity.

'He drove straight at me,' Miss Oliphant declared, her loud, hectoring voice booming round the police-station. 'Absolutely straight at me. And as for dipping his headlights — !' She snorted. 'If I hadn't kept my wits about me there'd have been a head-on collision. As it was — well, I just hugged the verge as tight as I could, and prayed.' Wilson wondered if she had considered braking or accelerating as alternatives to prayer. 'I thought I had just managed to scrape past, but no such luck. He caught the back of my car and swung it round, and I shot across the road and hit the bank and finished up broadside on to this gentleman.' She turned to look at Wilson. Perhaps it was the discoloured and swollen left eye that made the look malevolent. 'He just slammed straight into me. Couldn't stop, I suppose.'

She sounded as though she had considered the alternative — that Wilson had rammed the Vauxhall deliberately — and had reluctantly abandoned it.

The elderly station sergeant sighed. Wilson thought he looked tired. Or perhaps it was the drooping eyelids that gave him the appearance of a man long due for bed. His voice was brisk enough.

'Would you agree with that, sir?' the sergeant asked.

Wilson nodded. In his opinion the woman, far from keeping her head, had lost it. But he was worried and depressed, and he did not care sufficiently to argue the point. His head ached, his knee was stiff and swollen. There was a nasty bruise on his chest, although the doctor had assured him that he had suffered no internal injury. And added to his own discomfort was the damage to the Anglia. He could guess what the company would have to say about that.

'You say you followed this chap from Lewes. How had he been handling the car prior to the accident?'

Wilson sighed with relief, ignoring the sudden stab of pain in his chest. It was not the question he had feared.

'Abominably.' Temporarily forgetting his desire to figure as inconspicuously as possible in the police investigation, his smooth voice was suddenly transfigured with venom. 'It's a miracle he got as far as he did.'

They stared at him — Miss Oliphant, the sergeant, the tall mobile policeman who had been first at the scene of the accident. The sergeant cleared his throat noisily.

'Would you say he was drunk?' he asked.

'No. No, I wouldn't say that.' The brief outburst was over. Caution had returned.

'Why not?'

He shrugged, wincing at the pain. 'No particular reason. Just an impression.'

Miss Oliphant snorted. 'Of course he was drunk. Drunk or mad. No man in his right senses would drive the way he did.'

The sergeant ignored the outburst. He said quietly, 'You must have been pushing it a bit yourself, sir, wouldn't you say, to stay with him?'

Wilson ran a long, nervous finger round the inside of his collar (it was a detachable collar, oversize because he could not bear the pressure of a stud on his prominent Adam's apple), frowning unhappily as he sought for a non-committal reply. None came to him, and he contented himself with a vague shrug. The ill-fitting jacket (it had been bought off the peg, and his breadth was not proportionate to his height) slipped down one shoulder to give a lop-sided effect.

To the annoyance of Miss Oliphant the sergeant appeared to accept the shrug. Thrusting out chin and bosom, she said hotly, 'If you mean was he going too fast, then of course he was. Much too fast to avoid a collision, anyway.' She put broad, squat fingers to the bruised eye, probing the skin. Removing the fingers, she held them out in front of her, then lowered them to her lap. Wilson wondered if she had expected to see blood drip from them. 'He had not even the courtesy to come to my help after he'd hit me. He was far more interested in that crazy couple in the Morris.'

The sergeant was examining an insurance certificate on the counter before him. Without looking up he said, 'About that couple, sir. Did you get a good look at them?'

Wilson shook his head.

'I'm afraid not. Just a man and a woman — that's all I can tell you.' He turned to Miss Oliphant. He disliked the woman, but he had to placate her. To be faced now with a charge of dangerous driving could ruin him. 'I apologize for my apparent discourtesy,' he said, his voice smoothly ingratiating. 'It wasn't intended. It was just that I could see you were not seriously injured, and I feared the others might be.'

She snapped her fingers, indifferent to his apology.

'That's as may be. And there was no woman. Just the two men.'

'You're sure of that, madam?' asked the sergeant.

She assured him emphatically that she was. Hadn't they both worn trousers? The sergeant pointed out that nowadays trousers were no indication of sex, and looked at Wilson. 'But I'd like to know why you thought one was a woman, sir.'

'I couldn't say. Just another impression, I suppose.' If they preferred to look for two men that was all right with him. 'I've no doubt Miss Oliphant is right. My eyesight isn't too good.'

Technically, he supposed, that was an incriminating admission for a motorist to make. Neither policeman took him up on it. There was something about the documents laid out on the counter that seemed to intrigue them. But at least he had gone some way towards mollifying Miss Oliphant. She looked at him and nodded.

'My eyesight is excellent,' she informed him. Adding as an afterthought, 'It's only a question of training, you know. Training and self-discipline. Any healthy person can do it.'

The constable muttered under his breath. He had been watching the sergeant's finger as it moved from document to document. Now the finger had stopped. It was anchored firmly on Wilson's insurance certificate, as though determined that it should not escape.

'It would seem that you haven't been entirely frank with us, sir.' Wilson sensed the change in the man's voice, and braced himself. Miss Oliphant sensed it too. She swivelled in her chair to gaze with sharpened curiosity from one to another of the men. 'According to this, the car you were driving belongs to London and Provincial Properties. Now, that's quite a coincidence.'

'Coincidence?'

'Yes, sir. You see, they also own the wrecked Morris. Or isn't that news to you?'

It was not in George Wilson's nature to be flippant. He wanted to dismiss the question with an airy 'So what?' but he knew the words would sound foreign to his lips. He said faintly, 'I don't quite see what you're getting at, Sergeant. I mean — well, how does that affect the accident?'

'I don't know, sir.' He looked down at the counter. 'There was a suitcase in the back of the Morris belonging to a man named Banning. Arthur Banning. Is he a colleague of yours?'

'Yes.'

'You are both employed by London and Provincial Properties?'

'Yes.'

A large and belated bluebottle was buzzing lazily round the naked light bulb. Wilson watched it. He had to look somewhere, and he was afraid to meet the gaze of his questioner. The mild policeman had suddenly become the stern inquisitor.

'So you knew whom you were following, then.' The sergeant hesitated. 'Some

34

sort of a chase, perhaps. Was that it?'

There was a sharp hiss from Miss Oliphant. Reluctantly Wilson abandoned the bluebottle. He knew that he had to make a show of indignation if he were not to be browbeaten into defeat.

'That's a most improper suggestion. I resent — ' His eyes met the sergeant's, and he blinked nervously. 'Of course I wasn't chasing him. At least — '

They waited in silence for him to continue. He could feel the pulse hammering in his temple, there was perspiration on his forehead and in the palms of his hands. The sergeant eyed him steadily, rasping a coarse hand across the stubble on his chin. The bluebottle smacked heavily against the light bulb and fell to the floor. After a moment of inertia it began to crawl slowly towards the wainscoting.

'It's difficult to explain.' Wilson kept his eyes on the bluebottle. 'I was following him, of course, but only because he happened to be going my way. The Morris passed me as I was leaving Lewes, and I recognized the number. I supposed he was also making for Croydon. Only — '

He paused. 'Only what, sir?' asked the sergeant.

'Well, it seemed so unlikely. Only this afternoon Banning had told me he would be leaving this evening for a few days' holiday in Yorkshire. Westwood — he's the branch manager — had told him he could take the car.' There was a tickling sensation in his nostril, and he knuckled his nose vigorously and sniffed. 'So I couldn't understand what he was doing in Sussex. And then there's the way he was driving. Quite unlike Banning; he's a teetotaller, and a most careful driver.' He drew a deep breath, choking it off abruptly as pain shot through his chest. 'That's why I hung on to him. I wanted to find out what he was up to.'

The sergeant considered this. So did Miss Oliphant, though less mutely. In his desire to satisfy the police Wilson had temporarily forgotten the woman. Her voice ruptured the silence like an alarum.

'Well, to my mind, Mr Wilson, you ought to be thoroughly ashamed of yourself. Fancy tearing along the highway like a maniac merely to satisfy an idle curiosity! Criminal, I call it. Downright criminal.'

He was too weary, too dispirited, to protest.

The sergeant frowned at the interruption. It disturbed his train of thought; he was getting somewhere, but as yet the 'where' eluded him. Perhaps the man would talk more freely if the intimidating Miss Oliphant were removed.

He said politely, 'I don't think we need keep you any longer, madam. I have your address; we'll be getting in touch with you in due course.' He nodded to the constable. 'Constable Martin here will take you home.'

She rose reluctantly to take the documents he proffered. She would have preferred to stay, but already the constable was at the door. With a nod to the sergeant and a look of mingled curiosity and malevolence at the unfortunate Wilson, she departed.

'A bit of a tartar, that one.' The sergeant's voice sounded more friendly.

'Now, sir — let's get this sorted out, shall we? Why didn't you say straight out that you knew this chap Banning? It would have saved us quite a bit of time and trouble, don't you think?'

'I just couldn't believe it was Banning,' he said slowly. 'It seemed so improbable.'

That wasn't true. He had never doubted. He knew well enough why Banning was in Sussex, why he had tried so desperately to elude him. But he could not tell that to the police. The departure of Miss Oliphant had given him time to think, to plan a way out. Would the sergeant follow the line at which he had hinted?

'I appreciate that, sir. Nevertheless, it doesn't quite fit, does it?' The sergeant hesitated. 'Let's put it this way. Miss Oliphant thought the driver was drunk, you said he was sober. An impression, you said. But it wasn't an impression, was it? It was based on your knowledge of Banning. So you still thought it was Banning when you came into this room, despite the evidence to the contrary. Isn't that right?'

'I suppose so.' He looked for the bluebottle, but it had disappeared. 'Does it matter?'

'I fancy it does, sir.' The sergeant was beginning to enjoy himself. Traffic accidents usually demanded only routine police work. This one looked like being quite a lulu. 'From your knowledge of the facts, everything indicated that Banning was not the driver. The natural assumption, then, was that the car had been stolen. Yet that doesn't seem to have occurred to you.' He took a deep breath. 'It might be inferred that you knew Banning was in Lewes and had followed him there.'

'And why should I do that?'

'You'd know best about that, sir. But not for any friendly purpose, obviously, or he wouldn't have been so set on losing you. Driving like a maniac, haring off across the fields after the accident! Looks like he was real scared, wouldn't you say?'

'I would not.' He smoothed a damp hand over his greying, balding head, where the hair receded sharply from an acute peak on his forehead, and tried a slight laugh. It was not a success. 'You seem to be gifted with a very vivid imagination, Sergeant. Maybe that goes with the job. The plain fact is that I had had a heavy day and I just wasn't thinking straight. The crash didn't help. But of course it wasn't Banning; I see that now. As you say, the car must have been stolen.' He managed a sickly smile. 'Poor old Banning! That will have put paid to this holiday, I imagine.'

The sergeant did not echo the smile, the steely gaze from under the drooping lids did not waver. As though Wilson had not spoken he said, 'And then there's your assumption that one of the fugitives was a woman. Was that because you expected Banning to be with a woman?'

'I suppose so. He was going on holiday with his wife.'

The sergeant picked up a pencil, examined the point, and reached for his notebook.

'Could you give me a description of Mr and Mrs Banning, sir? It might help us in our inquiries.'

He had met Ruth Banning only once,

but he did his best to comply. The sergeant said thoughtfully, 'She doesn't sound like a woman who'd go chasing across country in the dark on her husband's say-so.'

He had to admit that she did not. Ruth Banning was no hare; that was something the police could easily verify. But he had to head the man off. He said earnestly, 'You're making a mountain out of a molehill, you know. All these sinister suggestions — they're completely without foundation.' He put a slim hand to his forehead in a gesture of fatigue. 'My fault, of course. I should have put you in the picture earlier. But that damned accident was more of a blow to me than perhaps you realize.' He leaned forward, winced at the extra strain on his swollen knee, and gingerly straightened the leg. 'The truth is, Sergeant, that I had to come down here in a hurry, and I borrowed the Anglia without the company's permission. After what has happened they're going to take a dim view of that. There's going to be one hell of a rocket, with me on the receiving end.'

The sergeant said he had his sympathy. He sounded as though he meant it. Encouraged, Wilson said eagerly, 'That accident was no fault of mine. You know that. So does my part in it have to come out? If it could be suppressed — '

The sergeant shook his head.

'You'll be needed as a witness, sir. And you can't suppress the Anglia, can you? Not with the front stove in.' He gathered up Wilson's papers and came round from behind the desk. 'I'm sorry to have kept you so long, sir. We'd have got on better if you'd been more co-operative at the start.' He held out the documents. 'I'll arrange for a car to run you to the station. You'll be able to get a train back to Croydon from there.'

Wilson stood up, cautiously testing his knee. He knew that the sergeant was right, that he could not hide what had occurred. And Westwood would make the most of it. Westwood had had his knife into him for years, he would probably use this to try to get him sacked.

'If you don't mind my asking, sir,' the

sergeant said, 'what was the urgent business that brought you to Lewes?'

Wilson sighed. There, if the man but knew it, lay the root of the whole wretched affair.

'I'm sorry.' Dignity did not come to him naturally — it was a pose he had seldom been able to afford — but he did his best to assume it now. 'It was a personal matter which I am not prepared to discuss.'

'Fair enough, sir.' The sergeant's composure was unruffled. 'Here! Don't forget your raincoat.' He lifted it from the back of a chair. 'My word, but that's heavy! What have you got in the pocket? A load of old iron?'

Wilson went rigid. He had forgotten the raincoat, had forgotten what lay hidden in its pocket. If the man should decide to investigate . . .

His stomach felt sick. A cold shiver snaked down his spine, and he pressed his knees firmly together to stop the trembling. Then, very slowly, he walked the few paces forward, each step seeming a league, each second an age.

With an unsteady hand he took the raincoat and draped it over an arm.

'That's just about what it is.' He forced his lips into a smile that was as shaky as his voice. 'A load of old iron.'

3

Hugh Westwood was a dapper man in the early forties, deep-voiced and short-necked, and fond of good living. He had been manager of LAPP's Croydon branch for three years, and during that period he had succeeded in antagonizing most of the older members of his staff. The fact did not displease him. He could be genial and charming with those who might be of use to him, but he saw no reason to waste his charm on subordinates.

To the two policemen who called at his office that Thursday morning he was distant but polite. The police were public servants, but they possessed power of a kind. Sergeant Redman he knew, but the tall man in civilian dress was a stranger. Redman introduced him as Detective Inspector Kane of the East Sussex C.I.D.; a mild-looking man with a crooked nose and blond, wavy hair. Westwood approved the well-cut gray suit, the quiet tie, the

45

immaculately laundered shirt. But there was no warmth in his welcome, and he did not invite his visitors to be seated.

'Banning?' he exclaimed, when Kane had prefaced the reason for the visit. 'Yes, he's employed here. One of our rent-collectors. I had given him a few days off to attend to some private business. Is he badly hurt?'

'We don't know, sir. He's still missing.'

As he elaborated on the Morris's erratic journey from Lewes and the flight of its occupants after the accident, Kane examined the room. It was on the first floor, large and high-ceilinged, with tall windows overlooking the quiet street. Apart from the modern filing cabinets and the luxurious swivel chair in which the manager sat, the furniture was massively Victorian; thick Wilton carpeting covered the floor from wall to wall, there were rich velvet drapes at the windows. Mr Westwood, Kane decided, liked his comforts.

'We haven't yet established, of course, that Banning was the driver,' he said.

'H'm! Well, it sounds most unlike him.'

Westwood's tone was abrupt. The accident was trouble enough without this rather sinister aura of mystery. 'To my mind, the more probable explanation is that the car had been stolen.'

'In that case wouldn't Banning have contacted you? It's over twelve hours since the accident.'

Reluctantly Westwood admitted the truth of this. His high forehead was wrinkled in a frown as he fiddled with an expensive-looking fountain-pen. He had one of those faces, blue-cheeked and blue-chinned, that look permanently unshaven. With his heavy brows and long, slender moustache it gave him a sardonic appearance.

'What the devil is he up to? He left this office shortly after five o'clock. Didn't say where he was going; merely that the matter was urgent and personal, and that he'd be back early next week.' The pen's gold-plated cap winked as it moved in the shaft of sunlight illuminating the desk. 'You say the car was seen in Lewes around ten o'clock?'

'Shortly after. And with two people in

it. One of them may have been a woman.'

'H'm! If Banning was the driver that would be his wife.' Westwood leaned forward and flicked a switch on the intercom.

'Put me through to Mr Banning's home.'

Kane frowned at the terseness of the order, and looked for a chair. Redman pushed one forward for him and sat down himself.

'Mr Banning wouldn't be in any sort of trouble, sir, would he?' he asked politely.

'Trouble?' Westwood sat up sharply. 'What sort of trouble?'

Before the sergeant could reply there came a buzz from the intercom. Westwood leaned across the desk.

'Yes?'

'There's no reply from Mr Banning's home, Mr Westwood. Shall I keep trying?'

'It doesn't matter. Skip it.' He looked at Kane. 'Well, that seems to be that, Inspector. Presumably his wife went with him.'

'Yes, sir. Unless she's out shopping, of course. Tell me — what sort of a man is

Banning? We've been given a physical description, for what it's worth, but — well, would he be likely to panic under stress?'

Westwood took time to consider.

'I shouldn't have thought so. Dull, unimaginative type. No initiative, but reasonably co-operative. I'm told he's a teetotaller, and as far as I know he's honest. I doubt if he has the cunning to be otherwise, although he handles fairly large sums of money.' The protruding brown eyes seemed to jerk back into their sockets as the lids half closed over them. 'You say you've been given a description. By whom?'

Kane told him. He had withheld George Wilson's name on purpose, disliking to disburse information in bulk. He preferred to clear up each point as he came to it.

'Wilson?' Westwood dropped the pen, and it rolled slowly across the blotter. 'What the hell was he doing, driving around Sussex in one of the company's cars?'

'He declined to say.'

'I'm not surprised.' There was no mistaking Westwood's anger as he banged a slim, well-manicured hand on the desk. Once more he attacked the intercom.

'Vance? Has Wilson been in this morning?'

'Yes, Mr Westwood.' There was heavy deference in the disembodied voice.

'Did he say anything about his Anglia being damaged?'

'Not that I know of. He seemed to be in a hurry — in and out like a flash. Why? Is anything wrong?'

'Send him up immediately he returns. Immediately.' He picked up a pair of spectacles from the desk, rubbed the lenses vigorously with a white silk handkerchief, and placed the spectacles on his nose. 'Are the cars badly damaged, Inspector?'

'The Morris could be a write-off, I'm afraid. The Anglia's in slightly better shape; radiator cracked, headlamp smashed, near wing buckled.' Kane paused, eyeing the manager with disfavour. Obviously sympathy was not an overriding virtue in the man. 'At present, of course, we're not interested in Wilson except as a witness to the accident.'

'Maybe not. But I am.' He was writing busily, the pen forming smooth, bold characters on the memo pad. Then it stopped, and he looked up. 'At present? What does that mean?'

'Nothing, perhaps. But Wilson admits he was following the Morris deliberately. And despite some evidence to the contrary he assumed Banning was driving and that he had a woman with him. He didn't say what woman.' Kane hesitated, feeling his nose with his thumb. He had broken it playing football for the Saracens, and the kink in it had fascinated him ever since. 'Is it at all possible that Banning could be having an affair with Wilson's wife? That's outside my province, of course, but — well, it would add up.'

Westwood was in no mood for smiling, but he smiled now — a grim, fleeting stretch of the lips that straightened the moustache into a thin line.

'Quite impossible, Inspector. Wilson has been a widower for some years.'

'Oh!' It was a disappointment, but it did not substantially affect the issue. As a policeman his task was to trace the missing occupants of the wrecked Morris. 'Well, that seems to dispose of that. Have the Bannings any family?'

'A son, I believe.'

'Living at home?'

'I really couldn't say.' Clearly the manager took no interest in the private lives of his employees. 'And now, if you've no objection, I'd like to get back to my work. You'll keep me informed, of course.'

It sounded like a command. Kane nodded, and stood up. He said, 'We'll do that. And perhaps you'd be good enough to contact Sergeant Redman here if and when you hear from Banning?'

Westwood removed the spectacles. He said, pop-eyed, ' 'If,' Inspector? Why 'if'?'

Kane's hand was on the doorknob. He said, 'Doesn't it strike you as odd that you've heard nothing from Banning since the accident?'

'Extremely odd. I'll have something to

say about that when he returns.' Westwood stood up too. He was of medium height, but the massive desk dwarfed him. 'Of course, there is the possibility that he may have been injured. Seriously injured, I mean.'

The thought did not appear to distress him.

Redman said, 'If he'd been admitted to hospital the police would have been notified.'

Kane nodded agreement. Not without relish, he delivered a parting shot.

'All things considered, Mr Westwood, it looks to me as though your Mr Banning may have disappeared deliberately. People do, you know — and for a variety of reasons. Trouble at home, trouble at work — sometimes just an irresistible urge to get away from it all, make a fresh start. It might be worth considering, don't you think?' He paused, fingering his nose. 'And if you're looking for a reason in Banning's case I suggest you ask Wilson. I've an idea he might be able to supply one.'

★ ★ ★

Ruth Banning opened the door to them. She had just returned from shopping, and still wore her hat and coat. But she had exchanged her walking-shoes for slippers. That was always her immediate task on return.

The sight of the sergeant's uniform alarmed her. Her first thought was for Philip; something terrible must have happened to him if the police, rather than the firm, had to appraise her of it. When they had reassured her on that score her panic subsided.

'It'll be Arthur, then.' As she ushered them into the small sitting-room she removed her hat, and the blond hair burst from its confines like coiled springs. She did not attempt to pat it into order. 'Has he had an accident?'

She was concerned but calm. Kane was relieved; hysterical women worried him, and Ruth Banning had shown that she was not beyond hysteria. Briefly he gave her the facts concerning her husband's disappearance, and waited hopefully for her interpretation. But Ruth had none to give. Still in her coat, she sat down and gaped at her visitors.

'Lewes? I don't understand. He told me he was going to Yorkshire on business.' She had known since last night that he had lied to her. Perhaps now she would learn why. 'What was he doing in Lewes?'

'We were hoping you might be able to tell us that.' Banning, it seemed, had varied his tale freely. To his wife it had been a business trip, to his boss the call of urgent private affairs, to his colleague Wilson a holiday. Which, if any, was the truth? 'Has your husband any friends living in Sussex?' The gape widened into the preliminaries of speech, and Kane said quickly, 'I know he was all set for Yorkshire, but he might have decided to visit a friend first. I imagine he doesn't often have a car at his disposal for pleasure purposes.'

'We haven't really got any friends. Not close ones.' She sounded more resigned than bitter. 'He has a married brother living out Egham way, but we don't often see them. They've got money.' Coming from her the explanation sounded perfectly reasonable. 'Anyway, Mark's much younger than Arthur. They never — '

She broke off as the front door banged. There were footsteps in the hall, and Kane waited expectantly. Was this Banning? Then a stocky, fresh-complexioned youth came into the room, to stare with undisguised curiosity at the two policemen.

'Philip!' Ruth struggled from the chair. 'What's happened? Is anything wrong, dear?'

'No more than usual.' His brown hair was ruffled, there were cycle clips round his ankles. 'I just happened to be passing — doing a stint for old Wort-face — and I saw the police-car. What's up, Mum? Arthur in trouble, or have you been shop-lifting again?'

Ruth Banning flushed, the mottled patches on her cheeks darkening.

'You mustn't say things like that, Philip. Not in front of strangers.' She turned to her visitors. 'It's a family joke — please don't take him seriously. I picked up a packet of needles once in Grants — you know, absent-mindedly — and it wasn't until I was outside the store that I realized

I hadn't paid for them.' The flush began to fade. 'I went back, of course. But Philip's always pulling my leg about my 'shoplifting,' as he calls it.'

Kane nodded, smiling. He felt sorry for the woman. Tragedy could be just around the corner for Ruth Banning, and it always seemed more acute when it impinged on the ordinary and the humdrum. It might be nothing worse than a few lost illusions about her husband, but it could still be tragedy.

Redman said, 'Kids are all the same. No respect for their parents. My youngest — he's just nine — calls me 'Sarge.' It seems to amuse him no end.'

Philip scowled. Kane thought he looked overfed. His sports jacket was tight across the stomach, the single button by which it was fastened was pulling away from the cloth.

'Come on, Mum, let's have it. What's Arthur been up to?'

Ruth told him, glossing over details which appeared to reflect adversely on her husband. Philip received the news calmly. Kane had the impression that he

57

found it gratifying. He felt tempted to prick the youth's complacency by reminding him that his stepfather might be seriously injured, perhaps dead. That he did not do so was because he did not believe it. Banning had meant to disappear. That was the way it smelt to him.

'Apart from you and your son, Mrs Banning, who knew that your husband was going on this trip?'

'I couldn't say. Mr Westwood, I suppose; he's Arthur's boss. And some one rang up shortly after Arthur had left. He knew.' She opened her coat and fumbled in the pocket of her cardigan for a handkerchief. 'He didn't give his name, but he seemed to think Arthur was off on a holiday, and that I was going with him.'

But Arthur had not taken her. Arthur had gone alone, and now he was missing. If it had not been for the lies he had told her, and the locked drawer, and his strange behaviour before he left, she would have believed what the police seemed to believe — that he had met with an accident. An accident wrapped in mystery, perhaps — but still an accident.

Nothing planned. That was what she wanted to believe. An accident, provided it were not serious, would not disrupt her life irreparably.

But she could not believe it. It was unlike Arthur to make a big and dramatic decision, but she was sure he had made one now. He had gone — and presentiment told her he would not be returning.

Kane said gently, 'You didn't recognize the voice?' The blond tangle of hair swayed slightly in negation, and he asked, 'Do you know a man named Wilson? George Wilson? He's one of your husband's colleagues.'

It was not so much Arthur she would miss, but the tottering security he represented. They could not exist on Philip's meagre wages. It would mean leaving the house to live in some poky little flat — she would have to go out to work —

Tears stung her eyes, and she blinked furiously and turned away. She did not want Philip to see her cry.

'I met him once, I think.' Her voice sounded thick, and she sniffed and cleared her throat. 'Why?'

'It was he who spotted the car in Lewes. But it's not important.' Clearly he would get no farther with that line of inquiry, and he switched to another. 'At what time did your husband leave here, Mrs Banning?'

'After supper. About seven-thirty, I think.' Blowing her nose, she turned to her son for confirmation, then remembered that he had left the house before Arthur. 'It couldn't have been much later.'

'You wouldn't know if he had already filled up with petrol?'

'Yes, he had.' This from Philip. 'It showed 'full' when I switched on.' He saw the look on his mother's face. 'It's all right, Mum, I didn't drive the flipping thing. Just tried the engine, that's all.'

So Banning had left home at seven-thirty with a full tank and a full stomach. Kane considered what those facts could tell him. If the man really had been making for Yorkshire they implied no stops for fuel or food for at least two hundred miles. Not for a drink, either;

Banning was a teetotaller. And presumably he had attended to the calls of nature before leaving.

Two hundred miles. A good five hours' driving, then, before he would have reason to stop and give some chance thief the opportunity to pinch the car. But that was way out. The Morris had been seen in Lewes around ten o'clock, two and a half hours after Banning had left home.

So Yorkshire had been a blind and Banning a phoney. That was at least a reasonable deduction. But not particularly enlightening, since it was a fact he had already assumed.

'Would you gentlemen like a cup of coffee? I usually have one of a morning.' Ruth's voice was back to normal. She turned to her son, gently touching the sleeve of his jacket. The joints of her fingers were badly swollen — through too much immersion in water, Kane suspected. 'How about you, dear? You're not in a hurry, are you? It won't take a second.'

No, Philip said, he was in no hurry. Kane wondered how urgent was the stint on which 'old Wort-face' had dispatched him. But he accepted the offer of coffee. So did Redman. The sergeant was accustomed to his elevenses, and it was already past midday.

When the woman had left the room Kane leaned back and closed his eyes. A messy, untidy case, he decided, and one that would probably drift on for days. Weeks, maybe, if the missing Banning chose to remain missing. Which meant that Brands Hatch was out for yet another week-end. The third this year — and the Healey had never been running so sweetly!

Sergeant Redman said, 'Sounds like your ma's got another visitor, young man. Isn't that her voice in the kitchen?'

Philip grinned. It was a lop-sided grin which revealed gaps in his teeth.

'She talks to herself when she's alone. Regular comic turn she is sometimes.' Philip lifted an arm to rub the back of his head, and the button on his jacket fell off and rolled under the settee. He frowned, but made no effort to retrieve it. 'What do you think the old man was playing at, running away like that after the accident?'

'I've no idea. Have you? You know him better than we do.'

Slowly, regretfully, Philip shook his head. Then his blue eyes rounded and his mouth gaped.

'Running! That's funny.' His face relaxed into a grin, and he giggled. Both grin and giggle suited the rather bucolic face better than the frown. 'Here's something'll make you laugh. Only don't tell Mum. She doesn't like me to make fun of the old man.' Kane nodded assurance. 'It was one evening last week. Me and Roddy Stone — he's a friend of mine — were trying out a car Roddy was thinking of buying. An old M.G. — rough, but a goer. Going up the hill past the old airport she smelt a bit hot, so we turned right at the top and stopped. And there was the old man. Guess what he was doing?'

Parked with a floozie, was Kane's immediate guess. 'Search me!' he said.

'Running.' Philip paused for effect. 'Haring up and down that sports' field on the left, all togged up in shorts and vest and puffing like a flipping grampus. Honest!' He burst into a loud laugh. 'Well, I ask you! Running! At his age!'

4

Vince Harding ate his lamb cutlets and watched the girl at the window table. She was as lovely as her photograph, he decided, although he had not expected her to be blond. Her hair had the sheen and glow of pure gold, and when she turned her head it swayed and glinted in the sunlight. She wore a dress of yellow silk with a jacket of the same material, and round her neck was suspended a dull bronze pendant in the shape of a many-pointed star. Her face was more square than oval, with a wide generous mouth, the lips picked out in a delicate shade of pink. Her ears were flat and well shaped; the large eyes, beneath clearly defined brows and lightly mascaraed lashes, were set well apart. When she looked his way — as occasionally she did — he saw that they were a clouded hazel. Her legs were hidden under the table, but her body was slim, her breasts small. An enormous bloodstone ring glowed on the middle finger of her left hand.

Her name was Doris Williamson.

He had learned that from the hotel register; her signature, written in a round, childish hand against the previous day's date, was the last on the page. He had looked for her in the bar before lunch; she would almost certainly be alone, and a hotel bar was a satisfactory place in which to make a girl's acquaintance. But she was not in the bar. She had already started lunch when he went into the dining-room.

It was unfortunate that he had been given a table so far from hers. The room was not crowded, he should have spoken firmly to the waiter instead of allowing himself to be shepherded. Now, instead of leaning across to ask for the salt or making some casual remark about the weather, he would have to invent a more subtle way of effecting an introduction.

Despite his excitement Vince enjoyed the lunch; dining in an expensive hotel was a new experience, and the sense of power, of completion that it gave him was stimulating. Occasionally he thought of Chug Wallis, and a faint smile twisted his thin lips. Chug would have made for Brighton, swearing blue murder and not giving Lewes a thought. He would go where the pubs, the cafés, the slot-machines and the pintables were plentiful. And birds. In his crude, indifferent fashion, Chug was a great one for birds.

The girl had been examining her face in a mirror affixed to the flap of her handbag; now she snapped the bag shut and pushed back her chair. Hastily swallowing a mouthful of biscuit and cheese, Vince reached the door first. As she passed him he said, 'I'd like to apologize.'

'Oh? For what?'

She did not stop, but walked across the hall to the lounge. Vince followed, his eyes on her legs. They were long and straight and slender.

'I was watching you all through lunch. Couldn't take my eyes off you.' He was beside her now, the crest of her golden head level with his eyes. 'I hope you didn't mind.'

'I didn't notice.'

That, he knew, was a lie. Her voice was disappointing; a high, childish treble, thin and unpolished. But it did not cool his interest. The rest of her was fine.

As she sank gracefully into an armchair, he said, 'Mind if I sit here? I'm fed up with my own company.'

She said aloofly that she did not mind. Vince grinned to himself. You can't fool me with your poses, my girl, he thought. I've read the letter, I know what you are.

He ordered coffee and liqueurs, and set himself to amuse her.

Doris watched him as he talked, as she had watched him covertly during lunch. She had been at the window of her room when he arrived — in a white Zephyr saloon, with two elegant pigskin cases on the back seat — and, after a quick look in the register to see if he were staying and to learn his name, she had gone in to lunch in hopeful anticipation. He was a handsome young man, willowy and erect, with a profusion of dark, wavy hair. His face was both distinguished and distinctive; thin and ascetic-looking, with high cheekbones and a proud nose. The

68

slanting eyes, dark and piercing, suited the face, although they were perhaps set too close. And he had good hands; long and slender, with well-kept fingernails.

Most important of all, he had money. The car, the cases, the clothes, the gold cigarette-case and wrist-watch, told her that.

He was on holiday, he said. 'It's dull, though, just mooching around. A friend and I were taking the car to Italy, but he let me down at the last minute. I couldn't face it on my own.' When she inquired about his job he told her, with a self-deprecatory shrug, that he was independent. 'My old man was loaded, and most of it came to me. But I'm not entirely idle. I write a bit, and I'm keen on photography. Figure studies, mostly.' He smiled at her. 'Editors don't exactly snatch at my stuff, but I keep trying.'

Figure studies, he thought, was an inspiration. It had tantalizing possibilities.

Doris was impressed. He had a quiet, pleasant voice — not entirely B.B.C., but did that matter? — his manner was assured without being brash. And it was obvious that he found her attractive.

She crossed her legs, allowing the hem of her skirt to ride up. Noticing how his dark eyes went at once to her knees, she smiled.

Vince saw the smile, knew that the aloof pose was to be dropped. The thaw was complete. He said briskly, 'It's a lovely afternoon. Why don't we pop down to the coast?'

She shook her head.

'I'd love to, but I can't. I'm here to meet my uncle; he's taking me to Paris to spend a few days with my aunt.' A slight frown corrugated the smooth, clear forehead. 'I can't think what's gone wrong. He should have arrived last night; we were supposed to be crossing this morning. But he hasn't even telephoned.'

'Why don't you telephone him?'

'I don't know where he is.'

'And if he doesn't turn up to-day? Will you go on your own?'

'I can't. He has the tickets. I'll have to go home.'

She seemed more puzzled than dismayed. Vince thought he knew why. He

70

said, 'Well, even if he turned up now you couldn't go until to-morrow. There's no ferry. So why waste the afternoon? Leave him a note; tell him you've gone to Eastbourne, and that you'll be back around six. O.K.?'

She held out a hand. 'O.K.,' she said gaily.

You're on your way, Vince boy, he told himself as he helped her up. Play it cool and you can't lose.

★   ★   ★

The men's surgical ward at Chawtry Memorial Hospital was in the west wing — a long, one-storeyed building erected in 1947 from funds provided by a group of Canadian businessmen in gratitude for the medical skill and attention received by wounded compatriots during the War. It was to Chawtry that many of them had come after the Dieppe raid. But as he walked down the long corridor Medwin's thoughts were neither of them nor of the gravely injured man whose bedside he had just left. He was wishing he had worn other shoes. Iron-tipped heels sounded wrong in a hospital. Not that a hospital was a particularly silent place. It was just that he seemed to be making the wrong sort of noise.

The house surgeon pushed open the door of a room and ushered his visitor inside.

'Sit yourself down, Inspector.' He waved his arm towards a large armchair covered in worn brown leather. 'Care for a cup of coffee?'

Medwin would have cared for anything that would still the rumble in his stomach; it was nearly three o'clock, and he had not yet lunched. On his acceptance the surgeon disappeared into the corridor, to return with the information that the coffee would be along shortly.

He was a big young man, and he made a tight fit of the armchair. Medwin said, 'Is he going to make it? He looks bad to me.'

The surgeon shrugged.

'He's bad, all right. He's got everything against him, poor chap. Concussion, temporal fracture of the skull, broken nose, cracked ribs — practically the lot. Not to mention hypostatic pneumonia from the exposure.' He frowned. 'It beats me why he wasn't found earlier. Chailey Common isn't that deserted.'

'He was tucked away among the bushes.' Medwin pressed a hand to his stomach to silence an incipient rumble. 'Some kids found him. He might be there yet if their dog hadn't nosed him out. Could his injuries have been caused by a car?'

'Not on your nelly!' The surgeon's tone was emphatic. 'The head wound was inflicted by something like an iron bar, but the rest was done with the boot. Unmistakable — I've seen it before. This was no accident, Inspector. If they didn't quite manage to kill the poor bastard it wasn't for want of trying.'

The children had found the man shortly after midday, on their way back from school. His noisy breathing had told them he was alive. To Medwin it seemed a miracle that he was. There had been a sharp shower of rain around midnight, yet the flattened grass under his body was dry. He must have lain there for more than twelve hours.

Everything pointed to robbery as the motive. There was nothing on the man to identify him; no wallet, no keys, no papers. A pale band of skin at his wrist showed where his watch had been removed; even the loose change in his pockets had been taken. It was Medwin's belief that he had been attacked and robbed elsewhere, and then taken to the common and dumped. Bracken and bushes showed where his body had been dragged from a clearing at the roadside.

'When is he likely to recover consciousness?' he asked.

'No knowing.' The surgeon proffered a cigarette, which Medwin reluctantly declined. He had given up smoking less than a month previously, and the craving still persisted. 'Could be hours — days — even weeks. If he lasts that long.'

'H'm! Well, I can't afford to take chances. Would it be all right with you if I post a constable by his bedside? He might say something which would give us a lead. Not knowing who he is or what happened — well, we're groping in the dark.'

The surgeon had no objection. 'But no questions, Inspector. Not without Sister's permission. You must make that clear to your chap.'

A white-coated orderly brought them coffee; lukewarm and rather bitter. Medwin sipped it gratefully, and wished it had been accompanied by a biscuit.

The surgeon said, 'I hear there was a rather odd accident a few miles down the road last night. Near Offham, wasn't it? Rumour has it that the occupants of one of the cars bolted. That sounds like car thieves to me. Any connexion with our chap, do you think?'

Medwin shrugged. 'I doubt it. However, we'll be putting in a report to headquarters. If they think there's a possible tie-up they'll send some one along. Jimmy Kane, most likely. He's handling the Offham case.' He finished the coffee. 'Do you know him? Tall, fair-haired chap with a bent nose. Natty dresser.'

The surgeon shook his head. 'I'm a new boy. However, we'll make him welcome. Care to have a look at the wet-plates? They'll be ready by now. We'll know then what we have to contend with in the way of internal injuries.'

'The brain, you mean?'

'And the abdomen. Could be rup-tured.' He took a final gulp at the coffee. Some of it dribbled down the side of the cup on to his white coat. He swore, and fumbled for a handkerchief. 'He is also under observation for a ruptured spleen. Blood pressure is reasonably high, but there's always the possibility that it may take a sudden plunge.' He dabbed at the coffee stain. 'Taken all in all, he's in a pretty bad way, poor devil. I don't fancy his chances.'

* * *

It was warm and close in the pier arcade. The sea breeze did not penetrate to that raucous place, and there were beads of sweat on Chug Wallis's scowling face as he put yet another penny in the machine,

76

twisted the handle, and watched the shining metal ball leap from pin to pin and finally disappear.

He dug his fingers into a trouser pocket and fished out a handful of coins. 'No more bleeding coppers,' he announced, and thrust the coins back.

'They'll give you change over there,' the girl said.

'They can bloody well keep it.'

The girl followed his short, stocky figure from the arcade. Both were ungainly in their walk. Chug had the rolling gait of a seaman and wore a fisherman's jersey, although this was the nearest he had ever been to the sea. The girl moved stiffly, not bending her knees or lifting her feet, her sneakers swishing over the wooden planks. She wore a black sweater, V-necked, above a tight brown skirt and black stockings; the sweater was cheap and thin like the skirt, and her young breasts stretched the weave so that the pointed cups of the brassière showed pinkly beneath it. The sun had left her white, spotty face untanned, her mouse-coloured hair lay lank and unkempt about her head.

'Don't you get tired of playing them things?' she asked. 'We been in there more'n two hours.'

'So what?' He moved to the pier rail and hung over it, scowling blankly down at the green crests rolling in to the shore. 'Nothing better to do, is there, till the pubs open?'

'There's places,' she said, thinking of the coffee-bars and the clubs. She had lived all her seventeen years in Brighton, and knew them all. 'You like dancing?' He shook his head without deigning to look round, and she moved closer to put a grubby hand on his broad shoulder. She was the taller by several inches. 'They've got cars and things on the West Pier. Let's try that, eh? It's better'n here.'

He stepped back from the rail on to her foot, and she squealed. He did not apologize. He said, 'All that bleeding sea. Makes me want to puke.'

They had met that afternoon. She had attached herself to him because, from experience, she had assessed him as a visitor to the town, and visitors usually had money. He was not an attractive youth. He had small eyes, set close beneath almost hairless lids and a receding forehead; he breathed noisily through his mouth, and the thick lips only partially masked the black, misshapen teeth. But that had not deterred the girl; she liked her men virile, the more blatant and brutal the better. Her eyes had noted the broad shoulders and the heavy thighs, the deep chest and the bulging forearms, the thick wrists and enormous, hairy hands. Even his surliness had had a masochistic appeal.

In silence they walked back along the pier. Occasionally Chug let fly with his foot at an empty carton on the deck; not an aimless, idle kick, but a vicious one, with all his considerable strength behind it. The girl guessed him to be in a mean mood; his dark pudding-face seemed incapable of a smile. He had managed a leer when they met, blatantly prodding her rotundities with a speculative finger. Since then he had practically ignored her.

She said, 'You got a place to sleep?'

'Nope.'

'What you going to do about it, then? A bed ain't easy to find in the summer. Most places is full.'

'I'll manage.' He looked at her, the leer back on his face. 'Or was you thinking I might kip down with you?'

She laughed — a tired laugh that scarcely moved her face.

'You got a hope! I can just see me Mum's face. Anyways, I sleep with me sister.'

'So what? Afraid I'd like her better'n you? Could be.' He threw a careless arm about her waist, sliding his hand down to pinch her thigh. 'Skinny, ain't you?'

He was catholic in his taste for women, but he did not like them thin and he did not like them tall. Tall women hurt his masculine pride. He had allowed this one to latch on to him because he was angry and bitter, and because he needed some one on whom to vent his spleen. She was also the first to offer.

She was not offended by the sneer in his voice. The cursory warmth of his hand through the flimsy skirt had excited her. She said huskily, 'There's a place up near the station where they'd give you a bed. Want me to show you?'

He hoicked and spat. 'Please yourself.'

They were near the entrance to the pier. 'What we going to do this evening?' she asked, taking it for granted that they would be doing it together. He shrugged but did not answer, and she proceeded to offer alternatives, keeping a watchful eye on his dark face for a sign of rebellion. To encourage him she said, 'It don't matter what time I get home. My Dad's that drunk of an evening I could stay out all night. He just ain't with it.'

He made no comment. Out by the kerb a man was calling the evening papers, and he ran off the pier and bought an *Argus* and stood scanning the front page. He seemed to have forgotten the girl, and after a moment of indecision she followed him.

'I'm hungry,' she said. 'What say we eat?'

He rounded on her, his face suffused with anger. 'Get lost, damn you!'

He flung the paper at her face. The

breeze caught it and spread it, blanketing her view. She brushed it away to see his stocky figure dodging the traffic as he sprinted across the road.

'Well!' she exclaimed, furious that her evening's entertainment should be so rudely snatched away. The afternoon had been a dead loss. 'You big slob! You dirty, rotten slob!'

* * *

Because each was intent on advancing a special relationship with the other, they enjoyed the afternoon. They drove up to Beachy Head, had tea at the Grand, and strolled along the promenade. Doris had taken off the jacket as they walked. The sleeveless dress hugged her figure, giving emphasis to the pointed breasts and the slim waist and the smooth flatness of her abdomen. Vince exulted in the envious male glances. Remembering the photograph, he suggested a swim; they could buy costumes in the town, he said. But he did not press the proposal when she declined. There would be other afternoons. The girl might not know it, but he did.

There was no uncle awaiting them on their return, and no message. Standing before the mirror in the deserted bar, adjusting the clip on her wind-blown hair, Doris considered her position. Aloud.

'I'll have to go home,' she announced, regret in her childish treble. 'To-night. There's no alternative, really. I suppose there's a train?'

'Plenty,' he assured her, and paused to enjoy her reaction. From where he stood he could see the frown that suddenly marred her pretty face, the petulant projection of her lower lip. 'Or you could wait till to-morrow. No hurry, is there?'

'I'm broke. I hadn't bargained on hotel bills.'

She was studying him in the mirror. He made the answer he knew she expected.

'Let me stake you, then. If you feel bad about it you can pay me back later, although it isn't necessary. I shan't miss it.'

She turned quickly, pink lips parted in just the right measure of reproach mingled with reluctant gratitude.

'Oh, I couldn't possibly! It's kind of you to offer, but — well, we're practically strangers, aren't we?'

He moved nearer. But not too near. A false move now, and pride might force her into living the part he knew she was playing.

'We could alter that if you stayed. And you'd be doing me a favour. I don't much fancy having to make do with my own company again. Not after yours.' He smiled. It was a charming smile, with just the suspicion of a dimple at the corners of the mouth. 'Besides, Uncle might turn up to-night or to-morrow. You could still get your trip to Paris.'

'Well — ' She hesitated, sucking at her lower lip as she studied him. 'You're sure you mean it?'

'Of course I mean it. And no strings, either.'

She breathed a deep sigh. 'Then I'll stay. And thank you.'

She had made no mention of repayment. He was glad of that, it proved he had not been mistaken. There was a sudden warmth about his loins; he wanted to touch her, to make his conquest tangible. He said thickly, 'Good for you. Come on, let's drink to it.'

Doris did not want a drink. With a soft word of gratitude and a touch of her hand on his that sent his blood racing, she went upstairs to change.

He followed ten minutes later, after a large gin. As he relaxed in the bath he tried to plan the successive steps to ultimate victory; but a vision of the girl kept intruding, and he abandoned planning for consideration of her as a person. That little scene in front of the mirror told him that he had assessed her correctly, yet she was as superior to others of her type he had known as a duchess is to a tramp. The crude technique to which he was accustomed would not work with Doris. He must learn to employ finesse, to play the game her way. She would expect that. It would not be easy — but then, that was why he was here. If he had wanted it easy he could have found it in the streets at home.

As he stood up to soap his lean body he

exulted again in his good fortune. A pity Chug could not see him with the girl. That would really be piling on the agony.

He was back in the bar before Doris. A copy of the *Evening Argus* lay on the counter, and as he ordered a gin and tonic he picked it up.

'Mind if I look?'

'Help yourself.' The barman placed tonic bottle and glass before him, and pointed to the headline. 'It's getting a bit rough around these parts. That's the second this week.'

The headline was in bold type. INJURED MAN FOUND ON CHAILEY COMMON. Vince stared at it for a moment, and then read on.

Children playing on Chailey Common early this afternoon came across the body of a man hidden among the bushes. He was later taken to Chawtry Memorial Hospital, where he was found to have extensive head and other injuries. He is still unconscious, and his condition is said to be critical.

Nothing is as yet known of the man,

or how he came by his injuries. A local resident has told the police that shortly after nine o'clock last night he passed a car parked off the road not far from where the man was found. But the common is a favourite haunt of courting couples, and he did not stop to investigate.

The paper then went on to give a description of the injured man, and concluded:

Last Monday night a fifteen-year-old girl was attacked near the same spot. Her assailant has not yet been found, but the police consider it unlikely that there is any connexion between the two crimes.

'Very nasty,' Vince said. 'Let's hope the poor chap recovers.'
'He won't,' the barman assured him. 'Critically ill' — that's what it says. 'Seriously ill' — well, he's got a chance then. But 'critically ill' — that's as good as dead, that is.'

'Is Chailey Common far from here?'

'About eight miles.'

Doris came into the bar. She wore a slip of a dress of lined blue lace, edged with a darker blue satin. To Vince she seemed to glisten. Her hair, clipped back now behind the ears, shone as though burnished; there was a golden spray of flowers at her right shoulder, a heavy gold bracelet on her wrist. Her perfume was subtle and provocative.

'A gin and French, please,' she said gaily. 'Anything in the paper?'

He pushed the *Argus* away. 'Nothing that would interest you,' he assured her.

5

Detective Superintendent Baker, head of East Sussex C.I.D., was due to retire in six months' time. He viewed the prospect with mixed feelings. When the department was not running smoothly, when he was tired and dispirited from overwork, it lay just beyond his mental horizon like Nirvana. But there were also occasions when the thought of retirement made him shudder. The Force had been his life. He had few interests outside it, and contemplation of the long, empty days that lay ahead filled him with dismay.

This was one of those occasions. Kane saw it on his face as soon as he came into the room, and groaned. That look of purpose, of downright gluttony for work, could mean only one thing. They were in for a stiff session.

He sat down heavily, knowing he had no right to complain and hoping his weariness was not too apparent. He had returned from Croydon to find a message from Jack Medwin awaiting him, and had rushed off to Chawtry Hospital to look at an unidentified man who might or might not be the missing Arthur Banning. Yet it was only six o'clock now, and ten hours on the trot was not a long spell for a copper. You want to watch it, James Kane, he told himself sternly. You're getting soft.

'Well?' Baker's voice was brisk. He sat very erect, his thick hair startlingly white above the bronzed face. 'Is it Banning?'

'I think so.' Kane placed a photograph on the desk. It showed a man and a woman and a small boy sitting on a pebbled beach. 'According to Mrs B that was taken fifteen years ago, shortly after their wedding; and it's a poor exposure at that. Nevertheless there's a distinct resemblance. He's put on a lot of weight since then, and after the rough treatment he received he isn't looking his best, poor devil. But I'd say it's the same man. Both Wilson's and Mrs B's descriptions were vague, but as far as they go they tally. And the Morris is lousy with his dabs.'

'The dabs only say he was in the car.

They don't say he's Banning. We need positive identification for that.' Baker picked up the photograph and studied it. 'When is his wife arriving?'

'In the morning.'

'Why not to-night?'

'The son says she's too ill to travel. Bowled over by the shock.' Kane thumbed his nose. 'Well, could be. I thought she took the news of his disappearance pretty calmly this morning, but I suppose this would be more alarming.'

'Why didn't the son come instead?'

'He told Redman he couldn't leave his mum. More likely he couldn't be bothered. He's an unpleasant youth, and definitely anti-stepfather.'

'They sound a united family.' The superintendent removed his spectacles and thoughtfully nibbled one end. 'All right. Assume the injured man is Banning. How does that tally with the accident at Offham?'

'Not very tidily. For instance, if Banning was in the Morris when it crashed, what happened to his companion

91

when they scarpered? Why didn't they stick together? Particularly if, as Wilson thought, the companion was a woman.'

'Wilson assumed it to be Mrs Banning,' Baker said. 'We know it wasn't. It could have been a man, and I can think of several reasons why they might have separated. So don't let's worry about the companion, Jimmy. Not at this stage. First things first. Stick to Banning.'

'All right. But there's also the time factor. Banning could easily have walked the five miles from Offham to Chailey by midnight, which is the absolute deadline. But Medwin reckons he was there earlier. It seems that at nine o'clock that evening one of the local residents noticed a Morris Thousand similar to Banning's parked near where he was found. Medwin argues that this fixes the time he was dumped.'

'And you agree?'

'Well — yes.' Kane looked his surprise. 'Don't you, sir?'

'Perhaps. However, if Medwin is right, then Banning wasn't in the car when it crashed. What's your alternative?'

To Kane the alternative was obvious. Somewhere between Croydon and Chailey Banning had given a lift to a couple of hoodlums who had attacked and robbed him, dumped him on the common, and driven off in the Morris. 'Don't ask me where they got to during the next hour, or why they didn't abandon the car sooner, or why they were apparently doubling back on their tracks when they crashed. I just wouldn't know. But it explains why they bolted, and to my mind that's the real puzzle.'

'Ummmm!' In general the superintendent disapproved of theory in crime detection. It tended to bend the facts. 'It doesn't explain what Banning was doing in Sussex, or why Wilson was chasing him. However, Banning can't talk and Wilson won't, so we'll have to let that ride for the present.' He frowned, swinging the spectacles like a pendulum between finger and thumb. 'Wilson doesn't seem to fit, does he? And yet he's right there, bang in the middle of the picture. I wonder — Yes? What is it, Dutton?'

A uniformed sergeant was at the door. He said, 'There's a man downstairs you might like to see, sir. Name of Worsfold. He claims to have information concerning the accident at Offham last night.'

'Does he, indeed! Bring him right up.'

Mr Worsfold was a burly man, bearded and bewhiskered, garrulous and confident. He explained that he lived in Plumpton, where he was cowman for a local farmer, and that his wife occasionally took in lodgers. 'Nothing permanent, you understand, sir. Just the odd bed-and-breakfast.' The cigarette he had accepted was burning perilously close to the beard. He did not remove it from his lips as he talked. Kane watched it jig up and down, and wondered when the conflagration would start. 'There's a young chap calls hisself Dick Smith been staying with us since Monday. Hitch-hiker from London. He saw the sign in the window and come in.' Mr Worsfold scratched a hairy cheek. 'I don't know where he got to Tuesday, but Wednesday morning he sort of hung around. Said he was a bit pushed for cash, and couldn't afford café prices for his dinner. So the missus give him some bread and cheese, and off he went.'

'Not to return, eh?' With one eye on the clock, Kane was ready to write off Mr Worsfold and his lodger as a waste of time.

'That he did, sir. Walked in about half past ten, just as we was going to bed. And a right proper mess he looked, too.' The cigarette ash curved and fell, bespattering the beard with grey. 'Covered in muck he was, with his clothes torn, and bleeding like a stuck pig. He said he'd been to Plumpton races, and that he'd spent the evening in Lewes. He'd missed the last bus, he said, so he had to walk; but instead of sticking to the road he'd tried a short cut across the fields what some chap had told him of, and got proper lost. He said the mud come from the ditches he'd fallen into, and that he'd torn his clothes and scratched hisself on barbed wire.'

Kane's weariness slipped from him, and he gave a quick look at the superintendent. This was more like it.

Baker shrugged. To Worsfold he said, 'Is Smith still with you?'

'No, sir. He left early this morning. Said he was going to spend a few days in Brighton, see a bit of life. We was kind of surprised at that, seeing as how we knew he hadn't much money. But he said he'd won quite a tidy sum at the races.'

He took the cigarette from his mouth, decided it was too small to replace, and continued to hold it. Kane passed him an ashtray.

'And what decided you to come to us, Mr Worsfold?' he asked.

'It was when we heard about the accident at Offham, sir, and how this couple had run off across the fields.' Mr Worsfold stubbed out the butt. His fingers were broad and squat, the nails square. 'The missus reckoned it couldn't be nothing to do with Dick, seeing as how he didn't know anyone in these parts and we'd heard there was two of them in the car. But I wasn't so sure. He'd spent the evening in a pub, you see, and young chaps like him soon get to talking when there's a drop of beer inside 'em. Maybe he'd met some one from out our way, I said, and when they found they'd missed the last bus they'd started to walk home together. But five miles is a tidy step to them what's used to London buses and tubes, I said, and a young city chap like Dick — well, I don't reckon he'd be above borrowing a car to take hisself home if he come across one what was just waiting to be driven away. I mean — well, they'd been on the beer, hadn't they? It might seem a bit of a lark, really. But the accident, now — that'd sober 'em up good and proper, that would. They'd be plumb scared of what would happen if they was caught. I reckon it was plain natural for them to run.' He looked from one to the other of the two detectives, seeking approval. 'Anyways, that's how I seen it.'

Kane nodded. Baker said, 'And very logical too, Mr Worsfold. And thank you for your co-operation. A pity there aren't more of your sort around. It would ease the work of the police considerably.' '

Mr Worsfold beamed his pleasure. He said, 'I'd have come earlier if I hadn't wanted to check up first.'

The superintendent stared at him. 'Check up on what?'

'Well, sir, there was that bit about the barbed wire. I mean, it didn't rightly seem to fit. That's hunting country, you see, and barbed wire ain't popular. So I made a few inquiries, and it seems as how there ain't no barbed wire. Not the way Dick said he'd come.' The beam broadened as he took a small green booklet from an inside pocket and started to thumb the pages. 'And then there's the buses. It says here that the last bus leaves Lewes for Plumpton at nine fifty-one, so if Dick missed it he couldn't have started walking before then, could he? But he was back at our place not more'n a few minutes after half past ten, and that's a good five miles from Lewes.' He shook his head, scattering ash from the beard. 'He couldn't have done it on foot, sir, and that's a fact. Not even if he'd taken all the short cuts — which he wouldn't, him being a stranger.'

Baker banged his fist on the desk.

'You're dead right he couldn't! Mr

Worsfold, you're not only public-spirited, you're a bloody genius. Right! So your pal Smith had transport. And not just a lift, or he'd have said so. Looks cut and dried, doesn't it?' In his enthusiasm he forgot his dislike of hasty conclusions. 'I expect Mrs Worsfold has already tidied the chap's room; but ask her not to do any more until we've had a chance to check for fingerprints, will you? They might tally with some of the assortment we got from the Morris.' He put on his spectacles and drew a memo pad towards him. 'Now, let's have a description of this Smith character, shall we?'

Listening to the description, Kane reflected that Mr Worsfold might be co-operative and possess a logical, intuitive mind, but he had a poor eye for detail. He could not bring his late lodger alive for them. Dick Smith remained a vague, shadowy young man.

If Baker was disappointed he did not show it. His thanks sounded genuine.

'I suppose you didn't see any of this money that Smith claimed to have won at the races?' he asked. 'How much was it, by the way? Did he say?'

'No, sir, he didn't. But I reckon he won it, all right. How else would he be able to afford an evening's drinking, buy hisself a watch, and then go off to Brighton for a bit of life?' He picked up his cap and stuck it on his head. The cap, thought Kane, looked incongruous above so much hair. 'Must have been quite a tidy sum, I'd say.'

Baker sat very erect, staring at him wide-eyed.

'He bought himself a watch? When? What sort of a watch?'

Mr Worsfold looked surprised at the question, at the intensity of the superintendent's tone.

'Just a wrist-watch. Nothing special. He was wearing it when he come home last night; said he'd bought it off a chap in the pub. And I reckon he must have done. He weren't wearing it before.'

6

They sat in the car and watched the moon on the water and listened to the waves breaking gently on the shore. It was a warm, still evening, and surprisingly quiet down by the King Alfred. Occasional cars and pedestrians drifted past, but the buildings screened them from the main noise and bustle of the town.

Doris leaned back and stretched her legs.

'Peaceful, isn't it?' She sighed contentedly. 'I've enjoyed this evening, Vince. That was a fabulous meal. I don't know when I've eaten so much. I must have gained pounds.'

It had been Vince's idea that they should dine out, although the girl's expressed preference for Brighton had at first caused him some misgiving. Chug would be in Brighton, and Chug was someone he did not want to meet. But on reflection he had decided that the risk

101

was small. Brighton was a big place, and Chug would not be eating in the more expensive restaurants; he hadn't the money, and it wasn't his line. It was a fair bet that they would not be bothered by Chug.

He tapped the ash from his cigar and turned to look at her. Her face was even lovelier in profile, with the too-square chin hidden, and the classical line of forehead and nose seen to perfection.

'You don't want to let a few pounds worry you,' he said.

'They don't. I'm feeling fine.'

He was feeling pretty good himself. The dinner, the wines, the girl's beauty, had combined to intoxicate him, to stimulate him to a sense of well-being, of importance, that he had not hitherto known. He had stridden through the evening like a king. But now, alone with the girl in the dark proximity of the car, he was a little less sure of himself. He knew what he wanted. The problem was how to achieve it.

Light (was it moonlight or lamplight?) glinted on the girl's hair and nylon-clad legs, her posture emphasized the long line of her throat and the upward thrust of her breasts. He said thickly, 'You look good enough to eat.'

She turned her head sideways to look at him, and laughed.

'Haven't you eaten enough for one evening?'

She had been sincere when she said she had enjoyed the evening. Vince had been a new and delightful experience. Other men had entertained her, had spent money on her; but not like Vince. Mostly they had spent grudgingly — yet ostentatiously, seeking to impress, in the expectation of a quick return for their money. They had spent for their own pleasure, not for hers; and when their expectations had not been realized they had stopped spending. Most unpleasant of all, they had been elderly, dull men, trying to buy with their wealth what in themselves they no longer had the power to attract. It had not been like that with Vince. Vince was young, he was handsome, he was gay, he spent money with the happy abandon of a man who enjoyed spending and with the bottom of his purse a long way off. He would not be a man, she thought, if he did not hope for something in return. But at least he did not make it so obvious a condition of his spending.

She opened her eyes wide, slid her head a little closer to his. A wild, roseate dream was already germinating in her mind — a dream of wealth and gaiety and illimitable possessions. Even the realization that to make the dream permanent she would have to marry Vince did not discourage her. Hitherto she had regarded matrimony with distaste, seeing it as a dull, grubby, even degrading way of life; it admitted defeat of oneself as a person, it marked the end of independence and the beginning of a thinly disguised form of slavery. But need it be like that with Vince? She was not in love with him, he aroused no ardent, sensual impulse in her. No man had. But she liked him, he made her feel good; he was young and he was rich. Wasn't that enough to make a marriage work?

'The wind's getting up,' Vince said.

It wasn't. But he had to say something; the silence was growing too long. He wondered if she could hear the way his heart was thumping. He had seen the movement of her head, had thought he knew what it implied. With any of the girls back home he would have been sure. But with Doris . . .

He threw the cigar out of the window and braced himself. They're all the same, Vince boy, he assured himself. This one is smoother and classier, but fundamentally she's like all the rest. So what are you waiting for? It's why you're here, isn't it?

Her body was soft and yielding as she slipped into his embrace, her lips cool. He was gentle with her at first, savouring the moment. But as his ardour mounted his hold tightened, his kisses grew fiercer. Had he been calmer he would have been aware that her response was passive, that he had touched no sensual chord; for the moment it was enough that she did not reject him. But not for long. His right hand found her breast, cupped it and held it, fingering its resilience under the soft lace. Momentarily her body stiffened;

then she relaxed and lay still. Emboldened by her acquiescence his hand shifted to her knee, stroking the soft, nylon-clad flesh, moving purposefully.

She caught his hand, to lift it and hold it tightly as she drew away.

'Don't, Vince.' Her voice was muffled. 'Please!'

He went suddenly cold, his self-confidence shattered by the unexpected rebuff. From the moment he had walked into the hotel at Lewes everything had gone his way, building up his assurance, giving him confidence. He had been riding on the crest of a wave. Now the wave had broken, and he was lost. Had Doris been a casual pick-up he would have fought her, tried to force her into submission; and if he had failed he would have slapped her face and left her, with the comforting reflection that there were better fish elsewhere. But they did not come any better than Doris. Not in his little pool.

Yet he could not be mistaken in her. Not after that letter, after that coy little scene in the hotel bar. It must be his tactics that were wrong; she was used to a certain technique, and without it she wasn't playing. In his ignorance he had made a mess of it. So what now? Did he try force, did he cajole, did he gracefully desist on the tacit understanding that this was merely a postponement, not an end? Or did he throw in his hand and start again later from cold?

He did not know. And in his indecision he did nothing.

'Don't be cross, Vince,' she pleaded. 'Don't spoil the evening.' She squeezed his hand with both of hers. 'I mean — well, this isn't really the place for that sort of thing, is it?'

He felt better at that. It was less damaging to his ego, it hinted at eventual surrender even if it did not actually promise. He withdrew his hand, and with trembling fingers lit a cigarette. His body felt weak, drained of all vitality.

'Sure you're not cross?' He shook his head, and she sat up and patted her hair and smoothed her frock down over her knees. 'Good. Now, may I have a cigarette too?'

He gave her his and lit another. Inhaling deeply to steady his nerves, he said, 'Sorry I got fresh. But it's your own fault. I told you you looked good enough to eat, didn't I? Well, I guess my appetite got the upper hand.' He turned to her and smiled, hoping he looked and sounded nonchalant and knowing he didn't. 'What say we go some place for a drink?'

She accepted the invitation with enthusiasm. She did not want a drink, but it offered a graceful exit from an awkward situation.

'Wait while I do my face,' she said.

A Brighton pub in the holiday season is no place for a quiet drink. But Vince did not want quiet. He felt like champagne gone flat; the sparkle had left him, and he needed noise and bustle and outside human contact to restore it. Above all, he needed a drink.

The pub had a horseshoe bar, with the saloon lounge on one side and the public bar on the other. A tip to the waiter got them a small table in the lounge, and after his third gin Vince felt more cheerful. He did not notice that the girl only sipped at hers. He supposed that her spirits were reviving with his, and he said, 'What say we move on? From Lewes, I mean. It's not all that gay for a holiday.'

'You know I can't. There's Uncle. What would I do about him?'

He finished his gin and beckoned the waiter. He had expected her to refuse, just as he expected her finally to accept. Her behaviour in the car was beginning to make sense. She was playing hard to get, raising the ante.

'Nothing.' Confidence was returning. 'If you haven't heard from him by morning you can scrub him. So where do we go? Eastbourne? Hastings? It's on me, don't forget. All you have to do is tag along.' The dimples were back as he smiled at her. 'How about it?'

'I don't know.' She leaned towards him across the table and touched his hand. Her long, tapering nails curved inward at the points, he felt them scrape lightly across his skin. 'It's sweet of you to offer, Vince, but — well, can we leave it till the morning? I don't have to decide right now, do I?'

He was prepared to wait. He knew what her eventual answer would be.

After his fourth gin he felt slightly light-headed. Beer was his usual tipple, but it had seemed inappropriate to the occasion. He moved his chair closer to hers, found one of her hands and held it, letting the back of his hand rest on her thigh. She did not object. He could feel the warmth travel up his arm and flood his body, and suddenly he was impatient of the pub and the people and the noisy chatter, he wanted to be back in the dark privacy of the car.

He squeezed her hand. 'Let's go, shall we? It's hot in here.'

'All right.' But she made no move to rise. She was gazing over his shoulder. 'Do you know anyone in Brighton, Vince?'

'No. Why?'

'A man in the other bar has been staring at us hard for the last five minutes.'

'At you, you mean. And why wouldn't he?'

He turned to follow her gaze. She could not see his face, but the sudden, involuntary pressure of his hand on hers caused her to squeal in protest. He made no apology. The pressure relaxed, and he drew his hand away. When he turned to her again there was a glitter in the dark, slanting eyes, the skin seemed to have tightened over the cheekbones, his mouth was a thin, hard line.

'Listen, Doris. And listen good.' He spoke in a hoarse whisper, although the watcher in the public bar was too distant to overhear. 'Remember I wasn't dead keen on coming to Brighton this evening? Well, he's the reason. I didn't know he was here, but I thought he might be. And he hates my guts. He's got it into his stupid head that I swindled him on a business deal — the details don't matter — and he's all set to get even.'

'Did you swindle him?' she asked, troubled.

'Hell, no! But that's not the point. He thinks I did, and when we leave here I'm damned sure he'll follow. He could turn real nasty. So we'll separate; I'm not dragging you into this. Give me a few minutes start, and then make for the car. You know where it is?' She nodded, and he slipped a key into her hand. 'Wait for me there. I shan't be long.'

'But why?' There was fear in her eyes. 'I mean — well, wouldn't it be better to call the police? He wouldn't dare molest us then.'

'Not us. Me. You're safe enough. And I don't want the police interfering. This is a private squabble.' He patted her knee. The contact made no impact on his senses. 'Don't panic, love. I can handle him.'

She glanced quickly across at the watcher, and then away.

'He looks an ugly customer,' she said, and shivered.

'He's ugly, all right. But he's slow. He hasn't got it here.' He tapped his forehead, gave her a wolfish grin, and stood up. 'Well, I'm off. Be seeing you.'

As he made for the door the man in the other bar put his glass to his mouth and tilted back his head, swallowing furiously. Vince did not stay to watch; Chug's

112

greedy thirst might give him the few seconds' start he needed. Out on the street he turned right, pushing his way impatiently through the pavement strollers; not looking round to see if Chug were following, accepting pursuit as inevitable. Now was the danger, with the crowds hampering him. He had to get clear; there was no protection in people. Once Chug caught up with him there would be no escape. Chug would stay with him; there would be an inexorable grip on his arm, he would be steered to some lonely spot with no witness to the inevitable retribution that would follow. It would be painful and thorough. There were no half measures about Chug Wallis when it came to exacting vengeance.

He turned right again. With relief he saw that the street was narrow and dark, and practically devoid of people. He broke into a run, knowing that in speed lay his safety. He could not match Chug for brute strength or ruthless savagery, but he had him beat when it came to speed. Chug would not catch him now.

Running swiftly and easily, his crêpe

113

soles padding softly over the pavement, he was well down the street before he heard the sound of Chug's footsteps behind him. It was an uneven, lolloping sound, with the weight coming down more on one foot than the other, and it brought him encouragement rather than dismay. It told him that already he was out-distancing his pursuer.

But it was not enough to out-distance Chug. He had to lose him completely before he dared make for the car. The mouth of a narrow alley yawned out of the darkness to his right, and he turned down it. This would be one of the famous Brighton Lanes. The area was strange to him, but he had heard enough to believe that in that maze of little streets and alleys Chug would have no chance of finding him.

He ran on down the Lanes, following one blindly until he turned into another, unheedful of the little shops with their displays of trinkets and glass and furniture and books behind bottle-green windows or dusty, open panes. It did not matter that he was lost. Eventually he must debouch on to a main street. He could find his way from there.

He dropped reluctantly to a walk, his stamina unequal to his speed. There was no sound of pursuit, and presently he leant against a wall, taking in gulps of the night air until his breathing slowed and his heart ceased to hammer. Above the buildings the sky glowed from the lights of the town, but the alley was narrow and dark. He wondered whether to go on or turn back. His hurry now was to return to the girl.

He went on. Walking swiftly, he came to a T-junction illumined by a lamp high on the wall, and he turned left in the general direction of the sea. The walls were high, but enough light shone from the scattered windows to show him, after several twists and turns, that this was a dead end. Cursing his ill luck, he started back. Doris would be getting impatient.

It was then he heard the footsteps.

He knew at once that they were Chug's. No one but Chug would be running down those Lanes, and there was no mistaking that uneven tread. Panicking, he broke into a run himself, the perspiration on his body no longer caused solely through exertion. In that dark, deserted maze an encounter with Chug could be murderous. And unless he reached the junction first he was trapped.

He did not reach it first. He rounded the final bend to see a stocky figure in jeans and dark jersey standing irresolute under the lamp. He was peering down the far branch of the alley, and with returning hope Vince realized his pursuer was as lost as himself, that chance alone had brought him there. If Chug should choose to go the other way . . .

He was moving back into the shadow of the wall when Chug turned and saw him.

For a brief moment both were still; the one from fear, the other from surprise. Then Vince turned and ran, and without a word Chug came after him, his awkward gait bringing an echoing tattoo from the close, high walls.

Vince had run because to run had been instinctive. Yet even as he ran he knew that he was merely delaying the inevitable. There was no escape that way. In a few seconds he would come to the end of the alley and would have to turn and fight. No, not fight — that was the wrong word; the encounter would be more in the nature of a massacre. Their short partnership had always been uneasy, with himself supplying the brains and Chug the brute strength. Hitherto brains had been predominant. Now it was the turn of strength.

And Chug would know it.

Or would he? With that doubt came a thin ray of hope. For Chug could not know that this was a dead end; he would expect Vince to go on running, perhaps even expect to lose him as he had lost him before. But what if flight were suddenly switched to attack? How would Chug's moronic brain cope with such an unexpected reversal of tactics?

It was a gamble of despair, but Vince took it. He slowed to a stop and turned. Chug was a few yards away; he ran leaning forward, so that his face was in shadow, and with dismay Vince saw the knife in his right hand. But it made no difference; he was already committed. Now Chug was so near that he could hear his loud breathing, could smell the rank odour that he emitted when agitated. Instinct told Vince how the attack would come, and as his opponent's arm swung back for the strike he braced himself against the wall and brought his foot up in a swift, vicious kick. It caught Chug full in the crutch, and with a howl of pain he doubled up, dropping the knife as he clapped both hands to his body. Vince gave him no time to recover. He kicked again, not caring where the foot landed, and smashed a fist into the dark, unshaven face. Chug went down, screaming.

Vince gloated over him as he writhed on the ground. He had always affected to despise the use of force and the infliction of pain, contemptuously dismissing them as barbaric. Even to himself he had been reluctant to admit the truth — that he shunned them because he was afraid. Yet he knew it was so; knew it from the vicarious pleasure he received as a frequent spectator at boxing and wrestling matches, from witnessing the bloody fights among his acquaintances and their savage use of the boot and the knife. Now his pleasure was so intense that it was almost pain to contain it. He wanted to shout it aloud, to hear it echo down the alley. That writhing creature at his feet was Chug; Chug the ruthless, Chug the indestructible. And he, Vince Harding, had put him there.

The writhing body stilled. A hand reached out, exploring the cobbles for the knife. Vince kicked the knife away, put his heel on the hand and screwed it into the ground. Then, breathing hard, he stood back and listened with delight to his victim's howls of agony.

'Go on — yell, you bastard!' He shouted the words viciously. 'Yell your bloody head off. Who the hell cares?'

Unable to resist the temptation, he lashed out again with his foot, careless of where he struck.

It was a full minute before sanity returned and elation turned slowly to doubt and doubt to fear. Fear that was cold and numbing in its intensity as, with terrifying clarity, he realized what he had done. For his triumph was also his condemnation. By a lucky stroke he had achieved victory to-night, but there would be no victory for him next time. And there had to be a next time. Chug would see to that.

He shuddered. Even in cold blood Chug had no inhibitions where savagery was concerned. With the hate that would be in him now violence would no longer satisfy; he would be consumed with a burning determination to destroy. Only the total annihilation of his enemy, of the man who had first cheated and then humiliated him, would satiate Chug's lust for vengeance now.

That was inevitable. Unless — unless Chug were himself destroyed.

Wide-eyed, Vince stared at the man on the ground. Chug lay on his side, hands still pressed to belly and groin. He had stopped groaning. A low babble of curses issued from his saliva-flecked lips, and even in the dark Vince could see the wrathful glitter in his eyes.

And a few feet away lay the knife.

As though impelled by some outside force, Vince bent to it, grasping the handle firmly. But it was the grip of fear, not of determination. His body was cold and his stomach sick at the thought of what he was about to do. What had gone before had been done in a flurry of despair, without thought or reason. But this — this was cold-blooded murder. Yet he had to do it. It was kill or be killed.

He took a step forward. Chug saw the movement, saw the knife in his hand. Still cursing, he rolled over on to his stomach, scrabbling at the cobbles with hands and feet in a frantic effort to get up. There was no appeal for mercy. It was not in Chug's nature to beg. Not even for his life.

Slowly, almost wearily, Vince bent his arm and leaned forward to strike. Chug's broad back was immediately beneath him, he could smell the rank sweat, see the red boils on his hairy neck. In a brief moment Chug would be on his feet and the opportunity would be gone. He had to strike now.

'Now!'

Even as he shouted the word aloud he knew he could not do it. There was something in him that would not let him take that final, terrible step to self-preservation. Sobbing with rage at his inefficacy, he dropped the knife and ran.

He stopped running when he left the Lanes. The car park was not far away, and he needed to regain his self-control before he reached it. Fear of Chug was still with him, would remain with him, but uppermost in his mind was anger. Anger at himself. He was weak, a coward. He had had his enemy at his mercy and he had let him go. His nerve, his manhood, had failed him.

Doris was standing by the car. Her relief at his return was great.

'I thought you were never coming,' she said. 'What happened?'

'Nothing much. We had a bit of a barney, that's all.'

He took her in his arms and kissed her; he needed her warmth, her closeness, to calm his distress. She did not protest, the pressure of her lips was firmer than before. But as she drew away she gave an exclamation and gripped his arm.

'He's followed you, Vince. Look! Over there. That's him, isn't it?'

He swung round. Chug was coming down the hill, his stocky figure and rolling gait unmistakable under the lights. He was less than a hundred yards away.

'Quick! Get in!' He ran round the back of the car and scrambled into the driver's seat. Chug might not have seen them, he could have come that way by accident. But Vince was taking no chances. It seemed to him then that he would never take chances again.

The two doors slammed almost simultaneously as the engine came to life. As they drove out of the park Doris said, 'Why did he follow you? Didn't you settle your argument?'

Vince grunted. With the Zephyr's acceleration his courage was returning.

'He's a difficult chap to convince. Pig-headed. Won't listen to reason.'

'He looks repulsive.' She shuddered. 'I hope we don't bump into him again.'

'That makes two of us,' Vince said.

7

'What particularly concerns me,' Hugh Westwood said, 'is the fact that you were following Banning. Why? Did you know his errand in Lewes?'

Wilson shook his head. 'It was just a coincidence, Mr Westwood. I followed him out of curiosity. I'd understood he was going to Yorkshire, not Sussex.'

'I see.' The manager's tone had been unusually mild. Now it sharpened. 'And what, may I ask, were you doing in Lewes?'

'It was a private matter, Mr Westwood. I'd rather not say.'

'You'd rather not say!' Westwood swung sideways in the big swivel chair and surveyed the tall figure of his employee from an angle, as though that might perhaps make him appear more personable. 'You borrow the company's car without authority, you smash the damned thing up after chasing round the country on the company's petrol, and you prefer not to say why!' His voice was bitingly sarcastic. 'You're not only a thief, Wilson, you're a fool. And there's no room in this company for either.'

George Wilson said nothing. His chest and his knee still hurt, but he lacked the courage to ask if he might be seated. Dejected and spiritless, he stood before the massive desk like a human scarecrow; thin and angular and drooping, his jacket looking as though it were about to slide from his sloping shoulders and down the length of his long body.

'Well?' Westwood demanded.

The grey eyes looked at him, then shifted to the desk.

'I know I should have asked your permission before taking the car. But I couldn't get hold of you, and the matter was urgent, so — ' He lifted his long arms, and let them drop in a gesture of despair. 'Well, I just took it. There was no alternative. I'll pay for the petrol, of course, and I'm sorry about the damage to the car. But the insurance will take care of that, won't it?'

Slowly the chair swung back. Westwood removed the heavy spectacles, leaning forward to rest his elbows on the desk. His bulging eyes glared at Wilson.

'You think so? You're wrong, you know. *You'll* take care of it, Wilson. In full. It is up to the company, of course, to decide whether or not to prosecute, but I know what my advice would be.' He paused. 'As for your future here — frankly, I doubt if you have one.'

'You mean I'm likely to be sacked?'

'Does that surprise you?'

It did not surprise him. He had known when he took the car that he was putting his future in jeopardy; the accident had merely shortened the odds. Now it seemed that in addition to dismissal he was also to bear the cost of the damage, that the company might even sue him. And at fifty-nine, and without a reference, he would be practically unemployable.

The knowledge gave him a new courage. In the past he had been servile, both from a sense of insecurity and because Westwood was the type of boss who demanded servility. Now, with his job as good as lost, there was no further need to grovel.

But the habit of years was not to be dropped like a cloak. He avoided the manager's eyes as he said quietly, 'That's rather uncalled for, don't you think? I mean — well, look at Banning. It's only a few weeks since his annual holiday, yet you give him a long week-end *and* the use of the car. And that was simply for pleasure.' As the sense of injustice grew in him his voice hardened. 'I gather the Morris is a complete write-off. No wonder he bolted, seeing that the accident was entirely his fault. So what happens to Banning? Does he get the sack too?'

Westwood was so startled that he forgot to be angry. With a slight wave of a well-manicured hand he brushed the question and its implication aside.

'Banning asked my permission. You did not.' He was reaching for the in-tray when a new thought occurred to him. Hand poised above the pile of correspondence, he stared hard at Wilson. 'Who told you he was using the car for pleasure?'

'He did.'

'H'm!' The hand dropped. 'Well, no doubt he did not want his private affairs made public. From what he told me I gather he had some urgent family business to attend to.' His eyes narrowed. 'Odd, wasn't it, that you should both be in Lewes at the same time and on apparently similar errands? Quite sure there was no connexion?'

Wilson wanted to tell him to go to hell, but his new courage was unequal to it.

'I told you — no.' He spoke with what dignity he could muster. But this was dangerous ground, and he could see that Westwood did not believe him. Seeking a new angle, he said, 'Have you heard from Banning yet?'

'Not yet.'

The carriage clock on the desk showed nine-thirty. To Wilson it offered an excuse to escape. He said smoothly, 'Well, I'd better get moving, Mr Westwood. It's late. Or was there anything else?'

'Just one thing.' Westwood transferred a pile of correspondence from tray to blotter, and reached for a side drawer. 'I gather you were in something of a hurry when you came in yesterday morning. In and out like a flash, according to Vance. Was that devotion to duty? Or had you another reason, perhaps?'

Wilson shifted his feet, wincing at the heavy sarcasm.

'I wasn't trying to avoid you, Mr Westwood, if that's what you're thinking. It was just that, being without a car, I knew I'd have a job to get through the day's work. As a matter of fact, it was after nine before I'd finished. That's why I didn't call back in the evening.'

'I see.' Westwood pulled open the drawer. 'Luckily for you it didn't rain; you left your raincoat downstairs. I found this in the pocket. It seems to demand an explanation.'

Like a conjuror producing a rabbit from a hat, he drew a heavy service revolver from the drawer and laid it on the desk.

Wilson gaped at it, startled as well as frightened. He had forgotten the revolver — an old four-five which had come into his possession after the War (he could not

129

remember exactly how or when) and which had become one of the many useless objects he had hoarded over the years. He could not even remember why he had gone to that particular drawer before leaving the flat on Wednesday evening. But there the revolver was — and on impulse he had thrust it into his pocket. He had had no clearly defined purpose in taking it, but at the back of his mind had been the vague thought that its possession was relevant to his errand.

He wished once again that he had left the damned thing in the drawer. It had been of more danger to himself than to anyone else. When the sergeant at Lewes had picked up the raincoat and remarked on its weight he had nearly had heart failure. But this — this could be worse. Westwood had him on the hook — and Westwood would see to it that he did not wriggle off.

His lips moved silently, reluctant to utter the words they framed. As the silence grew Westwood said, 'I imagine you don't make a habit of carrying this around, so you must have had a particular need for it on Wednesday. Had it anything to do with Banning?'

'No.' The denial was a mere squeak, and he cleared his throat. 'Honestly, Mr Westwood, I don't know why I took it. It was the sort of stupid thing one does without thinking.'

He knew it to be a thoroughly inadequate explanation, but Westwood seemed to accept it. He said, spinning the chamber, 'Does one? How odd. It's loaded, I see. Four rounds.'

'Good Lord!' Wilson looked shocked. 'I didn't know.'

'I'm sure you didn't. Have you a licence for it, by the way?'

'No. No, I don't think so. You see, it's been tucked away in a drawer for years. Ever since the War. I'd forgotten all about it until I came across it on Wednesday.' It dawned on him that here was a more plausible explanation than the one he had already given. He said eagerly, 'That's why I took it with me, you see. I was going to get rid of it.'

Westwood lit a cigarette. He took his time over it, watching the dejected Wilson through half-closed eyes. It amused him to see the man sweat.

'I'm not a fool, Wilson. Don't expect me to swallow a half-baked story like that. It's my belief you and your damned gun are connected in some way with Banning's disappearance. Isn't that so?'

'No, Mr Westwood, it isn't.' Wilson tried to match the other's unblinking gaze, but the task was beyond him. He said earnestly, 'I know no more of what has happened to Banning than you do. That I swear.'

Westwood continued to stare at him, letting the smoke drift slowly from pursed lips. Eventually he said, 'Well, if you say so.' He picked up the revolver and returned it to the drawer. 'All the same, I think I'll hang on to this. The police might find it interesting, don't you think?'

★ ★ ★

They were just finishing lunch when George Wilson called. Ruth said fretfully, 'Help me clear the table, Philip, will you? There's some one at the door. Just put the things in the kitchen.' She glanced at the ornate marble clock that stood on the sideboard; it was too big for the mantelpiece. 'Heavens! Nearly three o'clock! I didn't realize it was so late.'

The caller's appearance was vaguely familiar to her, but she could not place him until he introduced himself. 'We have only just heard at the office of your husband's accident,' he said, following her into the sitting-room with bent head. At six foot three, necessity made stooping a habit. 'Most distressing. I felt I must offer you my sympathy.'

Behind the visitor's back Philip grimaced; he found the smooth, unctuous tone amusing. But to Ruth its solemnity showed a proper solicitude; still wearing her apron, she thanked him and asked him to sit down. 'I'm all behind,' she explained, frowning at the sudden giggle which this ambiguous statement elicited from her son. 'Luckily Philip's been given the afternoon off. But I've only just got back from the hospital. The police called for me. They weren't sure, you see, that it was Arthur.'

Wilson nodded. He sat on the edge of the worn and faded chair, looking worn and faded himself, his long arms, cap in hand, dangling between his legs. The morning round had been an ordeal; still tormented by the fear that had prompted his sudden journey into Sussex, haunted by the threat of unemployment and trouble with the police over the revolver, he had been unable to cope intelligently with rent-books and figures and the quirks of tenants. But the threat of unemployment was not new; he had lived with it for years. He was uncertain how seriously the police would view his possession of the revolver, but there was the possibility that Westwood would not mention it to them; not out of consideration for an employee, but because it would be poor publicity for the company. The possibility became almost a probability when he learned at the office after lunch that Banning had been found — injured, but not by a bullet.

But the other, the most dominant anxiety — that he could not subdue. That was why he was here now.

'How is he, Mrs Banning?' he asked.

Ruth's eyes were red, and she looked flushed. But there were no tears.

'He's still unconscious. They say he's got a chance, but to me he looked terrible. So white and so — so empty. As though he were dead already.'

Her dishevelled state, her obvious distress, troubled him. But he could not leave it there. He had to keep probing.

'Do the police know how it happened?'

'Not really. Only that he was beaten up and left on the common. He was there all night, they say.' She sighed. 'I suppose some one thought he had money. But he hadn't, of course. Just a few pounds.' Pride forbade her to add that Arthur never had more than a few pounds in his pocket. 'None of his clothes and things were taken, although they must have searched his suitcase. The police say it was all mussed up when they found it.'

Banning's health as such did not interest Wilson; for all he cared the man could die of his injuries. It was Banning's secret that mattered, and that was one intimacy Banning was unlikely to have

135

shared with his wife. Wilson hoped that he had not. Yet there must be something the woman could tell him, even if she were unaware of its significance.

'He told me he was going to Yorkshire,' he said. 'On holiday. Have you any idea what he was doing in Sussex?'

Philip was by the window, peering through the net curtains. 'Take the afternoon off,' Wort-face had said. 'Your mother will want a bit of sympathetic company at a time like this.' And Philip had delightedly agreed. But he had no intention of wasting a free afternoon at home. His first task had been to telephone Roddy, who was on holiday and had bought the M.G. They had arranged to try it out that afternoon before taking it down to Brighton the next day.

'That's what he told us,' he said. 'Only it was business, not a holiday. I suppose he knew you wouldn't buy that lark. I didn't either; I knew it was a phoney. But Mum did.'

Ruth shook her head. It was a negation of what her son had implied rather than what he said.

'Was it you telephoned Wednesday evening, Mr Wilson, after my husband had left?' she asked.

'That's right. I can't remember why.'

'You said it was important.'

'Did I? Some office query, I expect.' He stroked his moustache, knuckling the drooping hairs away from the corners of his mouth. 'Did they tell you at the hospital when he might be expected to recover consciousness?'

She shook her head.

Philip had been watching an approaching car. As it pulled up outside the house he said quickly, 'Here's the Bannings, Mum. They've got a Jag., haven't they?'

The information put Ruth into a turmoil of confusion. She had wanted to prepare herself for the Bannings; change her slippers and dress, bring some order to her hair. There was no time for that now.

'Arthur's brother,' she explained, getting up and hastily untying the apron. 'I telephoned him. He said he'd be coming.'

She pushed the apron under a cushion and shuffled to the oval mirror that hung above the tiled fireplace. The fireplace, pink and square and with a bronze fire-box, was the sole improvement No. 27 had seen since she and Arthur had moved in. It had been won only after a hard tussle with the landlord.

Watching her pushing and pulling at her hair, Wilson knew that the opportunity for further questioning had gone.

'I'll be getting along, Mrs Banning.' Ruth turned quickly, started to wipe her palm down the apron that wasn't there, and took his outstretched hand. It felt boneless, although the skin was coarse and hard. 'I'm spending to-night in Lewes, and I'll make a point of calling at the hospital. I do hope I'll find your husband better. And if I can be of any assistance don't hesitate to call on me.'

Philip let him out, waiting at the front door as his adopted uncle and aunt decanted themselves from the shining grey Jaguar. His feelings towards them were mixed. He resented them for stressing, albeit unintentionally, the drabness of his existence and the lack of advantages it offered, yet he admired them for their smartness, their obvious prosperity, their social glitter. Alone with his uncle, admiration tended to be uppermost. Mark Banning, to whom it was manna to be liked, who had to be the centre of interest in whatever company he found himself, flattered the youth by treating him as an equal; he could be amusing in a direct way, and was addicted to wisecracks and dirty stories. But he was a nervy, highly strung man who relied on whisky to keep him at peak form; without it he could be moody and irritable, and usually this had its effect on Philip. The latter was quick to reciprocate; resentment welled up in him, and any friendly advance was immediately rejected as patronage. This was even more marked when his aunt was present. She made him feel awkward and inferior, and guiltily aware of the difference between herself and his mother. Since, in his selfish way, he was fond of his mother, he was ashamed of this disloyalty, and subconsciously blamed his aunt. He thought her arrogant and aloofly condescending, whereas she was in fact too shy, too narrow in her outlook, to know how to unbend. Within her own close circle, with those whose interests and way of life were similar to her own, she could be charming, at times almost vivacious. Yet even with them she had her inhibitions. Arthur, in one of his rare moments of insight, had said that Carol Banning could never be completely herself because neither she nor anyone else knew exactly what her self was.

And she had no sense of humour.

'Got the bailiffs in?' Mark Banning gazed after the departing Wilson as he shook hands with his adopted nephew. He seldom looked long at the person he was addressing. His hands were slender and supple, his grip half-hearted. 'Seedy looking type. But long. Definitely long.'

Philip's grin was forced. The query was too near the possible to be amusing.

'One of Arthur's mates.' He turned the grin to a nervous laugh. Only recently had he started referring to his stepfather by his Christian name. He was uncertain of the reception his uncle would accord such familiarity.

Mark Banning was twelve years younger than his brother, and as unlike him in appearance as he was in character. Around six feet in height, he had a large head set on narrow shoulders from which his lean body seemed to taper to slim hips and tiny feet — the leanness and the taper being accentuated by a well-fitting light-weight suit, long-jacketed and narrow-trousered. His face was oval in shape, pale and small-featured and with a narrow ginger moustache; his hair, carefully brushed back, had started to thin. He paid regular visits to his barber, his manicurist, and his masseur, was fastidious about his linen, and femininely fussy over accessories.

'Poor old Arthur!' He had a nasal voice, clipping the words as though glad to be rid of them. 'How's your mother bearing up?'

'All right, I guess.'

'Good.' Mark put a confiding hand on the youth's shoulder. 'Between ourselves, old lad, I've been dreading this moment. Hysterical women drive me up the ruddy wall.'

They stood aside as Carol Banning stepped past them into the tiny hall. Philip looked at her briefly and then away. His chief perception of her was olfactory — a delicate aura of 'Miss Dior.'

As she greeted her sister-in-law Ruth was once more nervously aware of the gulf between them. Carol at thirty-three was a beautiful woman, tall and elegant and slow-moving, and built on generous lines. That afternoon she wore a light woollen suit that blended with her creamy skin and accentuated her dark hair and eyes. A straw hat trimmed in green crowned her shapely head, her gloves and handbag were of green suède. Over one shoulder was draped a mink stole. The faint smile on her face as she shook hands, the gently raised eyebrows, were expressive neither of contempt nor condescension. They were the outward indications of her inability to communicate.

'I'm so sorry for you both,' she said, her voice a soft contralto.

She sat down, crossing one leg over the other and removing the gloves to reveal a scintillating display of diamonds. The hemline was just above her knee, and Philip, who always found difficulty in meeting her cool, unblinking gaze, stared at the knee, fascinated by the glimpse of a generous thigh in the shadow of her skirt. He had no girl friends. His adolescent sexual impulses were translated into uncomfortable dreams, and visual revelations such as those provided by short skirts and low neck-lines and borrowed art studies.

Lolling back on the settee, occupying almost the whole of it, Mark Banning listened impatiently to what Ruth had to tell him. He was a poor listener, and kept shifting his position — smoking incessantly, yawning occasionally. Once he burped, and winked at Philip. Carol sat very still. It was her first visit to No. 27, and her eyes roved slowly round the room, inspecting its contents but revealing nothing of her thoughts. It was a small room, and over-crowded: a three-piece suite bought by Ruth's first husband and clumsily covered (Ruth was a poor needlewoman) with cretonne from which the pattern had almost faded; a glass-fronted Victorian bookcase, reaching to the ceiling and filled with books that were never read (Arthur had bought most of them in job lots); a nest of occasional tables veneered in light oak; a mahogany pedestal-lamp, its plain parchment shade badly scorched. The corner china cabinet was Ruth's most treasured possession, although her taste in china was catholic; the cabinet was crammed with pieces ranging from seaside souvenirs to delicate porcelain. There were pouffes on the floor and pictures on what wall space was available, and an overflow from the dining-room in the form of two mahogany straight-backed chairs.

'Damned bad luck!' Mark could not wait for Ruth to finish. He sat up, resting the ankle of one leg on the knee of the other and grasping the ankle firmly to anchor it. He was impatient of detail, impatient of his own silence. 'It beats me what Arthur was playing at. Still, nattering won't help; we'd better get down there, see what's to do. How long will it take you to pack, Ruth?'

'Pack?' She gaped at him.

'You're coming with us, my girl. At a time like this a wife's place is by her husband. Trite, but true.' Disengaging his long legs, he stood up and stretched. 'There must be a handy pub where we can put up for a few days. How about you, Philip? Care to tag along? It's on me, of course.'

'Sorry.' To Philip the 'of course' sounded like patronage. 'I can't make it. Got things to do. Anyway, I'm working tomorrow morning.'

'Please yourself.' Mark Banning seldom cajoled unless it suited his purpose. If people did not care to accept his arrangements he ignored them. 'Come on, Ruth. Get weaving.'

She shook her head. 'I couldn't. Not without Philip. I couldn't leave him here on his own.'

'Nonsense!' He put a friendly but compelling hand to her back. He wanted Ruth's company no more than he wanted her son's, but it was necessary to his vanity. 'Philip can look after himself. He's not a baby.'

'I'll be all right, Mum.' Pride urged Philip to agree with his uncle. And the prospect of a few days without maternal supervision was not displeasing. 'You go.'

Ruth continued to protest; but she was already defeated, and she knew it. As she plodded wearily up the stairs she wondered at Mark's newfound concern for his brother. He had shown none before, not even when Arthur had nearly died from pneumonia. There had not even been a postcard then, let alone a visit; he had called at the house when Arthur was back from hospital, but only to discuss insurance. Yet now he was willing to devote several days to fraternal attendance at the hospital. Why the change? Could it be the mystery that attracted him, or had she misjudged him?

Downstairs, Mark was fidgety. 'There wouldn't be a drink in the house?' he said to Philip. And then, 'No, of course not. I forgot; Arthur's T.T.' He shook his head. 'A sad blot on the family escutcheon. Now, who the devil's that?'

'That' was the front door bell. 'Probably Roddy,' Philip said. 'I thought I heard a car.'

It was Hugh Westwood, not Roddy. He came into the room looking almost as immaculate as Mark. Westwood had been impressed by the grey Jaguar; he was even more impressed by the younger Bannings. It had not occurred to him that Arthur might have such attractive and apparently affluent relatives. In his most cordial manner he expressed regret for Arthur's misfortune and for his own intrusion.

'I just want a few words with Mrs Banning. I shan't keep her long.' He was looking at Carol as he spoke. Smiling, he made her a slight bow. 'The elder Mrs Banning, I should say.'

Carol's dark eyes surveyed him levelly. Her answering smile was perfunctory. Mark said, 'She's upstairs. You'd better fetch her, Philip.'

Philip went into the hall and shouted. There was no reply, and with an exclamation of annoyance he banged his way up the stairs. Westwood said, 'I knew yesterday, of course, that your brother had disappeared, but it was only an hour ago that the police informed me he was in hospital.'

'Did they say how he was?'

'Pretty bad, I gather. He's still unconscious.'

Ruth disliked Hugh Westwood. On their few previous meetings he had been curt to the point of rudeness. Now his greeting was friendly and sympathetic, and again she wondered at the change. First Mark, and now Westwood.

'I must apologize for introducing business affairs at such a time, Mrs Banning, but I'm afraid it can't be helped. Something has cropped up which makes it imperative for me to speak with your husband as soon as possible.' Irrelevantly, he thought how unlovely she looked. It was a warm day, and the exertion of packing had brought beads of perspiration to her brow, her round face was flushed. She gaped at him preparatory to speech, and he said hurriedly, 'I shall be going down to the hospital this evening — he may have recovered consciousness by then — and it occurred to me you might like a lift.' It had not occurred to him until that moment, but it sounded good. 'However, no doubt your brother-in-law will be taking you.'

Mark said impatiently, 'What's this urgent business that concerns Arthur?'

Westwood ran a finger along the line of his moustache, moving his head rather than his hand. His bulging eyes looked unhappy.

'It is rather personal. Mrs Banning might prefer — '

Mark interrupted him. He was fretting for a drink.

'I'm his brother, Mr Westwood. Anything that concerns Arthur concerns me. That's so, Ruth, isn't it?'

'I suppose so.' It never had, she thought. But she was glad that Philip was still upstairs. If there was anything wrong, anything that concerned Arthur, she did not want Philip to hear it.

'Well, if you say so.' Westwood was embarrassed by the large audience. Alone with Ruth he could have been blunt, direct, unapologetic. With the Bannings present he had to choose his words. 'You see, with your brother likely to be away for some weeks, Mr Banning, I had to make arrangements for some one to take over his work. I've been going through his books and — well, there appears to be some irregularity.'

Mark stared at him. 'Such as what?'

'Money.' He rapped the word out because he could find no way of glossing over what he had to say. 'No doubt your brother has an adequate explanation, Mr Banning. I'm still working on the books, but — well, quite a considerable sum would appear to be missing.'

8

Arthur Banning was not in the main surgical ward. He lay by himself in a small, bright room with light-oak woodwork, and tall windows that looked out on to green lawns and flower-beds gay with asters and antirrhinums. But there were no flowers in the room. The enormous sheaf of gladioli which Mark had brought had been whisked away by the nurse.

'He's so pale,' Ruth said for the third time, and gulped. It was not just seeing Arthur that made her feel ill; hospitals always upset her. 'And so still. Are you sure he's still breathing?'

It was odd that she should feel so detached. As though the man on the bed were a stranger. And he looked a stranger. He lay on his back with his arms outside the blankets, his bandaged head turned to one side, so that she could see his white face and the terrible bruise round his left eye and the naso-gastric tube attached to his cheek. A saline drip stood by the bed. She watched the slow movement in the glass filter and wondered absently what it did for him.

'He's breathing,' Mark said. Adding under his breath, 'Just.'

Three double whiskies at the pub had cheered him; but he had drunk them fast, and that made him sweat. He wondered whether there were hospital rules against visitors interfering with the ventilation. An open window might dispel some of the ether smell as well as the heat.

They sat watching the slight rise and fall of the blankets that was the only indication of life in the unconscious man. Carol wondered why she had come; Arthur Banning was nothing to her. But Mark had insisted. 'I need moral support,' he had told her. 'I'm sorry for Ruth, but she gives me the willies. I refuse to be stuck with her on my own.' When she had pointed out that there was no need for him to be stuck with Ruth, that he could drop her at the hospital and return for her later, he had vetoed that suggestion also. 'I want to see for myself,' he had said. 'It's important. You know that.'

There were voices and movement outside in the corridor. Mark looked at his watch. 'Visiting-time, I suppose,' he said. 'It's seven-thirty.'

Ruth sighed. Seven-thirty. By now Philip would have finished his supper, would probably be watching television. Had he had enough to eat? There had been the remains of a stew which she had told him to warm up, and some pressed veal and a treacle tart; but when he had got through those he would probably live on tinned food and fish and chips. Mark had given her no time to prepare anything, and never before had Philip had to fend for himself.

She worried about him until she could bear the suspense no longer. She said, 'I think I'll phone Philip, just to make sure he's all right. There'll be a call-box here, won't there? And he ought to know where we're staying, just in case. He might want to get in touch with us.'

Mark thought her a fool to fuss over the boy, but he did not try to dissuade her. Altruism was wearing thin.

The public telephone booths were in the main block. Ruth was always nervous of them. She never had the right change, she would make a mistake in dialling, press the wrong button. But Mark had given her change, and presently she heard the telephone ringing in No. 27.

It went on ringing. Listening to it, Ruth's anxiety grew. Except on his days for the Tech. (and Friday was not one of them) it was unusual for Philip to go out of an evening; his wages were too slim to permit of public entertainment. But that afternoon he and Roddy Stone would have been out in Roddy's new car. What if they had had an accident? Philip might be in hospital, seriously injured. He might even be dead! And no one in Croydon knew where she was staying. Not even Philip.

'There seems to be no reply,' the operator said. 'Shall I try again?'

'No. It doesn't matter.'

She walked slowly back to the West Wing, troubled in her mind. She would have to go home. Arthur did not need her. Lying there like a dead man, there was nothing she could do for him. Whereas Philip . . .

Coming towards her down the lighted corridor was a bare-headed young constable in uniform. Vaguely she recalled having seen him outside Arthur's room, but she was startled when he stopped her.

'I'm sorry about your husband, Mrs Banning,' he said. 'Is he any better?'

She shook her head, gaping at him. He smiled at her bewilderment.

'I'm on special duty here. We're hoping that when he recovers consciousness he may be able to give us information which will help us in our inquiries.' He paused to cast a suspicious eye on a blue-jerseyed visitor who shambled past them towards the main ward; a stocky, unshaven youth with a lop-sided walk. 'We won't intrude on you and your folks, ma'am. I'm to wait outside the room, the inspector said, while you're visiting.'

She thanked him. A nice young man, she thought; cultured and friendly and clean-looking. A pity Philip hadn't some one like him for a friend, instead of that

Roddy Stone. Roddy was loud-mouthed and flashy — and not, she suspected, entirely honest.

'Will you be here all night, then?' she asked.

'Some one will. Not me personally. I go off duty soon.'

She asked him if the police knew yet what had happened, if they were any closer to arresting the men responsible. But he could not tell her that. 'I'm not exactly in the inspector's confidence,' he explained. 'But we'll get them eventually, don't you worry about that.'

She did not worry about it. It could not affect her or Philip. It could not even affect Arthur; and with so many other anxieties to plague her it seemed relatively unimportant. More pressing was the fact that Arthur was dying — as she was certain he was. And there was Westwood's sinister suggestion — assertion, almost — that Arthur had done something wrong, something to do with money. What sort of repercussion would that have if Arthur died? If Arthur owed the company money (even to herself she would not permit the thought that he might have stolen it) would she and Philip in some way be held responsible?

She must ask Mark about that. But predominant among all her worries was the fear of what might have happened to Philip.

Outside her husband's room she paused to consider what she should say to her brother-in-law. Mark would disapprove of her intention to return home. How could she convince him that it was essential?

She had not noticed that the door was ajar until she heard Carol's voice. The words were unintelligible, but Mark's reply was horribly clear.

'If he's going to die, then I wish to Hades he'd hurry up and do it.'

Ruth gasped, and moved closer to the gap. In her soft contralto Carol said, 'And if he doesn't? What then?'

'You know damned well what then!' Mark's tone was bitter. 'We're in the ruddy soup, that's what!'

* * *

Chug Wallis did not attempt to fathom the impulse which drove him to visit the hospital, nor did he pause to consider what he should do when he got there. It was an impulse compounded of uncertainty and sadistic curiosity, and it originated in a man's name seen in the evening paper. Identified, the paper said . . . Arthur Charles Banning, a rent-collector from Croydon . . . taken to Chawtry Memorial Hospital . . . multiple injuries . . . still unconscious. That's what it said. But he had to make sure. He had to see for himself.

He had given no thought to visiting-hours, but he knew enough to inquire for the surgical ward. Half-way down the long corridor he nearly turned back. An elderly blond woman with fuzzy hair was talking to a bare-headed policeman, and instinct told him why the policeman was there. But he went on; it was less dangerous, and if the papers were right he had nothing to fear. Ahead of him the doors to the main ward stood open, people were moving about. All he had to do was walk in and look.

He went slowly down the ward, staring at the men in the beds, ignoring the visitors. No one stopped him, no one questioned him. People eyed him curiously, but he did not recognize their curiosity because it did not occur to him that he was some one to be curious about. But the man he sought was not there. Not unless he lay in one of the two screened-off beds.

Back at the main doors he hesitated, scowling at the floor, angry and frustrated. He wanted to search the ward again, peer behind the screens. But the policeman he had seen earlier was back in the corridor, watching him, thoughtfully stroking his smooth chin. It would be foolish to loiter.

He walked quickly past the policeman, averting his head but sure that the man's eyes were following him. Farther down the corridor a tall, lean man, cap in hand, was talking to a blond nurse. As Chug approached them the nurse said, 'Mr Banning is in a room by himself.' She turned to point to where the policeman stood, stared for a moment at Chug, and then back to the tall man. 'But his wife and brother are with him at present. I'm not sure whether — '

'No, no. Please don't disturb them.' The man's jaw twitched nervously. 'I merely wanted to know how he is.'

Chug paused by a trolley laden with bottles and medical equipment to hear the girl's reply.

'Well, he's still unconscious,' she said. 'And still on the danger-list, I'm afraid.'

The tall man thanked her and limped away. Chug followed. As he passed her the nurse said, 'Can I help you?'

She was plump and pretty, with large blue eyes. But for once Chug was not interested in women, no matter how seductive. He shook his head, forced his thick lips into a grin, and set off for the dark at the end of the corridor.

★ ★ ★

They watched the little blond nurse feed Arthur through the naso-gastric tube. She had followed Ruth into the room, and Ruth had been glad of her presence; it excluded private conversation, and Ruth knew that had the nurse not been there she would have poured out her indignation at what she had overheard. She knew too that she would have been unable to express it coherently. She could talk to Arthur and Philip — they understood her, they spoke the same words — but she could not talk to Mark. Not when there was something important to say. It was not so much that he intimidated her (as he did), but that she hesitated to start something she might be unable to finish.

For much the same reason she said nothing of her intention to return home; the intention remained, but the conditions, the atmosphere, were wrong. Mark had asked her casually how Philip was managing, and she had said that he was out. He had stared at her for a moment, surprised at the unusual brusqueness of her tone; and then the nurse had come in to divert his attention.

'How often do you feed him?' Carol asked.

'Every two hours,' the nurse said. 'I'm late, I'm afraid. But we're short-handed at present, and it's not easy to keep pace with the clock.'

She's a pretty little thing, thought Mark. Nice legs, and a figure that even a nurse's uniform can't hide. And those baby blue eyes don't fool me. Her interest in men isn't confined to the clinical.

'So you'll be back at ten, eh?' he said.

'Not me. I go off duty at nine; the night staff takes over then. I expect there'll be some one in here with him all night.'

Idly Mark considered trying to date her. It was a consideration made from habit; he was fond of Carol, but he liked variety. Yet he doubted whether he could do himself justice under existing conditions. Until he knew for certain about Arthur it would be difficult to concentrate on pleasure.

I'll tell him when we get back to the hotel, Ruth decided. They don't have to take me in the car; I can get a train from Lewes. But I won't refer to what I overheard. It was a terrible thing for a man to say about his brother, but what good can it do to accuse him? He'd probably deny it anyway. And Carol

162

would back him up. She likes me no more than he does.

With the entry of a white-coated surgeon the room seemed overcrowded. He was a dark young man, briskly efficient, and with a manner that did not lend itself to sympathy. He wasted no time in conversation. Together he and the nurse worked on the unconscious man, taking pulse, temperature, and blood pressure, listening to his respiration, making entries on the chart that hung at the foot of the high hospital bed. He was peering into the patient's eyes when Hugh Westwood came in. The nurse frowned at the interruption, but she made no comment.

Westwood looked even more worried than when he had left No. 27 that afternoon. He slipped into the room as though he knew himself to be an intruder, nodded nervously at the three seated people, closed the door quietly, and moved round to the window to be out of the way. His protruding eyes were red-rimmed, the blue of his chin had assumed a darker hue; his sleek brown hair stuck out at the back like wisps of straw on a hayrick. His staff, who knew him only as dictatorial and briskly confident, would have been startled by this new diffidence.

The surgeon finished his examination and stood up, to stare at the newcomer as though he were something the cat had brought in. He said, 'Four visitors at a time are too many. Are you a relative?'

'I'm his employer.' Even Westwood's voice seemed to have lost some of its depth and precision. 'But I'm not staying. I just called in to see how he is, and to have a few words with Mrs Banning.'

'Well, keep it short, please,' the surgeon said.

Still with a speculative eye on the nurse, Mark said, 'We'll all be going in a few minutes. Just sitting here looking at him, poor chap, seems pointless. I suppose the hospital will get in touch with us if there's any significant change? We're staying in the village for a few days. At the Anchor.' He arched his back, stretching his long neck. 'How do you reckon his chances, doctor?'

'Well, his breathing's easier and his pulse is more regular.' He stared thoughtfully at the man on the bed. Seen in profile, his face was remarkably clean-cut, as though it had been carved rather than moulded. 'And his blood pressure is reasonably steady. They are all hopeful signs, although it is too early to prophesy. The next twenty-four hours is going to be the critical time.' His eyes lingered on Carol and then moved to Ruth. With a slight smile he said, 'Don't lose heart, Mrs Banning. Go back to the hotel and have a good night's rest, and ring the hospital in the morning. There might be more definite news for you then.'

He nodded at the others and left. Mark said, 'It's hot in here, nurse. Any objection to a little fresh air?'

'You can open the window if you like.'

Westwood opened it for them. When the nurse had gone he said, 'I must apologize for intruding once more; but I had no option.' He looked at the bed and sighed. 'It would seem I've had a wasted journey. I won't get anything from him to-night.'

Mark said, 'Still haunted by that cash deficiency? How's it coming?'

'Not very well.' There was no vacant chair, and Westwood moved to the foot of the bed, deposited his bowler hat on the trolley, and gripped the iron rail with both hands. 'I've been working on it all afternoon. The amount involved is still uncertain, but it's even larger than I feared. Much larger.'

'How large?' Mark asked bluntly.

'Somewhere around six thousand pounds.'

Mark had been sitting cross-legged, holding his ankle. Now he shot up in his chair, releasing the ankle so that his foot slid to the floor, and stared at Westwood in incredulous amaze. Even Carol's smooth poker-face registered surprise. Ruth gaped, shook her head as though to clear it, felt her stomach heave, and clenched her teeth with a snap. When Westwood had earlier mentioned a considerable sum her mind had first registered an amount in the neighbourhood of fifty pounds and had later stretched it unhappily to a hundred. But six thousand pounds! It was a sum almost beyond her comprehension.

Mark gave his knee a vigorous slap. 'Damn it, man, that's impossible! You must have made a mistake.'

'I only wish I had.'

Mark took a cigarette from a slim silver case, lit it, and smoked a few vigorous puffs.

'I think it's time we had the story from the beginning,' he said. 'At present we know only the ending, and that stinks.'

The beginning, said Westwood, had occurred in January, just before he left for Switzerland on a ski-ing holiday. The company was in the process of reorganization, and Phelps, the area manager, had sent for him to explain how this would affect his branch. Mostly this concerned procedure, but there was one material change; certain properties in Streatham, consisting mainly of new blocks of flats, were to be transferred to the Croydon branch. Phelps had thereupon handed him the necessary documents, saying that the transfer was a personal decision which he would communicate to his staff in due course, but that Westwood should not wait for the company's written instructions before starting to collect the rents.

'I flew to Switzerland the next day,' Westwood said. 'Your brother was to be in charge during my absence, and I gave him the new documents and instructions and told him to get on with it. For the rest of that day I was busy ensuring that the new office procedure became effective immediately. It wasn't until I was actually in the air that I remembered I had said nothing to the branch cashier or the rest of the staff about the new properties. But I wasn't greatly concerned. If your brother didn't mention it the company's written instructions would put them in the picture.' He shook his head. 'Unfortunately that never happened.'

'No?'

'No. Your brother kept the information to himself, and the official instructions failed to arrive.'

'I see. And you, I suppose, had forgotten all about it by the time you returned.'

Westwood nodded. With his long curving nose and the hair projecting from the back of his head and his bulging eyes he looked like a busy cockatoo.

'Yes. It's incredible, I know, but that's what happened. I was away a month — broke my leg ski-ing, and spent a fortnight in hospital. Everything seemed to be running smoothly when I got back and, as I saw it, it went on running smoothly. As for the official letter — ' He sighed. 'Well, it still hasn't arrived. I can only assume that Phelps forgot, as I did, to inform his staff of the transfer, and that in the general upheaval of reorganization it simply got lost.'

Ruth remembered that January, and the bitter wrangle that had ensued between herself and Arthur. She had insisted that, with the added responsibility and extra work, he should ask for more money. It was Arthur's refusal to do so that had caused the bitterness.

Now she was beginning vaguely to understand the reason for his refusal.

'And Arthur?' asked Mark. 'Exactly what did Arthur do?'

That, Westwood said, was what he wanted to know, why he was there. But one could make a shrewd guess. The cashier had no record of any rents from the transferred property having been paid in. Yet the money had certainly been collected; Westwood had checked with the tenants. 'He signed the rent-books in my name,' he said. 'Not a good forgery, either.'

Mark whistled. 'Did he, though! The cunning bastard!'

'Not very, Mr Banning. Inquiries over rents are dealt with by the collectors concerned; only the more tricky problems are referred to me. A simple query from any one of those tenants during the past eight months would have blown the fraud sky high.'

'Six thousand quid would be worth a few risks.' Mark spoke with feeling. 'But what gave him the idea? That's what beats me. Arthur doesn't think big like that. He's a small man.'

Westwood shrugged. 'Those rents amount to nearly two hundred a week. He missed the first two weeks — probably forgot — so that by the end of the third he'd find himself with close on six hundred pounds. That's a lot of money to a man in your brother's position.'

'It's a lot of money in any position,' Mark said. 'And you reckon that's what triggered him off? He couldn't bear to part with it?'

Again the shrug. 'Only he can say. But the discovery that the new property was not on the office lists, and that Area were apparently completely indifferent, must have made the temptation very strong.'

'Irresistible, I'd say. Even to Arthur.'

Westwood frowned at the levity in Mark Banning's voice. Releasing the rail, he looked directly at Ruth. His tone was more peremptory as he said, 'I gather this has come as a surprise to you, Mrs Banning? But surely you must have had an inkling that something was wrong. Haven't you noticed a difference in him, for instance, over these past months?'

'No,' she said. 'He's been just the same.'

She reflected guiltily on how different life for herself and Philip might have been had Arthur decided to spend some of that stolen money on them. If he *had* stolen it;

that was something she still found it difficult to believe. For if it were true would he really have allowed himself to get behind with the rent (as he still was), or have let her skimp and struggle to eke out the housekeeping allowance? The only sign of affluence had been that three pounds for Philip's trousers. Three pounds! Out of six thousand!

'Just the same,' she repeated firmly. 'Except that perhaps he's been late home more often.'

Westwood said curtly, 'With all those extra rents to collect, I'm not surprised.'

'How about cheques?' asked Mark. 'He couldn't cash those.'

'Only a few would pay by cheque,' Westwood told him. 'It's not that class of property. But those who did — ' He shrugged. 'Probably destroyed them. Or perhaps he persuaded them to make the cheques out to himself, and paid them into his own bank account. Some people are very gullible.'

'He doesn't have a bank account,' Ruth said. 'He always said that if he had any money to spare he'd look after it himself.

He said a bank account was just an expensive convenience for the idle.'

Mark looked incredulous. He could not visualize life without his bank and the concomitant overdraft.

'Don't tell me he's hidden it under the mattress,' he said. 'Even Arthur couldn't be as naïve as that.'

Some of the colour drained from Ruth's cheeks as memory stirred.

Westwood said, 'He could have decided that six thousand pounds was enough, that it was time to get out. He could have been on his way to make a fresh start abroad when this happened.' He stared for a moment at the man on the bed before turning to Ruth. 'Forgive my saying so, Mrs Banning, but I had an idea you might be in on the scheme — that you were to join him later.' The apology was not reflected either in his eyes or in his tone. 'However, it seems I was wrong. The police telephoned me this afternoon — they had been unable to contact you — to tell me that your husband's wallet had been found in a field near Chailey Common. There was no money, but it did contain his passport and two return tickets to Paris.'

'Return tickets, eh? So this was merely *au 'voir*, not good-bye. Maybe he reckoned six thousand wasn't enough.' A new significance occurred to Mark, and he mouthed a whistle that failed to materialize. 'Two tickets! But that means — '

He glanced at Ruth and then at Carol, and left the sentence unfinished.

Ruth did not need Mark to tell her what it meant. Arthur had been taking a companion to Paris, some hussy he had met on his rounds and who was prepared to sleep with him in return for a gay week-end. It did not entirely surprise her. Men like Arthur, middle-aged men living dull, sober lives, were more likely to cut loose than the others. That he had shown no inclination to do so before was because he had lacked the means.

She felt no qualm of jealousy. She and Arthur had long since ceased to be lovers, they had stayed together because togetherness had become a habit and separation was a luxury they could not afford. They had nothing to give each other, and what he gave of himself to this girl he was not taking from her. But she no longer doubted Westwood's accusation that Arthur had stolen money from the company. On his meagre salary he could not have taken himself to Paris, let alone a companion.

One thought gave her some comfort. Her presentiment had been wrong. Arthur had intended to return, he had not meant to abandon his family entirely.

Mark said thoughtfully, 'He wouldn't take six thousand smackers on a week-end jaunt. A few hundred would be enough for that. So if it isn't in a bank or under the mattress, then it's tucked away somewhere. At home, presumably. Any ideas, Ruth? Where could he hide it so that neither you nor Philip would come on it by accident?'

It could have been loyalty to her husband (she did not blame him for taking the money, it was the company's meanness which had driven him to it), or anger against Mark, or her dislike of Westwood, which made her shake her head. It could even have been cupidity. She did not analyse the motive, but she shut her mind deliberately to the locked drawer in the bedroom.

She said, 'I don't know. The garden shed, perhaps, or under a loose floorboard. There can't be many places.'

Mark wondered at her apparent calm. The revelation that her husband was a thief and a libertine would seem to be of less moment to her than the fact that her precious son had been left to fend for himself.

'Maybe we'd better delay tearing the house apart until Arthur's been given the chance to come clean,' he said. 'And now that he's been rumbled he hasn't much choice.'

'I hope you're right,' Westwood said gloomily. His long, blue-chinned face lent itself to gloom. 'If the money isn't recovered I'm out of a job. I'm probably out in any case. It was my forgetfulness that gave your brother the opportunity.' He picked up his bowler hat from the trolley, examined it as though surprised to see it there, and then replaced it. 'Do you happen to know if there's a vacant room at your hotel? I feel I should be on the spot, so that I can question your brother immediately he's conscious again. I haven't informed head office, you see. I keep postponing it in the hope that I can gild the pill a little, tell them the money's been recovered. Or the bulk of it.'

'There's a room,' Mark said, lighting another cigarette. 'Or there was. Several. I fancy supply exceeds the demand in these parts.' He inhaled deeply, and looked at the man on the bed. There was still only that almost imperceptible rise and fall of the blankets to show that his brother was alive. 'You're in a right mess if Arthur dies without recovering consciousness.'

Westwood shuddered, shutting his eyes. Apparently it was a disaster he did not care to contemplate.

Ruth stirred uneasily. She was staring at her husband, her hands clasped in her lap and her plump face creased in sorrow. Suddenly aware of his lapse from tact, Mark touched her arm.

'Sorry, Ruth. I shouldn't have said that.

But it was only a hypothesis. Of course he's going to recover. The doc as good as said so, didn't he?'

Ruth scarcely heard him. His tactlessness had not troubled her. For once she had been thinking solely of her husband — and it had seemed to her then that it might possibly be better for Arthur if he did not recover.

* * *

From outside the curtained window Chug Wallis heard the scraping of chairs and the shuffle of feet. He could not see into the room; but he knew that the people were leaving, and he moved away into the shadows and leant against the wall and considered the next move.

Six thousand nicker! That was what the man Westwood, the one with the deep voice, had said. Six thousand bleeding nicker! Yet Vince had estimated the notes in the suitcase at a mere few hundred, and he had accepted that estimate. He'd had no option, really. Fivers and once-ers looked much alike in the dark, and Vince hadn't let him count them. Vince had snatched up the neatly bundled notes and stuffed them into his rucksack and told him to get weaving.

But had Vince been right? Had he deliberately fooled him, then as later? The thought almost paralysed him with rage, and he found himself sweating under the heavy jersey. Beads of sweat trickled into his eyes, and he knuckled them away, mouthing obscenities, trying to blot the image of Vince's possible treachery from his mind. It obscured all else — and now, if ever, he needed to think clearly.

Six thousand nicker! The man with the thick nasal voice, the one Westwood called Banning, had said that his brother wouldn't take all that money on a week-end jaunt; just a few hundred, he'd said, with the rest tucked away at his home. The man didn't know, he was only guessing. Yet if he were right . . .

Chug grinned wolfishly. If the man were right the thing was dead easy. He had the address and he had the key. No breaking and entering; just walk in through the front door any time he chose.

And no need for a rush job either; with Banning in hospital and the woman down at the pub the house would be unoccupied. He could take the bloody place apart, and none to stop him.

If the man were right. But suppose he were wrong? Suppose the whole bloody lot had been in the suitcase? The whole six thousand!

A car went slowly down the drive, its headlights bringing the tall trees at the roadside into sharp relief. Chug came away from the wall and started to cross the wide lawn that sloped towards the gates. The choice was a simple one; either the house or Vince. He wanted Vince, wanted him so badly that he had become almost as important as the money; and if Vince and the money were together so much the better. But where to look for him? Not in Brighton; not after what had happened Thursday night. Vince would have taken his bird some place else. But where?

With that impasse the choice vanished. He would try the house first; after that, money or no money, he'd look for Vince.

It might take time, but he'd catch up with him eventually. And when he did . . .

He was so absorbed in anticipation of what he would do to Vince when the moment came that he was almost at the gates before he realized that the moment might never come. For it depended on continued freedom — and freedom depended now on that man in the hospital bed. Banning had seen him, had seen them both; if Banning could speak he would describe him to the police, would identify him if they picked him up. From what Vince had said he had supposed that that could never happen; only when he had read that report in the evening papers had he suspected that Vince might have been wrong. Now suspicion seemed to have been confirmed. He had not heard everything that had been said in the room, but he had heard enough. Hopeful signs, the doctor had said. And if none of the others believed that the man would live, the brother certainly did.

Chug stopped, and turned to look back. Across the expanse of lawn the lights of the main ward shone brightly. Through the tall windows he could see figures moving, the high beds, even the men in them. Off to the right, glowing in the dark mass of the wall like portholes in a ship, were other lights; smaller and separate, the windows of private wards and offices and surgeries. Some were curtained, some were not. But Chug had eyes only for one — a dull, pink rectangle behind which lay the unconscious man whose recovery could mean the end of freedom.

9

Vince was no expert exponent of the waltz. He could manage the steps and the rhythm, but steering a girl round the crowded ballroom bothered him, made him feel hot under the collar. He preferred something like the Twist, where a couple could pick their spot and let themselves go. But Doris had wanted to dance, and right now anything Doris wanted he wanted also. Perhaps it was the champagne that made him feel that way — this was the first time he had drunk champagne in quantity — but he had the disturbing impression that he might also be falling for the girl. He would have to watch that; it wasn't so good if you fell for the girl. Or that's what they said. It destroyed the sense of power, it turned a man into a slave instead of a conqueror.

That's what they said.

She was not a good dancer, but he did not know that; when they stumbled he blamed himself, murmuring apologies into her ear. Her response was a quick squeeze of hand or shoulder to show that she did not mind.

They were dancing the encore now. He held her more tightly, brushed his lips against her cheek. She did not draw away.

'Enjoying yourself?' he asked.

'You know I am. It's a fabulous band.' Her high treble sounded unsteady, as though she too had been affected by the champagne. 'A fabulous evening altogether. But I wish this wasn't the end. I could dance all night.'

He clutched her to him to prevent a collision. 'But not with me, eh?'

She laughed, leaning back to smile into his face. He could see the swell of her breasts above the low-cut bodice.

'Even with you. It's that sort of evening.'

And so it should be, he thought, for what it cost. He had chosen the most expensive hotel in Eastbourne; chosen it deliberately, to impress her. Two days ago (was it only two?) he had thought himself a rich man, but at his present rate of spending the money would soon be gone. Not that he cared. Since the previous evening life had suddenly ceased to have a positive future; at any hour the reckoning might come, and he would have to face up to Chug and what Chug might do. It was an enervating and frightening prospect; yet he had somehow managed to accept it, and with a hitherto unrecognized fatalism. If the dark thought of Chug was seldom entirely absent from his mind, it merely hardened his resolve to squeeze from each day that was left the ultimate in pleasure that money (and Doris) could bring him — and to hell with the future!

It was with reluctance that he released her arm when they returned to their table. He wanted constantly to touch her. As she sat down he lifted the champagne bottle from the ice and held it against the light.

'We may as well finish this.'

'Not for me.' She put a hand over her glass. 'I've had enough. And if you'll forgive my asking — well, haven't you?'

Her smile robbed the query of reproof.

'I'll forgive you. But dancing is thirsty work.' He removed her hand, squeezing it gently, and filled his glass to the brim. 'I thought you looked wonderful at the beginning of the evening, and I still think you look wonderful. So at least the champagne hasn't affected my judgment.'

She did look wonderful. Her dress was of lawn, multi-coloured and strapless, with a short flaring skirt and a tight little bodice cut low at front and back. Her golden hair was clipped behind the ears, her large hazel eyes had a luminous look. The only jewellery she wore was a pair of jade earrings.

She gave him a mock bow. 'You don't look bad yourself,' she said. 'A dinner jacket suits you.'

Privately he agreed with her. His previous dinner jackets had been hired or borrowed. This one, although bought off the peg, was new and well cut and fitted perfectly, and he had spent some time admiring himself in the mirror before joining her. It had restored much of the confidence lost in his encounter with Chug.

He gulped the champagne down too quickly, so that the bubbles rose to his nose and he wanted to sneeze. He was not in fact thirsty, but he needed all the assurance, all the mastery that it could give him. For this was the night. It had to be. He had gilded the pill so thoroughly that if she did not swallow it now he knew she never would.

They had moved to the hotel that afternoon. There had been no protest from Doris, no more talk of uncle. Even Vince's seemingly lighthearted proposal that they should share a room, with the mock explanation that it would be more matey and less expensive, had been refused with no show of indignation.

'Now you are trying to tie strings,' she had said. 'That wasn't in the bargain.'

He had booked adjoining rooms overlooking the sea.

The ballroom had emptied, waiters were already clearing the tables. Doris sighed.

'Time to go,' she said, and stretched a hand across the table to touch his. 'Thank you, Vince. It's been absolutely terrific.'

He caught the hand and held it.

'Why end the evening here?' he said. There was a frog in his throat and he swallowed hard, trying to sound cool, hoping he didn't look the way he felt. This was the crucial moment. 'There's a bottle on ice in my room and all mod. cons. Come up for a night-cap and discuss what's to do to-morrow.'

Her eyes clouded again. She knew what was in his mind. The doubt lay in hers.

'I told you, I'm not thirsty,' she said, begging the question, hoping her nervous smile would tell him that this was mere prevarication, not a definite refusal — that the decision had still to be made.

'You don't have to be thirsty to drink champagne,' he said.

Gently she detached her hand from his and picked up the empty wineglass, twirling it absent-mindedly between finger and thumb as she studied him from beneath lowered lashes. He would not be the first. The first had happened over two years ago, when she was seventeen; not a bad-looking man, although she had guessed him to be

188

older than the forty-five years to which he had admitted. Avid for experience, bored with the young men of her acquaintance, with their cheap pleasures and their crude familiarities, the smooth sophistication of the older man had fascinated her. It had hardly needed his lavish entertainment and expensive presents to persuade her to go to bed with him. She did not regard it as a price she was expected to pay. It was all part of experience.

The experience had proved a failure. Where she had anticipated pleasure there had been only physical distaste. Worse still, there had been no profit in it. The free spender had soon become mean, seeming to think that the expensive treatment needed to promote the first surrender was superfluous to the second and the third. There had been no fourth. She had broken with him before that.

But the taste for luxury and good living remained. There had been other men since, all rich and most of them elderly. But she had learned her lesson; she had encouraged them to extravagance, but there had been little giving in return. Neither meanness nor morality had decided her in this; it was simply that she saw no reason to submit unnecessarily to an unpleasant experience. And unnecessary it undoubtedly was. When a man grew too importunate she discarded him. There was always another anxious to take his place.

The last had been Arthur Banning.

Arthur had been all that she despised in men; dull and fat and middle-aged and poor. She had told him so when, after several weeks of rejecting his infatuated pleading and petty gifts, his importunity had become a bore. What did he think she was? she had demanded. A charitable institution for elderly and frustrated husbands?

She had thought that was the end of it — until he had stopped her in the High Street one afternoon and told her he had inherited a fortune. She had laughed and walked away, telling him she had grown out of fairy-tales. But he had followed her, pleading insistently; and in a final attempt to be rid of him she had pointed to a pair of jade earrings in a jeweller's shop window and had told him that if he was so rich and so hot for her he could begin the seduction with those. She had expected him to refuse. But he had strutted into the shop, with her trailing incredulously behind, produced an enormous bundle of notes, and had paid for the earrings on the spot.

After that she had allowed him to take her out to dinner. He had made no immediate demands; it was not until some days later that he had suggested the week-end in Paris. To Doris, who had never been abroad, the proposition was alluring. Arthur himself was the only drawback; it would take a lot of cash to compensate for Arthur as a lover. But the cash was undoubtedly there, and he seemed eager to spend it; and where better to spend it than in Paris?

She hesitated only slightly before accepting.

It had been Arthur's idea that they should leave Croydon independently and meet at Lewes, to spend the night there before crossing to France; but it had been on her insistence that he had booked separate rooms. She had been frank with him. Her affections were not involved, and she would not sleep with him until they were actually in Paris. Perhaps not even then; she was making no promises, it depended on how Paris affected her. And if he didn't like the conditions he knew what to do.

He didn't like them, but he was too infatuated to refuse.

She had been puzzled by his non-arrival in Lewes, but it had not worried her. Even the lost trip to Paris ceased to matter after Vince had appeared. It was not until that afternoon, when she had been glancing idly through a paper while waiting for Vince, that she had discovered what had happened to Arthur; it did not greatly concern her, and she had hastily hidden the paper as Vince joined her. The name of Arthur Banning would mean nothing to Vince, he would be unlikely to connect him with the missing uncle. But, schooled though she was by now in sophistry and deception, she was taking no chances that by some inadvertent word she might give the game away. If Vince were to learn the truth about Arthur and the others he would never give marriage a thought. And she no longer doubted that marriage was what she wanted. Her only problem was how to persuade Vince to want it too.

'We'd better go, Vince,' she said. 'It's late.'

By the time they reached the landing she had made up her mind. Sex, it seemed, was important to men; they might be prepared to wait, some longer than others, but if it were not eventually forthcoming they lost interest. That had not mattered before, but it mattered now. Vince was too good a prospect to lose.

Detaching his arm from her waist, she said, 'I'll take you up on that drink, Vince. But just the one, mind.' She laughed nervously. 'I'd hate to find you with a sore head in the morning. And that's what will happen if you and that bottle get together without a chaperone.'

He wanted to make some brittle remark that would stress his self-assurance, his mastery of the situation.

But neither the thoughts nor the words would come.

'Get busy with the cork while I change into something more comfortable,' Doris said. 'I shan't be long.'

He sat on the bed, a glass of champagne in his hand and his head in a whirl. Tasting the champagne was his first conscious act since leaving her; he had no recollection of entering his room, of drawing the cork. Even the raising of the glass to his lips was automatic. Eyes fixed on the door, he could think only of the fact that in a few short minutes Doris would be in the room, that what he had schemed and paid for so lavishly was actually about to happen.

He put down the glass, went over to the wash-basin, and rinsed his face in cold water. Fully awake now, he suddenly panicked, terrified that she would find him unprepared. He began to strip, formulating in his mind the way he would act, the things he must and must not do or say. Impetuosity had ruined the previous opportunity. That must not happen to-night.

He was in pyjamas and dressing-gown, schooling himself as he wandered aimlessly about the room, when the knock came. It was a soft, tentative knock, barely audible; yet he heard it and halted abruptly.

'Come in,' he called hoarsely.

She leant against the closed door and stared at him through eyes that looked enormous. Her hair was a golden aureole about her face, her lips were full and inviting. The powder-blue dressing-gown was tied loosely at the waist, and where it parted he could see the transparent nightdress and the warm, seductive glow of flesh beneath.

It was too much for his self-control; the schooling and the planning were forgotten. Filled with an almost agonizing desire, so that his body quivered and jerked uncontrollably, he ran to the door and seized her hungrily, covering her face, her neck, her throat, with kisses.

'Vince!' She sounded tearful. 'Please! You're hurting.'

Without a word he picked her up in his arms and stumbled across to the bed.

* ★ ★

The superintendent had not intended to call at the station on his way home. But Kane's light was on, and he wanted to know why. Jimmy Kane was a good chap, but overfond of his bed. Only a national emergency, the superintendent reflected as he climbed the stairs, would keep Jimmy at his desk after midnight.

'Catching up on the paperwork,' Kane explained. There were dark shadows under his eyes, his blond hair was rumpled. 'I've been unable to get down to it lately. Too much hither and thither. How did the dinner go, sir?'

'Nicely, thank you.' Baker sat down and stretched his legs. His dinner jacket was old-fashioned and his trousers too full, but somehow they looked right on him. 'It's the drive back from these long-distance functions that I dislike. Where have you been hithering to-day?'

'All over the place, from Hove to Croydon. Regular Cook's tour — plus a pub crawl in Lewes. It got me nowhere.'

'Why Hove?'

'Dainsford had picked up a character who seemed to fit Worsfold's description of Dick Smith. I took the old boy along to have a look at him. No go.'

Baker produced a packet of cigarettes, took one, and pushed the packet across the large, flat-topped desk.

'A pity.'

'I'll say it's a pity.' Kane reached for a cigarette. He had run out of pipe tobacco. 'A few words with Mr Smith, and I might have slept soundly to-night.'

'I don't believe it.'

Kane grinned, and lit his cigarette. He had white, regular teeth.

'He's a very, very likely customer, sir. The Morris was lousy with dabs — most of them Banning's, of course — and quite a few checked with those found in Mrs Worsfold's spare room. Banning lost a wrist-watch, Smith acquired one. If you add to that his new-found wealth shortly after Banning was fixed — well, it's food for thought, anyway.'

'Don't let it give you indigestion. How did the pub crawl go?'

'Complete wash-out. The beer-pullers

thought I was crazy. I was, too. I should have known that Worsfold's description was too vague. It must fit half the youths in Lewes.' Kane sighed. The sigh turned to a yawn, and he put a hand to his mouth. 'Sorry. But it's been that sort of a day. The only positive scrap of information I managed to glean was that Dick Smith actually did go to the races on Wednesday. We found a couple of bookies' tickets in his room, and I checked the numbers with the bookies concerned. But they'd be losing tickets, of course. They don't tell us if he picked a winner or two.'

'He'd have been something of a wandering boy, wouldn't he?' Baker said. 'If he slugged Banning, I mean.'

Kane nodded gloomily. He knew what was in the superintendent's mind. Why should Smith go north from Plumpton (on foot, presumably) leaving his lugagge at the Worsfolds' — and then, somewhere north of Chailey, thumb a lift in a car heading south?

'Of course, if it's theory you want one can always find one to fit,' Baker said.

'Suppose Smith has a bad day at the races, loses every cent. That means the holiday is over. He can't return for his baggage because he owes for his room, so he decides to make for home and send for the baggage later. Being broke, he has to hoof it or hitch-hike, and around nine o'clock he finds himself on Chailey Common.' Baker scratched his head, and a little shower of scurf dotted his lapel. He brushed it away. 'How am I doing?'

'I'm with you so far,' Kane said cautiously.

'Good. Now, suppose Banning has parked on the common to attend to nature. Smith comes across the car, Banning returns from his bush or what-have-you, Smith slugs him and takes his wallet. So now there is no need to curtail his holiday; he has money, he even has a car. He drives back to Lewes, does a round of the pubs, chums up with some other character who also lives out Plumpton way, and offers him a lift.' The superintendent took a deep breath. He had rattled off the items without pausing. 'No doubt he intends to abandon the

Morris near his lodging, but the crash upsets his plan. As they clamber out he tells his companion that the car was hot, and they remove themselves in haste. Next day Smith clears off to Brighton; only now he isn't Smith, he's Brown or Jones or Robinson. As for his companion — well, he's the sort of moron who doesn't want any trouble, so he keeps his mouth shut.' Another deep breath. 'Now dig holes in that.'

Kane shook his head. 'I can't, sir. It looks like concrete to me.'

'Just a knack,' Baker said modestly. 'But don't get sold on it, Jimmy. It's only theory, and probably bad theory at that.'

He agreed with Kane that the passport and tickets found in Banning's wallet indicated that the man had been all set for an illicit week-end on the Continent. 'And entertaining a floosie in Paris costs money,' he said. 'Real money. If my flight into fantasy were correct, then friend Smith would have collected quite a packet. A celebration booze-up would certainly be indicated.' He stretched and stood up. 'What were you doing in Croydon?'

'Trying to contact Wilson. He seems to have vanished.'

'Don't make too much of that. An Englishman is entitled to his week-end. Unless he happens to be a policeman, of course.'

The telephone rang. Kane picked it up, listened, and said, 'O.K., put them through.' And to the superintendent, 'The hospital, sir.'

He listened without comment until the caller had finished. Then he said, 'Yes. Yes, quite right. And thank you.' He put the receiver back on its cradle and looked across at Baker.

'Banning's dead, sir. Died about half an hour ago.' He planted both elbows on the desk and propped his face between his hands. After a moment he added, 'And that makes it murder.'

'It had the shape of murder from the start,' the superintendent said gravely. 'It's filled out, that's all.'

10

They sat at a round oak table in the inn parlour. The table was large, the wooden chairs straight-backed and hard, so that only Ruth seemed able to sit still; the others, and Mark in particular, were continually fidgeting. Yet of the four it was Mark who seemed the most cheerful, although dark shadows under the eyes hinted that both he and Westwood had slept little. Westwood sat scowling at his coffee, stirring it with a smooth, circular motion of the battered hotel spoon; Arthur Banning's death appeared to have shaken him badly, although so far he had not referred to it since Mark had broken the news. He had retired to his room immediately after breakfast, and had stayed there until they had called him for coffee. As for Carol, her conversational repertoire was unequal to the occasion. Carol had acquaintances, not friends, and among her acquaintances the death of a relative was not discussed. A stilted condolence for Ruth was all she had been able to manage.

Ruth welcomed the coffee. It made the day seem less cataclysmic, it was a brief return to the mundane; a mid-morning cup of coffee was one of her few indulgences in the daily routine. Ruth too had slept only fitfully. At home she was a heavy sleeper, but in a strange bed and on a mattress not moulded to her protuberances it was not until near dawn that she had ceased to toss and turn.

'Well, what now?' Mark said briskly. He had had a large brandy with his coffee. 'Home, I suppose. There's nothing more to be done here, and I've quite a bit of business to attend to. How about you, Ruth? Carol and I will be moving on after lunch. Croydon is rather out of our way, but we can run you home if you like. Or how would it be if we dropped you at Haywards Heath? You could get a train from there.'

Ruth said it would do very well. She did not want them with her when she got home. Mark had telephoned Philip's employer for her after breakfast, to be told that Philip had reported for work as usual; and with that source of anxiety removed she had been able to concentrate on Arthur's death and its possible effect on her future. The news of his death had shocked but not surprised her. She had already made up her mind that he was to die.

Mark picked up his glass, saw that it was empty, contemplated ordering another brandy, and decided to wait.

'This has more or less forced your hand, hasn't it?' he said to Westwood. 'You have no alternative now but to bring in the police.'

Westwood gloomily agreed. But not, he thought, the local police; it was out of their province. In any case he would have to advise head office first. With a feeble attempt at humour he added, 'I suppose none of your business friends needs a manager guaranteed to keep losses down to six thousand a year?'

Mark did not think it funny. Other men's jokes seldom were.

'Don't be such a damned pessimist,' he

said, twirling the stem of his glass between long, supple fingers. 'Most of that six thousand may be recoverable. Arthur can't help you now, but you should get together with Ruth. Search the house. If the money's there — well, the wicket won't look quite so sticky, will it?'

'No!' Ruth said sharply.

It was an involuntary exclamation. She could never have refused so flatly had she paused to think first. But then reaction came, and she flushed and tugged nervously at the swollen joints of her fingers.

'I — I'd rather do it myself. There's no need for Mr Westwood to help.' Even to herself that did not sound sufficiently convincing, and she added, tugging the harder, 'I don't want Philip to know, you see. Not unless he has to. And if Mr Westwood were there he'd be bound to ask questions.'

They stared at her. Westwood looked as if he were about to protest. Then he shrugged, picked up his coffee cup, and drained it. Delicately mopping his lips and moustache with a silk handkerchief, he said, with a return to his former curtness, 'It's your house, Mrs Banning, so I can't insist. But I hope you'll make the search a thorough one. Everything depends on it — for me, anyway.'

Relieved, she nodded vigorously. Almost from the moment she had learned that Arthur was dead the money had seldom been absent from her thoughts. LAPP, in the guise of Hugh Westwood, had put temptation in Arthur's path, their meanness had conditioned him to succumb. In a sense Arthur had died because of that money, for had he not taken it he would have been nowhere near Chailey Common on Wednesday evening. Brooding on all this, it seemed to Ruth that LAPP were morally responsible for her husband's death. Yet they would make no restitution. Quite the reverse. They would brand Arthur as a thief, and demand that she meekly return to them whatever money she recovered.

Well, she would not do it. Arthur had paid for that money with his life, and if you paid for a thing it was yours. To Ruth that was logic; and since there was none to disagree with her because none knew the way her mind was working, it did not occur to her that it was false logic. The money was hers — hers and Philip's. If, as the men seemed to think, there was something like five thousand pounds hidden in the house, it would provide for their future, give Philip a proper start in life and herself some security. She would put it in a bank; and then, if the company did not believe her when she said there was no money, they could search the house themselves.

But she had to find it first. And alone. That was why she had agreed so readily to return home by train, why she had rejected Westwood's offer of help. Even Philip must not know. A sudden access to wealth would go to Philip's head, he might boast of it to his friends. That Roddy Stone, for instance.

She was planning for the future — they would leave Croydon, perhaps move into the country or down by the sea — when George Wilson came in. The parlour was an L-shaped room, dark-panelled and low-ceilinged, with the entrance at the far end, so that they did not know he was there until he had turned the corner of the L. Ruth wondered uneasily how much he had overheard. He stood with his head a bare inch from the low beams, the inevitable cap in his hands, looking hangdog and miserable.

'Wilson!' Once more the employer, Westwood barked the name at him. 'What the devil are you doing here?'

'I've only just heard the news.' Wilson was looking at Ruth. 'I'm terribly sorry, Mrs Banning.'

Ruth said nothing. She was too deep in her plans to respond either to sorrow or sympathy. But Westwood was clearly annoyed. His high forehead wrinkled in a frown.

'You seem to have a fondness for this district, Wilson,' he said. 'Don't tell me you're here merely to inquire into Banning's health. The telephone would have been just as efficient, and cheaper and quicker. What's the attraction?'

His voice was loaded with sarcasm. Wilson wanted to tell him to mind his own business, that this was Saturday and he had a right to use it as he wished. But he had not yet been handed his notice. Until that happened there was always the faint hope that he might be reprieved.

'I spent last night with friends in Lewes, Mr Westwood. Right now I'm on my way home. But I told Mrs Banning I would look in at the hospital, and I did.' From habit his tone was deferential. He tugged at his tie to relieve the pressure on his Adam's apple, and glanced again at Ruth. 'I really am sorry, Mrs Banning. A dreadful thing to happen.'

He shifted his feet in a moment of indecision, then turned with a muttered good-bye and walked away, his long body as uncoordinated as a marionette.

''And Melancholy mark'd him for her own.'' Mark grinned. 'Now, who said that? Before me, I mean.'

'Thomas Gray,' his wife told him.

'Did he? Well, I reckon he must have had our friend Wilson in mind. But I'll say this for the poor chap — his distress seemed genuine. Were he and Arthur buddies?'

Westwood shrugged. Intimacies between employees were outside his ken, but now he would have given much to know what had existed between Wilson and Banning. Certainly from Wilson's attitude the previous morning it had not sounded like friendship.

'I wouldn't know, I'm afraid. Were they, Mrs Banning?'

'No. Arthur didn't like him. He thought he was shifty.'

Mark laughed. 'Well, I may be Arthur's brother, but to me that sounds like the pot calling the kettle black.'

Ruth bridled. She had given little affection or credit to her husband while he was alive, but already he was assuming a more prepossessing aspect in her mind. After so much mental scheming she had almost forgotten that he had stolen; it was the money, not its source, that was important. It would be waiting for her at home (she had no doubt of that), and she felt a tremendous gratitude towards Arthur for having provided it. In Ruth's biased and single-minded view he had become the thoughtful husband insuring his family's future against his death.

She disliked Hugh Westwood, but she could not blame him for his angry bitterness. His job and his future had been jeopardized by Arthur's action. But there was no such excuse for Mark. Mark should have sought to vindicate his brother, not disparage him; yet he had shown neither concern for Arthur's suffering nor sorrow at his death. His haste to reach the hospital had been occasioned by self-interest, not compassion, and he had brought her with him only because to Mark it was important that he should at least appear to be acting correctly. The little she had overheard outside Arthur's room the previous evening had been enough to tell her that.

Mark said cheerfully, 'Poor old Arthur. All those months of earnest fiddling, afraid every day that he was about to be rumbled — and then to get himself killed just when he's heading for the big pay-off. That's irony for you.' He shook his head. 'Well, he always was incompetent. Destined for failure was Arthur — though I never thought he'd turn crook.'

Ruth could contain her indignation no longer. The belief that she was now a rich woman, that financially at least she was the equal of her brother-in-law, gave her a new temerity. She said breathlessly, 'You ought to be ashamed of yourself, talking about your dead brother like that. If Arthur was a thief it was the company's meanness drove him to it; they practically forced him to take that money. You're far more wicked than ever he was. I heard what you said last night — how you hoped Arthur would die quickly. You thought you and Carol were alone; you didn't know I was listening. But I was. The door wasn't shut.'

Mark fingered his moustache, then moved the hand to scratch his cheek. It was a nervous and uncustomary gesture. He was not often disconcerted.

'You've got me wrong, Ruth,' he protested, aware that Westwood was regarding him with curiosity. 'Of course I didn't want Arthur to die. What I said was — '

'I heard what you said.' She was not prepared to listen to excuses and evasions. 'What's more, I know why you said it. It's because of the insurance policy, isn't it? The one you took out on Arthur's life after he'd had pneumonia. You said it would provide something for Philip and me when he died, but that it was to be in your name so that you could make sure the money was put to the best use. I know you asked him to say nothing about it to me — that would have made it difficult for you, wouldn't it? — but he did. You weren't fooling anyone, Mark. We both knew the use it would be put to, that neither Philip nor I would ever see a penny of it.' She puffed out her cheeks indignantly, so that the mottled patches looked like dark land masses on a pink globe. 'And now I suppose you're in some sort of a hole, and poor Arthur couldn't die quick enough to help you out.'

The slight change of expression on Carol's lovely face showed that she was worried. Westwood looked from accuser to accused and wondered which to believe. But before Mark could find words with which to refute the charge a voice from the L said quietly, 'Is that true,

Mr Banning? I'd be interested to know.'

Kane walked farther into the room and stood regarding Mark. The two had met for a brief moment at the hospital earlier that morning.

His composure now thoroughly adrift, Mark said angrily, 'What the hell has it to do with you, Inspector? I'm not aware that private family matters are any concern of the police.'

Kane shook his blond head in a gesture of reproach rather than negation.

'They often are, you know. Very often. Particularly when murder is involved.'

'Murder? But this isn't — ' Mark paused, and nodded. 'Yes, of course. Arthur was murdered, wasn't he? I was forgetting that. But I still don't see — '

'I hope you don't, sir.' Kane was looking at Ruth. He did not like what he had to say. 'The pathologist has carried out an autopsy on your husband, Mrs Banning. That is the normal procedure in cases of unnatural death.' He hesitated, fingering the kink in his nose. 'I'm afraid this will come as a shock to you, but it seems that death was not the result of the

214

injuries he sustained prior to his admittance to hospital. At some time last night — probably around midnight — he was deliberately murdered.'

* * *

Jimmy Kane was shy with women. Young women in particular seemed to find him attractive, and this embarrassed him. Charm, he thought, was an attribute inappropriate in a policeman; in a detective inspector pushing forty it was almost indecent. So he was wary of the blond nurse's friendliness, uncertain whether her obvious interest in him was personal or vocational. To establish a rapport with a person from whom he was seeking information often made the job easier, but he was not risking it with Nurse Gracey. He would keep the interview strictly official.

'Visitors? Well, his wife and his brother and his sister-in-law came just after seven,' she told him. She sat perched on the arm of a chair, one leg swinging. Kane kept his eyes averted. 'His employer joined them later, while the doctor was there. I don't think he had any other visitors.' She leaned forward, her blue eyes wide. 'What happened to your nose?'

'I broke it playing rugger. When did these people leave?'

'I don't know. Some time before nine.' She smoothed back a strand of hair. 'That's when I go off duty.'

Ignoring this gratuitous piece of information, he snapped his notebook shut and stood up. Nurse Gracey did not take the hint. Still swinging, she said cheerfully, 'Your job's rather like ours in a way, isn't it? I mean, we both deal with people in misfortune. Do you like it?'

'Some of it.' He was beginning to thaw. She was very pretty, and her friendliness was infectious. It was also, he thought, ingenuous. 'Not all, I'm afraid. Do you?'

'The work, yes. It's fascinating. But the people — well, some of them are odd, to say the least. There was a young man last night — a visitor — ' She shuddered deliciously. 'I think he was responsible for my nightmare.'

'What did he do?'

216

It wasn't what he did, she said, but the way he looked. Tough and rough. 'Like something out of the Stone Age. You know — thick lips, piggy eyes, a receding forehead, and his face and hands covered with hair. But no eyebrows. And when he smiled — at least, I suppose it was a smile — his teeth looked dreadful. All black and broken. Oh, yes — and he had boils. Lots of them.'

'Sounds a handsome fellow,' Kane said, smiling for the first time. 'Who was he visiting?'

No one, said Miss Gracey. That was the odd thing. She explained how the youth had wandered up and down the ward, how he had stood by the trolley listening to her conversation with a gentleman who was inquiring after Banning, and had hurried away when she spoke to him. Kane found this interesting; not only because of the Stone Age youth, but because of the other visitor. Tall, lean, and drooping, was how Nurse Gracey described him — with a straggling moustache and grey hair coming to a pronounced peak on his forehead. To Kane that description fitted George Wilson exactly.

'He didn't ask to see the patient,' the girl said. 'He only wanted to know how he was progressing.'

'What time was this?'

'About ten minutes to eight.'

For Kane the interview was over, but Nurse Gracey appeared to be in no hurry to leave. He wondered what had become of the nursing shortage, and was relieved when Baker arrived with the ward sister. Nurse Gracey did not wait to be told. She left immediately, with a rustle of starch and the merest nod to Kane.

'We'll walk to the pub,' Baker said. 'The car can follow.'

As they set off briskly down the hospital drive Kane wondered again at the superintendent's energy; for a man in his sixties he was surprisingly fit. But outside the gates they slowed. 'Take it easy,' Baker said. 'There are nuts to crack before we arrive.'

The first concern of the police had been to discover how, with a nurse and a detective constable at Banning's bedside, the killer could have got into the room unobserved. Now Baker thought he had the answer. Shortly before midnight Parsons, the detective constable, had left the room to go to the lavatory, and while he was away the nurse had discovered that there was insufficient 'Complan' for the patient's next meal. On reporting this to the ward sister she had been told that the nurse on duty in the main ward had gone to supper, and that she would have to fetch the 'Complan' herself.

'Which means that Banning was alone for from five to ten minutes,' Baker pointed out. 'Unfortunate, but no one's fault.'

'Very unfortunate,' Kane agreed. That, he thought, was something of an under-statement. 'Chummy must have been waiting outside the window, and grabbed his chance.'

'Or hers,' Baker said. 'Unlikely, I grant you, but let's have the facts right. A woman could get through that window as easily as a man.'

But Kane was off on another flight of fancy.

'No doubt the types who attacked Banning on Wednesday thought they had killed him. When they learned from the newspapers that he was still alive they decided to finish the job before he could recover consciousness and pass on their description. Something of a panic performance, perhaps — but wouldn't you say that's what happened, sir?' Baker grunted. 'They took a hell of a chance, though. They may have overheard the discussion between the nurse and the ward sister, but they couldn't know where Parsons had gone. He wouldn't have mentioned it to the girl. For all they knew he might have been back at any moment.'

A smile creased the superintendent's bronzed face. Parsons, he suspected, did not share Kane's bashfulness with women.

'Keep a sense of proportion, Jimmy. As you said yourself, it would have been something of a panic performance, not a coolly calculated operation; and when men panic they take chances. However, I don't accept your hypothesis. Not just like that. There are others who could have had an interest in Banning's demise. His brother, for one — if Mrs Banning has her facts right. It might be interesting to learn his present financial position and the amount of that policy. And then there's this fellow Westwood. With the mess he's in right now he must hate Banning's guts.'

'Maybe. But he wouldn't kill him, surely. Not until he had recovered the money. That would take priority over revenge, and he couldn't have both.'

'True.' Baker kicked impatiently at an empty beer can. It rattled down the highway for a few yards and then rolled back to the verge. 'But how about Wilson? Now there's a man who positively courts suspicion. He pops up all along the line, shrouded in mystery and unco-operation. He must know something; if not of the actual murder, then certainly of the events preceding it. The question is, how do we persuade him to talk?'

They turned off the main road. Ahead of them lay the church and the inn and the small cluster of other buildings which formed the core of Chawtry village. Kane, impatient of the superintendent's verbal spanner, reverted to his original theory. He was even prepared to name as the killer the uncouth youth Nurse Gracey had seen in the hospital corridor. Why else would he be there? Kane wanted to know. He had visited none of the other patients.

To the more cautious superintendent this was a dangerous assumption. It was a possibility, perhaps even a probability. But no more than that.

'There was another youth visited the hospital last night,' he said. 'Around half-past eleven, according to the night sister. She came out of her room to find him in the corridor. He didn't give his name, but told her he happened to be passing and had called to inquire after Banning. A short, plump youth, she said, with brown hair and a rather bucolic face.' Baker walked a few paces in silence. 'Does that description fit anyone you know?'

'Not personally,' Kane said. 'It has a vague resemblance to Worsfold's Dick Smith, if that's what you had in mind.'

After a pause for thought he added, 'Maybe the two youths are connected. The first spies out the land, the second does the killing. If the sister had not disturbed him he might have walked in through the door, all unsuspecting — and that would have been that. Parsons would have nabbed him. But as it was — ' He shrugged. 'I suppose the window was the obvious alternative.'

'You and your theories,' Baker said.

A police-car passed them and stopped. The driver was already out on the road as they drew level.

'A message from Lewes, sir,' he said, saluting. 'They're holding a man they think you want to interview. Name of Dick Smith.'

11

One look at Dick Smith was enough to tell Kane that this was not the youth whom the ward sister had seen in the corridor the previous night. His hair was more ginger than brown, and although he had a certain plumpness he was neither fat nor stocky. Nor was his face bucolic; it had the shrewd perkiness of the Cockney, although now it looked as though he had dived head first through a hawthorn hedge. And if he bore a faint similarity to Worsfold's description, so did thousands of others.

But he did not deny his identity, and Kane wasted little time in preliminaries. He told the youth bluntly what he knew, what he suspected. Smith had been cooling his heels at the station for over an hour, and some of his natural cockiness had deserted him. The knowledge that he was suspected of murder quickly dispelled the rest.

'But I never done it, mister,' he said desperately. He had a mobile face that reflected his moods. 'Honest, I didn't. This geezer you say was croaked — I never even heard of him. He don't mean nothink to me.'

'No? Where were you last night?'

He was confused about that. At the flicks earlier; that at least he knew. But later he had started on a round of the pubs, and from then on the evening became hazy. He could vaguely recall odd incidents: a girl who had cheeked him — a coffee-bar — a ride in a taxi. 'I reckon I was good and sloshed. When I woke up this morning I felt like me loaf was full of little hammers, and all of 'em knocking hell out of it. They ain't stopped yet.' He stroked his forehead with a hand on which the creases of the knuckles were grey lines of dirt. 'But I never done no murder. That I'll swear to.'

'Will you?' Kane eyed him steadily for a few silent moments. 'H'm! Well, let's go back to the beginning, shall we? Finger-prints found in your room at the Worsfolds' tally with those in the dead man's car. Most of them were on the steering-wheel. Any comment?'

Smith shrugged. 'O.K. So I was in a car. I been in lots of cars.'

'I'm sure you have. How about a Morris Thousand that was involved in an accident near Offham on Wednesday night? Were you driving that?'

Smith said cautiously, 'I may have been.'

'Suppose you tell me about it.'

Reluctantly, Smith told him. He had had a good afternoon at the races — 'Won close on thirty nicker' — and had spent the evening celebrating in the Lewes pubs. In one of these he had met a youth who lived out beyond Plumpton, and together they had put in some solid drinking. Being a Londoner, it did not occur to Smith that the last bus might leave before closing-time; when his new friend had announced that they had two minutes in which to catch it they had downed their beer and run — to see the bus pulling away from the still distant stop.

There had been no alternative but to

walk. But Smith was no walker, and when they found the Morris with the key in the ignition switch he had not hesitated. Neither had his friend. They had climbed aboard and driven off.

'Drunk,' Kane said succinctly.

'We wasn't drunk,' Smith retorted, some of his cockiness returning. 'Just wet.'

'The way you drove says you were drunk.' But to Kane this was less important than the result, and he said, 'Couple of heroes, weren't you? For all you knew the occupants of the car you hit might have been seriously injured. Yet all you thought of was saving your own dirty little hides.'

The sneer was wasted on Smith. He nodded, lank hair falling over his forehead.

'Sure. But me, I couldn't think proper. I'd cut me face on the glass, and I was all shook up. But this other chap, he says as how if we don't scarper we'll find ourselves in the nick. So we scarpers.' Smith sighed at the memory. 'And a bleeding do it was an' all, running across them flipping fields. Jumping ditches, we was, and climbing gates and busting through hedges. It made a right proper mucker of me duds.' He ran a hand over his battered cheeks. 'And look at me face.'

'I'm looking.' There was no sympathy in the inspector's voice. 'What happened to your friend?'

Smith shrugged. 'Last I seen of him was outside me digs. He said he lived another couple of miles down the road.'

'What was his name?'

'Search me, mister. We just called each other Bud.'

Kane wondered how much of this was truth. If Smith had indeed stolen the Morris in Lewes, then he had not robbed Banning; and if he had not robbed him he would have had no reason to kill him. He could be just a little fish caught up in the net.

Only one factor denied it. The watch.

'That's a nice ticker you've got there,' he said, staring at Smith's wrist. The youth's jacket was short in the sleeve. 'Where did you get it?'

Smith lifted his arm, so that the sleeve

228

rode up to show a dirty expanse of shirt-cuff. He too stared at the watch.

'I bought it,' he said, after a pause.

'Where?'

'In Brighton.'

'Now we're back with the lies,' Kane said. 'You told the Worsfolds you bought it in a pub Wednesday evening.'

'O.K. So I bought it in a pub.'

'In Lewes?' The youth did not answer. Kane said sharply, 'All right, Smith — take it off. You'll get it back if it's yours. But if Mrs Banning identifies it as having belonged to her husband — ' He took a deep breath. 'Well, you're in the muck, lad. Right up to the ruddy eyebrows. Come on, hand it over.'

Smith obeyed. 'It was in the pocket of the Morris,' he said sullenly. 'I seen it there and — well, you know how it is, mister.'

'I'm beginning to,' Kane told him.

But he wasn't. Why would Banning remove his watch and put it in the glove pocket? Or if he hadn't — why would his assailants? If they had taken the trouble to unstrap it from his wrist it was because they wanted it. They would not leave it in the car.

Prior to this final improbability Kane had been inclined to accept the youth's story. Now he doubted it. But he could not shake it, and eventually he abandoned his efforts and took Smith down to the charge-room.

'Book him,' he said to the station sergeant.

Smith was voluble in his protests. 'I never done it,' he almost shouted. 'I tell you, I never done it. You ain't pinning no murder on me, mister.'

'No? Then we'll have to make do with other charges.' Kane enumerated them on his fingers. 'Taking and driving away a motor vehicle without the consent of the owner: using a motor vehicle without a policy of insurance being in force: driving while under the influence of drink: failing to report an accident: driving without due care and attention: stealing by finding. Those will do for a start. Give me time and I'll think up some more.'

Dick Smith disposed of, Kane telephoned Baker at divisional headquarters.

'I'm off to Croydon, sir,' he told him. 'Wilson-wards. And I'll check the watch with Mrs Banning. I might also make a few discreet inquiries about the missing cash.'

'Go easy on that, Jimmy,' the superintendent warned. 'It's not our baby. By the way, we've matched the dabs found on the hospital window.'

'It wasn't clean?'

'No. We've got several. Some were made by a ward orderly, the others by our friend Westwood.'

Kane whistled. 'Good Lord! Westwood!'

'My own reaction exactly,' Baker said equably. 'But unfounded. According to Nurse Gracey Westwood opened the window from inside while she was there. The only factor of possible interest is that it was done at Mark Banning's request.'

★ ★ ★

As he relaxed in front of the television-set Philip decided that he had eaten too many baked beans for lunch. He liked beans, but they gave him wind; his stomach felt like an inflated balloon, and he kept belching to relieve the pressure. He and Roddy had finished the stew and the pressed veal and the treacle tart the previous night, on their return from Brighton. Now there was nothing in the larder. Come supper-time he would have to go out for fish and chips.

He had turned down the volume some ten minutes ago. No football fan, he was not interested in the players as people and teams; but one had to watch something on a Saturday afternoon, and he found the pattern of movement pleasantly soporific. Now he sank farther into the armchair and closed his eyes, blotting out the vision also. It had been after two when he got to bed. He needed to catch up on sleep.

His head lolled on the padded head-rest. He was almost asleep when the closing of the front door, the sound of footsteps in the hall, returned him to consciousness. But his eyelids felt too heavy to lift, and he called out drowsily, 'That you, Mum?'

There was no answer. For a full minute he waited, listening to the silence, wondering what she was doing but too lethargic to make the effort to investigate. He yawned and stretched, pressing back against the head-rest and arching his spine. Then he slumped down into the chair with a deep sigh, and opened his eyes.

A stranger had come into the room; a heavy, dark-visaged youth with stubble on his chin and boils on his face. He stood near the door, one hand sunk in the pocket of his jeans, the other puckering his woollen jersey as he scratched his chest.

For a brief moment neither youth spoke nor moved. Chug Wallis was as startled as Philip. He had known that the man and the woman were in Chawtry, and it had not occurred to him that there might be others in the family. He had entered the house on the assumption that it was unoccupied. But dismay had no part in his surprise. The overfed slob gazing at him open-mouthed from the armchair presented no problem.

'What the devil — !' Philip sat up with a jerk, gripping the arms of the chair. 'How the hell did you get in? Who are you, anyway?'

Chug took his hand from the pocket and held up a slender bunch of keys, swinging them on a ring held between a stubby thumb and forefinger.

'Your old man give 'em to me. And it don't matter who I am.' He advanced farther into the room. 'Come on, get up.'

Philip got up. He was frightened, but he was also angry.

'You've no right to come busting into the house like this.' His voice sounded disconcertingly reedy to his ears. 'Give me those keys and scram, or I'll call the police.'

Chug's thick lips stretched in an evil grin. He returned the keys to his pocket and shambled forward, slapping the balled fist of his right hand against the palm of the left. Philip backed away; he was all fear now, anger forgotten. He felt the seat of the chair against his calves and stepped sideways, hoping to put the chair between himself and the menacing intruder. But the movement delayed his retreat. Chug took advantage of it. Still grinning, he took a quick stride forward and sank the balled fist viciously into the pit of the other's stomach.

Philip grunted and folded, fighting for breath, tears starting from his eyes. He felt as though the balloon had burst, draining the air from inside him. And there seemed to be none outside. He gasped for it, clawed for it, without avail. In the dread conviction that his lungs were about to burst, he clutched his tortured stomach and sank slowly to his knees.

Chug too seemed to find difficulty in breathing. The air whistled through his blackened teeth with an ugly, convulsive sound, his broad chest heaved. But not from exertion. Physical violence excited him. Unable to resist the temptation, he shot out a foot and landed it full on the kneeling youth's rump.

Philip did not cry out; he had no breath for that. Still gasping, still clutching his stomach, he toppled forward to hit the floor with his head, and rolled over on to his side. Chug gave him a kick in the ribs, poised his foot for another, and decided against it. He might need the slob's assistance.

'Get up, you,' he said. His jaw felt stiff, set. He was quivering with excitement.

Philip blinked at him with tear-filled eyes. His ribs were sore, but the air was returning to his lungs. Chug's right foot was moving, scraping the carpet, and he took his hands from his stomach and propped himself up on them, trying to rise. There was an expression of menacing purpose on the dark face above him.

'Get up!' Chug said again, spitting out the words. 'If you ain't up pronto I'll boot you round the bleeding room.'

Somehow he managed it. He got slowly and painfully to his knees, grabbed at the chair, and pulled himself up. There were tear streaks down his plump cheeks, and he rubbed them with the back of a hand.

'W-what do you want?' he sobbed.

'Your old man's lolly,' Chug told him. 'The lolly what he pinched from his firm. It's here somewheres. Or didn't you know?'

Even in his fear Philip was able to feel surprise. What on earth was the brute talking about? Arthur might be a wet, but he was no thief. This was some terrible mistake.

'There's no money here,' he said dully.

'That's where you're wrong, mate. Five thousand nicker is what his boss reckoned there'd be. So you'n me's going to find it, see? Got any bright ideas where to look?'

Philip had none. The afternoon had developed into a nightmare, and he had little thought for anything except how to evade further punishment. Of one thing he was sure, however; there was no money, and there never had been. But to insist on this now would be to invite another hiding. Let the brute discover it for himself.

'No,' he said.

Chug clucked impatiently, and turned to the massive bookcase. Five thousand pounds was a lot of money, and he had no knowledge of how large a space would be needed to conceal it. But the bookcase was as good a starting-point as any, and he said roughly, 'Get them books out. All on 'em. And get 'em out quick.'

Philip did not argue. The sooner the search was done the sooner he might be rid of his tormentor.

He started to remove the books, piling them neatly on the floor.

Chug wandered round the room, looking under cushions and behind curtains and pictures, peering into the china cabinet, exploring fireplace and chimney, sounding the floor with his foot for a loose board. Satisfied that the money was in none of these places, he returned to the bookcase.

'For crying out loud!' With an impatient foot he sent a pile of books flying into the fireplace. 'Just bung 'em down. You ain't sorting no bleeding library.'

Philip bunged them down. Soon the floor was littered with books. Chug kicked them around in the hope that money might be concealed between the leaves. A few loose pages slipped from between the covers, but no notes. Disappointed, he picked up a heavy volume bound in worn leather and hurled it at the china cabinet, shattering the glass and most of the contents. The sight and sound of this wanton destruction relieved his ill-temper. Almost cheerfully he said, 'Well, it ain't here. We'll try some place else,' and cuffed the frightened Philip from the room.

They searched the hall, the kitchen, the dining-room. From the kitchen window Chug saw the garden shed, a derelict construction in need of paint, and remembered that the woman had named it as a possible hiding-place. But the adjoining houses were too close to risk a walk down the garden in daylight. Next door a man was mowing the lawn; the slob might be tempted to call for help. If the house did not yield what he was seeking he would try the shed after dark.

'Upstairs,' he told Philip. 'Your old man's room first.'

Philip obeyed without argument, anxious to conclude the search. His ribs still ached and he had a bad headache, but there had been no further violence; only a trail of disorder and wanton destruction. He wondered unhappily how Chug would react when the search finally proved fruitless. Would he vent his spleen on him, as he had vented it on the china cabinet?

It was a terrifying thought.

In the main bedroom Chug made first for the ottoman, hauling out blankets and towels and linen and piling them on the floor, and cursing obscenely at his lack of success. Philip stood by the bed, silent and watchful, relieved that for once he was being ignored. As Chug started to rummage through the wardrobe he even considered the possibility of escape. The bedroom door was open. He had only to run down the stairs and out through the front door. There would be people in the street . . .

But even as he considered it he knew he could not do it. His legs weakened at the knees at the thought of what Chug might do should he fail to make it.

Chug was at the chest now, tugging at a drawer that would not open. Impatiently he tried to wrench it free. Then, realizing that it was locked, he produced the bunch of keys and fitted one into the lock.

As the drawer came out Philip edged

cautiously nearer, fear momentarily submerged in curiosity. He could hear the other's loud breathing, sensed his sudden excitement. Some of that excitement was even communicated to him. There would be no money, he knew that. But a locked drawer was always intriguing, and he was curious to know what this one contained.

''Struth!'

He regretted the exclamation immediately, knowing that it would attract the other's attention. But it had been involuntary, wrung from him at the sight of what Chug held in his hand. He had been wrong, there *was* money in the drawer — a bundle of treasury notes that to Philip looked like a fortune.

Chug turned quickly. To Philip's astonishment he was scowling.

'The bleeding swine! The ruddy — '

Mouth agape, he was suddenly silent, listening. Philip listened too. There was the sound of the front door closing, of footsteps in the hall, followed some minutes later by a feminine exclamation of horrified dismay.

'Philip! Where are you, Philip? What on

earth's been happening?'

The fierce grip of Chug's hand on his arm made Philip wince.

'Who's that?' Chug whispered gruffly.

'My mother.'

'Philip!' Ruth's voice was tearful. 'Where are you?'

'Tell her to come up.' Chug tossed the notes on to the bed and whipped a knife from its sheath at his back, to hold the point menacingly at Philip's throat. 'And no funny business, see? Just say to come up.'

Philip jerked his head back, tucking in his chin. The knife followed. It had a razor-like edge.

'I — I'm up here, Mum.' As he swallowed hard it seemed to him that he could feel the sharp point pricking his Adam's apple. 'Come up, will you?'

12

George Wilson's lean fingers wandered over his face; brushing back the peak of his hair, knuckling moustache and nose, poking into his ears. If the inspector's visit had not frightened him he was certainly ill at ease. Tieless, dressed in a loose fawn pullover and grey slacks, with felt slippers on his feet, he stood by the window staring across the Croydon rooftops. On a low, glass-topped table near the fireplace were tea-things and a tin of biscuits. He had poured tea for himself and his visitor, but his cup remained untouched.

'You can't opt out of this, Mr Wilson,' Kane told him. 'You're involved, whether you like it or not.'

Wilson turned slowly. He looked tired and unhappy.

'But I didn't kill him. You must know that.'

'Must I? Innocent men don't usually

act the way you've acted. Not in my experience.'

'I had my reasons.' Wilson left the window, to seat himself in an old armchair near the tea-tray. With a touch of spirit he added, 'What business is it of yours, anyway? Why should the police poke their noses into my private affairs? And they are private. They have nothing to do with murder. Nothing.'

Kane leaned forward. He said earnestly, 'Let's stop playing games, sir, shall we? If you didn't kill Banning — if your trips into Sussex were in no way connected with his death — then we're not interested. But you can't expect us to take your word for it; we need proof, Mr Wilson, not protestations. How we get it is up to you. We can have you watched, dig into your private life, make inquiries of friends and colleagues and employers. That could be laborious for us and disagreeable for you, but it would probably get results. The alternative is for you to volunteer the information. We would have to check, of course, but it would be done discreetly.' He shrugged.

'As I said, it's up to you.'

Wilson picked up his cup, sipped and grimaced.

'It's cold.' He felt the teapot. 'So is that. I'll get some hot water.'

In his absence Kane studied the room. It was at the top of a large Georgian house which had been converted into flats; spacious and high-ceilinged, with ornate cornices and a heavy marble fireplace, and wallpaper that looked as though it had been there for a long, long time. So did some of the furniture. But not all. There was a fair proportion of the modern — of Scandinavian design, Kane thought. The glass ornaments on the wide mantelpiece were definitely Swedish.

Wilson shuffled back into the room, steam wisping from the spout of the kettle. He topped up the pot, poured milk and tea into the two cups, and returned to the window to stand with his back to the room.

'I can't stand the thought of publicity,' he said.

Kane guessed his train of thought. 'There doesn't have to be any,' he said. 'It depends on how deeply you're involved.'

Clouds were darkening the sky to the south. Wilson watched them, stirring his tea. Presently he turned, looked at his visitor, and then down at his cup.

'What do you want to know?' he asked.

'Well, now — ' Kane's voice gave no hint of the relief he felt. 'Shall we start with the reason for your trip to Lewes Wednesday evening?'

'I was looking for my daughter.'

Kane had not known there was a daughter, but his immediate impression was that this piece of information could hardly be relevant. How did Wilson's daughter tie in with Banning? It was only when he recalled his original assumption — that Wilson had been following Banning because he suspected the latter of having an affair with his wife — that he thought he had the answer.

'You thought she was with Banning? Is that it?'

Yes, said Wilson, that was it. He had known for some weeks of the man's infatuation with his daughter, but the knowledge had not troubled him. Not

246

after he had spoken to Doris. Doris, while acknowledging the infatuation, had made it clear that Banning was wasting his time. She had even joked about it; 'that funny, fat little man, with the red face and the turkey-cock walk,' was how she had referred to her would-be lover. 'I can do better than that, thank you.'

Kane smiled. 'Banning was certainly no Apollo,' he agreed. 'Have you a photograph of your daughter, Mr Wilson?'

'Only a snapshot.' He took a wallet from his hip pocket. 'That was taken last year, I believe.'

Kane studied the bikini-clad figure with approval. Miss Wilson, he thought, had been right to aim higher than the luckless Banning.

'A remarkably pretty girl,' he said, returning the snapshot. 'How old is she?'

'Just nineteen. But you'd think she was older. She's got this streak of restlessness — and a terribly mercenary outlook on life, I'm afraid. Perhaps that's partly my fault; having seen poverty at home she decided anything was better than that.' There was sadness, not bitterness, in his voice. 'And who can blame her? I never have. I've given her what help and guidance I could, but like all young things she's impatient of parental control. Thinks she's outgrown it.' He sighed. 'It might have been different if her mother had lived. Alice would have known how to handle her.'

He went on talking about the girl. Kane listened, wishing to appear sympathetic but inwardly impatient. Wilson was clearly obsessed by his daughter. Devoted to her too. If he criticized (as he did) he was quick to excuse or find a quality to praise. Kane got the picture of a doting father and a spoilt and wayward daughter, and wondered what all this had to do with him.

'I can't imagine her with Banning,' he said quickly, when Wilson paused. 'What made you think she had changed her attitude towards him?'

He had seen them leaving a restaurant together one lunch-hour. When he taxed Doris with it later she had told him that they had met by chance in the foyer, but Wilson had doubted that. It was an expensive restaurant, not the sort of place Doris would have chosen had she been paying. Nor did it explain the smugly triumphant expression he had seen on Banning's face, or the almost proprietary air with which the man had taken her arm to help her unnecessarily down the steps.

'I can always tell when she's lying,' Wilson said. He sounded unhappy about it. 'Practice, I suppose. Although I'm sure the lies are invented to spare me.'

'Could we move on now to last Wednesday?' Kane suggested. He had had enough of preliminaries.

It was on the Wednesday morning that Doris had left. 'She told me she would be spending a few days in London with a friend,' Wilson explained. 'I was uneasy about it, but I didn't try to stop her. I knew it would be useless. What really shook me was hearing that Banning had been given a few days' holiday. It was too big a coincidence. Yet what could I do? I tried to telephone Banning, but he had already left — without his wife, which increased my suspicion. He had told her he was going on business for the company, but I knew that to be untrue. LAPP don't send men like us on that sort of errand.'

Kane wondered what he meant by 'men like us.' Was it character or business standing he was referring to?

'But why Lewes?' he asked. The man could not have gone there by chance. He must have had some indication of where to look for his daughter.

Yet in a way it had been chance. After his abortive attempt to contact Banning on the telephone Wilson had gone downstairs, intending to garage the car, and had met one of the three men who shared the basement flat. The man worked in the station booking-office, and had mentioned that he had sold Doris a ticket to Lewes that morning. So Wilson had gone to look for her. And it was in Lewes that he had seen the Morris go past.

'I just followed them,' he said. 'What else could I do?'

'Not much,' Kane agreed. He felt sorry for the man, but he had no consolation to give. 'Why didn't you explain this to the station sergeant after the accident? Why all the mystery?'

Wilson stared at him. 'And have her name plastered across the newspapers? With his?' There was a depth of scorn in that last query. 'Good God, no!'

'That wouldn't necessarily have happened,' Kane told him. He wondered if the man were entirely sane where his daughter was concerned. 'Not unless Banning and your daughter had been in the Morris when it crashed. Did you think they were.'

'Of course.'

Wilson brought his cup back to the table, and collapsed rather than lowered himself into the chair. To Kane it seemed that his defences had collapsed with him.

'Why did you call at the hospital Friday evening?' he asked.

'I hoped Banning might have recovered consciousness. I wanted to ask him about Doris.'

'You didn't go back there later that night?'

'No.' His tired brain read no more into the question than the literal. 'It would have been pointless. Even if he were conscious I knew I wouldn't be allowed to see him.'

'H'm!' Kane stood up. 'Well, that about wraps it up, I think, sir. Thanks for the cuppa. Perhaps I might have a word with your daughter later? What time does she get home?' There was an odd expression on Wilson's lined face, and he added hastily, 'I'm not doubting your word, sir, but we'll need her side of the story as well. Not that it will help us much, I'm afraid, seeing that Banning was attacked before he reached Lewes and they never actually met.' He hesitated. 'That's true, isn't it? They didn't meet?'

'I wouldn't know,' Wilson told him. 'I haven't seen her since Wednesday morning. She hasn't been back.'

Kane frowned. 'That's odd, isn't it?'

Wilson gave a half-hearted shrug. 'I've tried every hotel in Lewes,' he said wearily. 'She isn't there. I thought of listing her as missing, but she wouldn't thank me for that. Maybe when Banning failed to turn up she really did go to London. Your guess is as good as mine.'

As he drove to Croydon police-station Kane reflected that Wilson's story contained much that was puzzling, even contradictory. His assumption that his daughter had gone to meet Banning had apparently been based on just one glimpse of the couple leaving a restaurant together, plus the coincidence of a ticket to Lewes and the injured Banning being found a few miles away. And that last fact had not been known to him until after he had made his assumption.

Was that enough? Why should Wilson believe that his daughter, to whose mercenary outlook even his devotion could not blind him, could so suddenly change her attitude towards Banning? Didn't it presuppose that he had known of the money Banning had stolen; for how else would a man in Banning's position get money for that sort of caper? And if he had known, why had he not warned Westwood?

George Wilson, Kane decided, might still have much to explain.

★　★　★

'Criminal negligence,' Phelps said wrathfully, tone and manner in keeping with his massive bulk. 'There are no other words for it. I wouldn't credit it in a junior clerk, let alone a branch manager.' Sentences of more than a few words left him breathless, and he paused to recover. 'You say Banning is dead?'

'Yes, sir.'

Standing there in the area manager's study, with the man's bloodshot eyes brooding on him angrily, Westwood was reminded of how George Wilson must have felt the previous morning. But he was no Wilson. That old fool in the armchair was not going to trample on him as he, Westwood, had trampled on Wilson. Meekness was well enough for a start, it would allow Phelps to get the initial wrath out of his system the sooner. But once that was over he must be made to see that his own position was not entirely enviable, that he too had some responsibility for what had occurred. They were in this together.

'H'm! A pity. I'd like to have taught the bastard a lesson.' Death, apparently, was not sufficiently severe. 'Six thousand, you say?'

'Something like that.' He knew Phelps. Excuses and protestations would merely whet the old man's anger, serve as fuel to keep him going. Which was why he had offered none. Without them Phelps would run down the sooner. 'I haven't yet got the exact figures.'

Phelps shifted his big body in the chair. He was worried as well as angry. Head Office were going to be difficult about this. It was he who had recommended Westwood for the branch managership; how far would they hold him responsible? And he was due for retirement in a few years. A fine way to finish!

It did not help his temper that Westwood had chosen a Saturday afternoon to break the news. The man had had no choice, of course, but it made a mess of the week-end.

'I gather you haven't informed the police?'

'No, sir. I thought it best to consult you first. I believe they've got wind of it, but they are unlikely to take action until the company asks for it.'

'And you say there is a possibility that the bulk of the money may be recovered?'

'Banning's relatives seem to think so.' He spoke precisely, his deep voice measured. On his way to Phelps's house he had been nervous; he held a minor trump, but he had been uncertain how and when to play it. Now he had regained his confidence. The trump might not take the trick, but he had nothing to lose by playing it. And at least he would deflate that bag of wind opposite. 'I went along with the idea at first — wishful thinking, perhaps — but now I doubt it. It's my guess Banning had invested the money abroad and was on his way to collect.'

'Was his wife in the know?'

Westwood shrugged. 'Could be. But unlikely. There's a school of thought which says that another woman is involved.'

There was a long silence. Westwood took a cigarette from an expensive silver case, tapped the end, and lit it. Leaning back in his chair, he blew a smoke-ring and watched it circle upward and vanish.

His composure irritated Phelps. The man should have been making excuses, pleading for leniency. Not calmly blowing smoke-rings.

Phelps heaved his bulk into a more upright position and leaned forward, his enormous hands gripping his knees.

'Dammit, man, don't you realize what this can do to you?' His voice was a breathless growl. 'You're still comparatively young, you might have gone far.' Westwood knew this to be untrue, knew that Phelps knew it too. As far as LAPP were concerned he had reached the top. An area managership was not for him, he hadn't the right background. 'But now — ' Phelps shook his head, his long jowls flapping. 'I don't understand you, Westwood. I knew you were a cool fish — that's partly why I recommended you for the job — but if I were in your shoes right now I'd be sweating blood.' He struggled for breath. 'Haven't you anything to say in your defence?'

Westwood caressed his chin. It was smooth to the touch. He had shaved a second time that afternoon, and had taken particular pains over the rest of his appearance. Not to impress Phelps, but to bolster his own assurance. To look good was to feel good.

'One can always make excuses, sir, but it doesn't shift the responsibility. I don't have to tell you that.'

Phelps frowned. 'What excuses?'

'You may remember that the transfer of the properties involved occurred the day before I went on holiday. It didn't give me time to wrap things up properly. And then there was that damned accident; it kept me away for a month, instead of the fortnight I'd planned. As a result I was thoroughly out of touch when I returned.' Westwood pulled thoughtfully at his long nose. It pleased him that Phelps was still frowning. 'Because of that it was particularly unfortunate that your verbal orders to me were never followed by the usual written instructions. Subconsciously I may have relied on them; I wouldn't know. The fact remains, there was nothing on paper to put my staff in the picture, nothing to jog my memory when I returned.' He shrugged. 'But none of that excuses my forgetfulness. It merely explains it.'

The area manager's frown had given way to an expression of bewilderment tinged with mistrust.

'Are you telling me that you had no confirmation from this office of the transfer?'

'None at all.' Westwood hesitated. Should he show his hand boldly, or should he content himself with a broad hint? The latter course might be the more politic; it would enable Phelps to save his face if nothing else. Much as he despised the man, he needed his co-operation. 'You will want to check with your staff, of course, but I assure you that is so.' He twisted his thin lips into a smile. 'I suspect my neck won't be the only one to feel the chopper.'

'And just what do you mean by that?' Phelps's voice had become a rumble.

Westwood's grin vanished, his eyes hardened. Phelps had got the message, he thought. But he had to make sure, and he had to do so without coming completely into the open. If Phelps

259

were to disregard his own interests, choose to turn nasty . . .

'Well — ' He paused to consider. 'Who's responsible for seeing that such instructions are passed to the branches concerned? Your secretary? The chief clerk, perhaps?' Phelps stared at him without reply. Apart from his heavy breathing he was motionless. 'Anyway, whoever it was, he missed out on this lot — and, as you said yourself, such neglect amounts to almost criminal carelessness. He might try to pass the buck, of course, swear you gave him no such instructions. But that wouldn't get him far, would it? You'd have a copy of the memo. That's company rule, isn't it?'

The chair creaked as Phelps moved in it. Westwood moved too. He stubbed out his cigarette and stood up, smoothing the hair at the back of his head, adjusting jacket and tie. He hoped he looked more confident than he felt. For Phelps was watching. The bloodshot eyes followed his every action, as though seeking in them a clue to Westwood's intentions.

'I'm sorry about this, sir,' Westwood

said eventually. 'I feel I've let you down.' That was true enough, although he felt no sorrow for Phelps. I don't owe him anything, he thought. He gave me the job because I was the best man for it, not out of regard for me. 'Obviously the directors will insist on a full inquiry into the facts. Do I put in a written report, or do I leave that to you? Not that it can make much difference. To me, I mean.' His laugh was shriller than intended. 'I'm for the push — no doubt about that, eh?'

Phelps said nothing. As Westwood suspected, he had got the message. They both knew that there was no memo, that he had forgotten to inform his staff of the transfer. What Westwood could not know was that he was already in bad odour with the board. John had rescued him from previous lapses, but even a brother-in-law as chairman would be hard put to it to save him from this one.

Slowly he hoisted himself from the chair. It was a laborious process, and he was breathing hard as he stumped across to the fireplace and stood with one hand on the mantelpiece and a foot on the old-fashioned brass fender. He took a cigarette from a silver box, and lit it. Then he turned to look at Westwood through tired eyes.

'You had better leave it to me,' he said, his voice flat, expressionless. 'I'll see what I can do.'

★ ★ ★

Immediately she opened the front door Ruth realized that something was wrong. It was not the stale atmosphere or the odour of burnt fat from the kitchen that disturbed her; Philip would never bother to open a window, let alone clean up after his amateur attempts at cookery. But at the far end of the narrow hall the linoleum had been torn back, and there were books scattered over the floor. Not the lurid paperbacks that Philip occasionally read, but books in hard covers. And what would books be doing in the hall?

She put down the suitcase, slipped out of her shoes, and padded to the sitting-room door — to halt abruptly at the scene of confusion and destruction that met her eyes. With dismay she looked round the room; blinking at the empty bookcase, its doors open and the glass cracked, at the litter of books and cushions on the floor, at the disarranged pictures and ornaments and the torn chair-covers. But it was the wrecked china cabinet which grieved her most. Tears filled her eyes as she bent to gather up the pieces of a Dresden shepherdess and clumsily tried to fit head to body. A china fish lay on its side, its tail smashed, its glass eye winking at her. Philip had bought the fish for her on a day trip to Brighton two summers back, and she had treasured it because a present from Philip was a rarity in her life.

Philip! It was unthinkable that he could have done this. But where was he?

'Philip!' she called, her voice tearfully shaky. 'Where are you, Philip? What on earth's been happening?'

There was no answer. Still clutching the broken shepherdess she went down the hall to the dining-room. That too was in confusion, and she crept fearfully into the room, half expecting to see Philip's mangled body asprawl on the floor. But there was no body and no evident damage, and she went back to the hall.

'Philip!' she called again. This time her voice was shrill. 'Where are you?'

At first there was only the thumping of her heart to break the silence in the house. Then she thought to hear voices; urgent, whispering voices that seemed to come from upstairs. So Philip was not alone. He was in his room. Suddenly she was filled with the dread premonition of who his companion might be. A girl! Some dreadful little tart he had picked up in the street and had brought home in her absence to experiment with sex.

An involuntary shiver possessed her plump frame as she imagined what might be happening at that moment. Was she in time? What stage had the experiment reached? Then she caught sight of the book-strewn floor, and remembered the wrecked sitting-room and the china cabinet. A girl could not be responsible for that. It had to be a man — and with mingled relief and anger she guessed at who the man might be.

Roddy Stone.

She had one foot on the bottom stair when Philip called to her.

'I — I'm up here, Mum.' His voice sounded strange. 'Come up, will you?'

She went up. She had never liked Roddy Stone. Philip knew that: Roddy had an evil temper and was a no-good Ted, she had warned him, and sooner or later Philip would regret the friendship. It looked as though he might be regretting it now. Presumably he had brought Roddy back to the house and they had quarrelled and fought, and in a temper Roddy had deliberately wrecked the place. Physically Philip would be no match for Roddy. Now he was in his room, lying on his bed; hurt, perhaps badly. Only who was up there with him? Not Roddy. Roddy Stone would not stoop to help a man after he had knocked him down.

So — who?

As she reached the landing she called out again. Philip answered from the main bedroom, and she wondered why he should have chosen her bed to lie on rather than his own. The door was ajar and she pushed it open, feeling it bump against some one. That surprised her too. Why would Philip be hiding behind the door? She might be angry, but he knew he had nothing to fear from her. He never had.

Then she was in the room, and there was no more need for wonder. White faced and trembling, his hair dishevelled, Philip stood against the bed. And beside him, holding the point of a knife against Philip's throat, stood a blue-jerseyed, stocky youth, whom she did not know but whose scowling face seemed vaguely familiar.

'Oh, no!' Her hand flew to her mouth in a gesture of horrified disbelief. 'No!'

'Shut up!' Chug took the knife from Philip's throat and grabbed her arm, kicking the door shut as he pulled her into the room. He did not waste time on preliminaries. 'That money your old man nicked. Where is it, missus? What's he done with it?'

'Money?' For every moment of the journey home she had been eagerly anticipating the fortune that awaited her,

266

but now it had temporarily lost its significance. She could think only of her son. 'Are you all right, Philip?' she asked anxiously. 'He hasn't hurt you?'

He shook his head. 'I'm all right,' he muttered, too fearful of physical retaliation to say otherwise. He had not moved since her entrance.

Apart from his strained expression and dishevelled appearance he looked all right, but she needed to be sure. She would have gone to him had not Chug's vice-like grip restrained her. Furiously she turned on him, fear forgotten in her anxiety for Philip.

'Let me go, you brute!' she stormed, struggling to free her arm.

He swung her round and threw her on the bed. He still held the knife. Tapping it against the palm of his hand, he glared at her through small, close-set eyes.

'I ain't here to play games, missus. Like I said, I want that money.' She could smell his sour breath as he leaned over her, hear it whistling through his black, misshapen teeth. 'And if I don't get me hands on it quick you and that punk son of yours is going to be real sorry. I'm impatient, see?'

He drew away, still tapping the knife. Ruth sat up, frightened now for herself as well as for Philip, but too limp to attempt any positive action. Blankly she stared round the room, seeing the tumbled pile of linen and blankets on the floor, the rumpled clothes in the wardrobe. But confusion had suddenly become the norm. It was not until she saw that the locked drawer was now open that she realized the significance of what this brutal, terrifying youth had said, and became aware of what was happening.

He wanted Arthur's money. But she had been sure, absolutely sure, that it would be in the drawer; why else would Arthur have locked it, what else had he to hide? Yet now the drawer was open — which meant that she had been wrong, that the money had never been there or this young thug would have taken it and gone.

'I — I don't know what you're talking about,' she said. 'There isn't any money.'

'Don't you come no bleeding lies with

me,' he told her angrily. 'I heard, see? I was outside the winder. There's five thousand nicker somewheres in this house, and I want it.' He scratched with stubby fingers at a boil on his cheek. 'So you tell me where it is, missus, before some one gets hurt.'

Because his face looked familiar she had thought at first that he must be an acquaintance of Philip's, and that Philip had foolishly mentioned the money to him. But Philip had not known. He was upstairs when Westwood had broken the news to her and the Bannings; she remembered being glad of that, she had not wanted him to know that Arthur was in trouble. Even had he been listening he would have learned little. Westwood had mentioned no particular sum, no one had suggested there might be money hidden in the house. That had come later, at the hospital.

The hospital! That was where she had seen the youth — in the corridor, while she was talking to the young policeman. The knowledge was somehow comforting. At least Philip was blameless.

Chug was searching the other drawers in the chest. She moved quietly along the bed and squeezed her son's limp hand. His body shivered at the contact.

'How did he get in?' she whispered.

'He had Arthur's keys.'

He took his hand from hers, not looking at her, his eyes on Chug's broad back; afraid that Chug might turn on them, give him another taste of his ferocity. But Chug ignored them and continued the search. Once again Philip contemplated escape and rejected it; not through a desire to stay and protect his mother, but because his legs felt too rubbery. He knew he could never make it. Not with the door shut.

'He opened the drawer with them too,' he said, his voice a hoarse whisper, and pointed behind her. 'That money was in it.'

Ruth turned her head, exclaiming at sight of the notes. But before she could move her plump body to reach for them Chug had whipped them away.

'Two ton,' he growled, riffling the notes close to her face so that a faint breeze fanned her cheek. 'If that. Two ton out of six thousand! Where's the rest, missus? What's your old man done with it?'

There was both denial and perplexity in the shake of her head. What *had* Arthur done with it?

'I don't know,' she said.

Chug stared at her. She could be telling the truth. Back there in the hospital room they had talked a lot about the money, but no one had come right out with where it would be. Only that it was somewhere in the house. Yet if any one knew it should be the woman. And even if she didn't she must know best where to look. But these old bags could be stubborn. She had to be shown he meant business.

'Then find out, damn you!' he shouted. And gave her a vicious slap on the face.

Tears sprang to her eyes as she cried out and put a hand to her cheek, pressing in the pain. But they were tears of rage and frustration. She knew now that there was no money; that bundle of notes in her tormentor's grubby hand was all that Arthur had left her. And now she was to lose even that.

271

'You beast!' The red patches in her cheeks showed darkly as she took her hand away. 'Even if I knew where the money was I wouldn't tell you. Get out of here before I call the police.'

Her anger communicated itself to Chug. The slap had loosed his taste for violence; his breathing was quicker and heavier, his hands were clammy, there were beads of sweat on his brow. He wanted to lash out with boot and fist, to feel the satisfaction of impact, to gloat on his victim's agony. But the money was more important, and even Chug's small brain could appreciate that uncontrolled brutality would not bring him that. It had to be slow and deliberate; enough to make the woman talk, but not enough to numb.

And she had shown him the way.

Philip was still near the door. Even the assault on his mother had not moved him to action or protest; he had flinched at the sound of the slap and somehow his plump face managed to look pale and drawn, but he had not spoken. He did not speak now, when Chug turned on him.

He shrank a little deeper into the angle between wall and bed, and waited as a rabbit waits for the snake.

Almost casually Chug walked the few feet which separated them, and stood regarding him, thick lips parted in an evil grin. Then he shot out a hand to grab Philip by the hair, and with the other laid the sharp blade of the knife against his terrified victim's cheek.

He looked at Ruth, still sprawled on the bed.

'See what I mean, missus?' He pressed lightly on the knife, and Philip gave an anticipatory whimper of pain. 'Either you find that money, or I start carving sonny boy here.'

Ruth's anger drained away, to be replaced by fear. Fear for Philip. At the sight of that shining blade against her son's cheek she cried out in agonized protest, urging her plump body to its feet.

'No!' she cried. 'Stop it, stop it! There isn't any money, I tell you. It's all a mistake.'

She spoke without thought, believing that to be the truth and therefore the more convincing. But to Chug it sounded like a deliberate attempt to deceive. He had heard them talking, hadn't he? The bloody woman was stalling, she didn't believe he meant business.

He had to show her.

With a heavy finger he tapped the knife blade sharply, giving a grunt of satisfaction as he felt the keen edge bite into flesh. The shrieks of mother and son rang musically in his ears as he drew the knife slowly downward and watched the skin furrow. The blood seemed slow in coming; first a thin red line, then a trickle, and finally a steady gush that ran eagerly down the smooth cheek to drip on collar and coat.

Reluctantly he took the knife away. As he released his grip on his victim's hair he felt rather than saw him sag on to the bed. But he was not interested in Philip. It was the woman who mattered.

'See what I mean, missus?' he said again, his voice thick. 'Don't look so pretty now, does he?'

He frowned in annoyance as he saw that she had fainted.

13

When a second knock on Vince's door evoked no response from within, Doris walked a few uncertain paces down the corridor, slowed, and came back. What was she supposed to do? Vince had said to wake him at six-thirty, and it was after that now. Yet despite their intimacy of the previous night she was reluctant to enter his room uninvited.

A middle-aged couple came from the room next to Vince's. The woman looked at her with curiosity as they passed, the man gave her an admiring smile. Doris smiled back, hoping she did not look as silly as she felt. Loitering outside a man's hotel bedroom was no crime, but to be found at it had a dampening effect on her dignity. She lingered until the couple had turned the corner, knocked once more and, when there was still no response, opened the door quietly and went in.

Vince was asleep on the bed, curled up

on his side, his face towards her. He was still in the clothes he had worn that afternoon; fawn linen trousers and a striped fawn and black shirt, short-sleeved and open at the neck. Doris thought how young he looked; was that an attribute of sleep? One hand was under the pillow, the other lay along his side; occasionally the fingers curled and his body twitched, and she wondered if he were dreaming. His dark hair was tousled. She had not previously noticed how long were his lashes.

For a full minute she leaned against the closed door, considering him, wondering why their intimacy had made no impact on her senses, why she could still feel for him no more than a mild affection — an affection which, she suspected, was inspired more by his wealth and looks than by his character or personality. His love-making had been no more welcome than that other's; and although Vince himself was not physically distasteful as the other had been, he had lacked the older man's subtlety. He had been brutally demanding, vigorously passionate. But for her there had been no excitement, no passion. Only sufferance. She had not complained, but it had been a relief when at last he had slept.

I must be fundamentally frigid, she thought; there's something lacking in me. I tried, but it wasn't any use. Perhaps it never will be. But I hope it was all right for him. He said it was — but then I imagine men always do. Only if it wasn't he'd be having second thoughts about marriage. He'd want some one more responsive, more passionate. To men sex is important.

She went across to the bed and shook him by the shoulder. He groaned, muttered something in his sleep, and curled into a yet tighter ball. Despite her anxiety, Doris smiled. He's like a child, she thought. It would be a shame to wake him.

But wake him she must. She shook him again, more energetically this time, and he opened one eye and looked at her suspiciously.

'Time to get up, Vince,' she told him.

'It's a quarter to seven. You promised me a drink before dinner, and we're eating early. Remember?'

'Uh — huh!' He rolled over on to his back and opened the other eye, regarding her impersonally. Then he put both hands behind his head, arched his body in a stretch, and grinned at her.

'I can think of something more inviting than a drink,' he said. 'Come on down. It'll give us both an appetite.'

'I already have an appetite, thank you. Also a thirst.' Despite the repugnance which his suggestion evoked in her, she managed a smile. She was still possessed by a sense of sexual inadequacy, in which there was less guilt than anxiety for her own future. 'Get up, Vince, there's a dear. I want that drink.'

He sighed lugubriously. 'Give me a cigarette, then, and I'll see if I can make it.' He jerked a thumb at the far side of the bed. 'They're in my jacket.'

The jacket was draped on a chair. As she leaned across him to get it he stretched out both arms and clasped her round the waist, pulling her down. With a shocked little cry Doris dropped the jacket on the floor, but she made no other protest. She lay passive, allowing his lips to nuzzle her neck, his hands to fondle her. Only when he grew more ardently insistent did she pull herself away and stand up.

'Not now, Vince. Please.' She smoothed her frock and patted her hair into place. 'Your timing is way off, darling. I have just spent an hour trying to make myself look beautiful for you, and now you want to muss me up. It's not fair.'

'That's not quite how I'd put it.' He sighed again. 'But have it your own way. How about that cigarette?'

She went to the other side of the bed and picked up his jacket from the floor. His wallet and some papers had fallen from an inside pocket, but she left them there while she sat on the edge of the bed and put a cigarette between his lips and lit it. He caught her wrist and pulled her towards him. But this time she resisted.

'You have a one-track mind,' she told him, freeing herself. 'Hurry up and dress. You've got your cigarette.'

'I still have to smoke it.'

She did not want to nag. She smiled and nodded, and bent to pick up the wallet and papers. The wallet bulged, and as she pushed it back into his pocket she noted with satisfaction the thick wad of green notes protruding from its edges. The papers followed the wallet. But the last was a photograph, and as she looked at it she exclaimed in astonishment.

It was a snapshot of herself.

Vince gave no sign that he had heard her. He still lay on his back, puffing smoke and gazing at the ceiling. Temporarily he seemed to have lost interest in her. Doris wondered if he were annoyed by her rejection of his love-making. The thought would have troubled her before. At that moment she did not care.

The snapshot showed her in a bikini. She had never liked it — it had been taken from an angle that to Doris seemed to emphasize her curves almost to grossness — but she had found that it was a winner with her elderly admirers. It titillated their senses, nudged them into renewed extravagance. She suspected it encouraged them to dream dreams which she had no intention of helping them to fulfil.

She had given the last copy to Arthur Banning.

Vince stirred on the bed. Doris shivered as she felt his fingers travel slowly up her spine.

'Gone a bit quiet, hasn't it?' he said.

She nodded — glad, despite the travelling fingers, that her back was towards him. She could not trust herself to speak. She was gripped by a sudden terror. It was foolish and illogical — Vince could have got the snapshot from one of the others, it did not have to be Arthur — but she could not help it. She had sent the snapshot to Arthur last Tuesday, in a letter confirming that she would wait for him at the Lewes hotel. But Arthur had never arrived; he had been attacked and robbed on the way, and had later died. Was it coincidence that Vince should have booked in at the same hotel the next day? And that Vince had had money — and the snapshot?

'What have you got there?' he asked.

She shook her head, not trusting herself to speak. Intrigued, he rolled over, raised himself on one elbow, and peered round her arm. The snapshot lay on her lap, and when he saw it he drew in his breath sharply. After a pause he lay down again.

'So that's it.' His laugh sounded forced. 'Stunned you, did it, finding it like that? Well, I'm not surprised. It's a stunning photograph.'

Doris cleared her throat. 'Where did you get it?' she asked, her childish treble reduced to a whisper.

'Found it, of course. How else?' He inhaled deeply. 'It was with a letter I picked up on the road. That's how I knew where to find you. You didn't think I turned up at that hotel by chance, did you?' He put an arm round her waist and squeezed it. 'What's biting you, love? Why the jim-jams?'

A letter he had picked up on the road. So it *was* the photograph she had sent to Arthur. It had to be. There had been others, but she had handed them over personally.

'What was the address on the letter?' It was an unnecessary question, but she felt impelled to put it.

'Don't ask me. There was no envelope, and anyway I wasn't that interested. All I wanted was your address.' He yawned. 'Pass me the ashtray, will you? I'm burning my fingers.'

She passed him the ashtray. Eager as she was to believe him, she knew that somewhere he was lying. It might be true that there was no envelope; and the letter itself would have given little away, it was no more than a brief note with initials for names. She could not remember the exact wording; but since it was the confirmation of a meeting, and she had told Vince that she was in Lewes to meet her uncle, why did he make no mention of the uncle now? Was it because, both from the snapshot and the letter, he had decided that *she* was lying? Was he being tactful? Or was it because he had found neither letter nor snapshot on the road, but had taken them from the unconscious Arthur after striking him down?

Either way she was lost. The rosy

dream was over. If the first supposition were true Vince would not be thinking of marriage, he was merely out for what he could get. Whereas if it were the second . . .

A chill ran down Doris's spine, and she shivered involuntarily.

Vince felt and saw the shiver. He drew up his legs, swivelled on the bed, and moved to sit beside her.

'That's enough of that.' He took the snapshot from her, emitted a low wolf-whistle as he looked at it, and reached to put it on the chair. 'Give us a kiss and I'll get dressed.'

It was a challenge she could not refuse, but her lips were cold and dry, the kiss perfunctorily brief. If he noticed her reluctance he did not comment. He squeezed her thigh as he stood up, collected the packet of cigarettes, and sauntered away to the bathroom.

Doris stayed on the bed. She knew she had to make a decision, but she was too confused to make it now. A false move would be disastrous. Perhaps he would say something during the course of the evening which would clarify the position.

She was still on the bed when Vince came out of the bathroom. 'Shan't be long now,' he said, with a cheerful smile.

Doris smiled back, her mood brightening. With his thin, ascetic face and the proud nose and the well-kept hands he looked the antithesis of a thief and a killer. Maybe he *had* found the letter on the road. And if he was what he purported to be he might well have been too fastidious to read it.

It was only later, when they were having drinks in the bar and she was reminded of their visit to the Brighton pub, that she remembered that, if Vince himself possessed neither the manner nor the aspect of a criminal, he had at least one acquaintance who did.

* * *

No. 27 was in darkness. As Sergeant Redman knocked on the door for the third time Kane said irritably, 'What's happened to the damned woman? It's

285

after seven. She should have been back hours ago.'

Redman moved away from the porch and tried to peer through a gap in the drawn curtains. A lamp on the far side of the street was reflected in the glass, and he flattened his nose against the window and cupped his face in his hands.

'See anything?' Kane asked.

Redman stepped back, adjusting his cap.

'The telly's on,' he said. 'I can see the glow. But either it's turned right down or the sound has gone.'

'Any one in the room?'

Redman shrugged. 'Could be, I suppose. But it's my guess they've gone out and left the set on. Television is a disease with some people. They never think of switching the damned thing off once they've switched it on.'

Out in the street two boys were walking admiringly round and round Kane's Austin Healey, watched by the driver of the police-car behind it. A group of adults had collected at the gate, following the movements of the two policemen with curiosity. Kane glared back at them, more from a sense of frustration than annoyance at their presence; custom had inured him to spectators. Officially his only reason for visiting No. 27 was to check the ownership of the watch Dick Smith had been wearing. Unofficially it was curiosity; he wanted to learn more about the money Banning was supposed to have stolen. Westwood had been reluctant to discuss it or to disclose the amount, insisting that his directors must initiate any police action. Kane had hoped the woman would prove more communicative.

Now it seemed that neither official nor unofficial curiosity was to be satisfied.

'Damn the woman,' he observed, with no great heat, and turned up the collar of his jacket. The threatened rain had started. 'What do we do now?'

'Why not leave the watch with me?' Redman suggested. He knew nothing of the missing money. Kane had not mentioned it; Baker had said to tread warily. 'I can check with her later. You won't want to hang around on a routine job like that.'

Reluctantly Kane agreed. He was moving away from the door when a loud thud sounded within the house. Startled, the two men looked at each other.

'Round the back,' Kane said. 'Come on.'

It was dark at the back. Kane bumped against a metal dustbin, and swore as the lid clattered to the ground. Too late the sergeant switched on a torch. Kane looked down at his shoes and trousers and saw that they were grey with ash.

'Bloody stupid place to put a dustbin,' he said feelingly.

Redman was peering into the kitchen, his torch against a pane. 'Looks empty,' he said, and moved past the door to the next set of windows. But here the curtains were tightly drawn, the windows fastened. 'Probably a cat.'

'Listen!'

They listened. From behind the curtained windows came a new sound — a dull, irregular thumping, as though someone in slippered feet were trying to kick down a door.

'That's no cat.' Kane moved to the

window and put his mouth to the jamb. 'Hello, there!' he shouted. 'Can you hear me? I'm a police officer. Is anything wrong?'

There was no answer, but for some seconds the thumping ceased. Then it recommenced; slow, missing an occasional beat, sometimes loud, sometimes faint.

'We'd better get in there,' Kane said, worried. 'Try the back door.'

Redman grasped the handle, rattling it to gauge the strength of the lock preparatory to exerting force. But no force was needed. The door was unlocked.

They hurried through the kitchen, where dirty crockery and pans were evidence that a meal had recently been prepared, switching on lights as they went. As he saw the disorder in the hall Kane frowned. But the thumping continued. It came from the back room, and he moved to the open doorway and ran his fingers down the wall, seeking the switch.

''Struth!' exclaimed Redman, as the lights came on.

A coloured handkerchief gagging her

mouth, Ruth Banning sat on a chair, facing them. Her wrists were bound together behind the chair back, her ankles tied to its legs. She blinked at them in the sudden glare of the light, her blond hair spread like a sweep's brush, her cheeks red. In the struggle to free herself her clothing had become disarranged; the voluminous blouse had slipped from one shoulder, her skirt had twisted round her waist and ridden above the knees. But her first thought was not for herself. She gazed at them imploringly, nodding her head violently in the direction of the fireplace.

It was not until they moved farther into the room that they saw Philip. He too was bound to a chair and gagged; but the chair had fallen, and he with it. He lay on his side, his slippered feet thudding heels first against the heavy sideboard. The grey woollen rug beneath his head was stained with blood.

They picked him up with the chair, exclaiming at the gash in his cheek, from which a piece of sticking plaster hung limp and red. While the sergeant freed him, Kane did the same for the woman. The rope had cut deep into ankles and wrists, and when he took the gag from her mouth he saw that there were furrows in her cheeks.

Tears sprang to her eyes as she felt herself free. Her lips moved, but she seemed unable to speak. Kane fetched a glass of water and held it to her lips. She sucked greedily, but had difficulty in swallowing, screwing up her eyes and contracting her neck.

There came a groan from the other side of the room. The woman heard it. Impatiently she pushed Kane's hand aside, splashing water over them both. She tried to rise, found that her legs were not functioning properly, and flopped back on the chair.

'Philip!' Her voice was a croak. 'Philip, darling, are you all right?'

He groaned again in answer. With both hands Ruth clutched at Kane's arm. Interpreting the action, he helped her gently to her feet.

'Been in a bit of a rough-house, hasn't he?' From across the table Redman turned to smile reassurance. 'But not to worry, ma'am. I've seen worse, and no harm done.'

Kane's hand at her elbow, she moved slowly round the table, grasping at it occasionally for support as she felt her legs buckle. Kane stifled the many questions he longed to put. She had to be pacified, restored, before she could be expected to tell them what had happened.

Philip looked all in. Shoulders hunched, head bowed, he sat on the hard wooden chair with Redman supporting him. One eye was bruised and rapidly closing, his lips were swollen. Blood still seeped lazily from the gash in his cheek, despite the sergeant's efforts to staunch it.

The woman gave a sharp cry of anguish as she saw him. Too stiff for hasty action, she put out a hand to stroke his face, lifting his chin gently so that she might see him the better.

'Oh, Philip! You poor darling!'

She burst into tears. Kane put an arm round her waist, and she sagged against him, shapeless and heavy. He could hear her snuffling against his jacket. The suit was new, and he hastily sought for a handkerchief and gave it to her.

'Take it easy, Mrs Banning. There's no real cause for alarm. He looks bad, I know, but the damage is superficial. Give him a few days, and he'll be right as rain.' While the sergeant went in search of water and a sponge, he helped her back to her chair. 'Just you sit there and relax while we tidy him up.'

He put the glass of water into her hand, watched her sip, and went to take another look at Philip.

'Got yourself in a right mess, lad, didn't you?' He spoke cheerfully, and bent to peer at the swollen mouth. 'Lost any teeth?'

Philip searched his gums with his tongue and shook his head, wincing at the pain. Returning, Redman said, 'I gave him a thorough going over, Inspector. Nothing broken. Everything seems to work.'

'Feel like telling us what happened?' asked Kane, getting busy with the sponge.

The youth stared at him through the one eye that was open. He looked dazed

293

as well as bruised.

'I was watching the telly, and he just walked in and hit me.' His swollen lips distorted the words. 'He said he wanted the money Arthur had stolen.'

'Who did?'

Ruth said hoarsely, with increased strength to her voice, 'Please, please, leave him alone! Can't you see how it hurts him to talk? You ought to get a doctor instead of asking all these questions.'

Kane knew she was right. He said, 'I'm sorry, Mrs Banning. But we won't send for a doctor. The sergeant here will run him to the hospital. That cut in his cheek may need stitching.'

She was on her feet, hovering round them anxiously as they helped him to the front door. He limped slightly from a kick on the shin; but he scarcely needed their help, and his mother's solicitude seemed to irritate him at the same time as he obviously considered it warranted. It occurred to the inspector that once the young man had recovered from the initial pain and shock his mother would come to regret the evening's happenings even more. Master Philip, he thought, was not the type to make light of his injuries.

The thin drizzle of rain had not dispersed the expectant onlookers, and there were craned necks and exclamations of shocked surprise as the three men came down the path. Sergeant Redman waved them aside. Despite his injuries, Philip eyed the Austin Healey with interest.

'That's not a police-car, is it?' he mumbled.

'No. That's mine.' Kane pointed ahead. 'You're going in the one behind.' To Redman he said, 'Get him back here as soon as you can, Sergeant. And send round the print-and-picture boys.'

Ruth was quick to recover. While she made a pot of tea Kane tidied the sitting-room, replacing the books in the bookcase and sweeping the broken china out of sight. He did it partly because he was genuinely sorry for the woman, but also because he suspected she would talk the more coherently if her mind was not constantly distracted by the sight of the damage.

As they drank the tea he got the story from her. She broke down again when she told how Chug had taken the knife to Philip's cheek, and he waited patiently while she recovered. He was uncertain how this young thug fitted into the Banning affair as a whole. Ruth Banning was sure she had seen him at the hospital, and her description of him fitted the Stone Age youth Nurse Gracey had encountered in the corridor; what was more, his possession of Banning's keys seemed to indicate that it was he who had attacked Banning on Chailey Common. Had he, as Kane had suggested to Baker, gone there to kill, and learned of the money as he waited his chance outside the open window?

He went into the hall and telephoned Baker. The latter was interested, but demanded more facts. 'And be quick about it,' he snapped. 'Stop holding the victims' hands and get down to business. Be brutal, Jimmy. It may hurt, but you do it.'

He's got C.C. on his back, Kane

decided. The old boy isn't usually so testy.

Back in the sitting-room he asked, 'What happened after you came out of the faint, Mrs Banning?'

'He was still there.' She shuddered, her large bosom quivering. 'I thought at first it was a nightmare, but he was still there. And because he hadn't been able to get anything out of me he'd tried to beat it out of Philip.' She shuddered again and put her hands to her face, screwing up her eyes to shut out the pain of memory. 'His poor face! It was horrible. Horrible!'

He nodded sympathetically. 'Who put on the plaster?'

Chug had allowed her to do that. When eventually he had decided that they were speaking the truth, that neither of them could tell him where the money was hid, the steam had gone out of him. He had lounged in an armchair in the sitting-room, staring morosely at nothing in particular, while she had attended to Philip. But he would not let her telephone for a doctor. She could do that after he left, he said, and that wouldn't be till it was dark.

'So you just sat and waited?'

'Yes.'

'Did he tell you anything about himself?' She shook her head. 'What did he talk about?'

'Nothing. He wouldn't let us talk either. I wanted to ask Philip what had happened earlier, but he told me to shut up. Said he wanted to think. And after what we'd been through I was taking no chances.' Her hand shook as she put down the teapot. 'He's going to be all right, Inspector, isn't he? Really all right, I mean? He won't be permanently disfigured?'

An odd woman, he thought. No sense of values. The trivial damage to her son seemed to weigh more heavily on her mind than the murder of her husband and the discovery that he had been a thief.

He assured her that the scars would soon heal and vanish, and showed her the watch. She examined it with no great interest. 'It looks like Arthur's,' she said, handing it back. 'But I couldn't be sure. Where did you get it?'

He told her briefly. 'What time did your visitor leave?' he asked.

About half-past six, she thought. 'He said he was hungry. He made us go into the kitchen, and I cooked some bacon and eggs. Then we came back here, and he switched on the telly and watched it while he ate.' She sat up, suddenly alert at the sound of a car slowing to a stop. 'Is that them?'

'Probably.'

It was them. Philip's face was still unsightly, although the gash in his cheek had been stitched and neatly covered with plaster. Ruth fussed over him, plumping cushions behind his back, replacing his outdoor shoes with slippers, pouring him tea. Redman and Kane waited patiently, listening to the rather one-sided conversation. Kane had not the heart to be brutal, to interrupt this outburst of maternal solicitude.

Content that she had done all she could for her son's comfort, Ruth said, 'I tried to telephone you yesterday evening, dear. From the hospital. I wanted to make sure you were all right. But there was no reply.'

'I was out with Roddy,' he mumbled.

She nodded, as though that was what she had expected. 'Where did you go?'

'Brighton.' Suddenly remembering, he said, 'How's Arthur?'

To Ruth, so much had happened since her husband's death that already it belonged to the past. She stared at her son, bewildered. It seemed impossible that he did not know. Her eyes wandered to the grave faces of the two policemen, and then back to Philip.

'He's dead,' she said flatly.

'Dead?' He sounded more surprised than dismayed. 'But they told me at the hospital last night that he was getting better.' Realizing that a more sympathetic comment was demanded of him, he added, 'Poor old Arthur! I'm sorry, Mum. Really I am.'

Ruth gave him a sad smile.

'Thank you, dear. And I'm glad you telephoned.' Her voice was thick with sentiment. Kane felt slightly sick. 'Arthur would have been pleased.'

'I didn't telephone. We called in on our way back from Brighton.'

The inspector's interest was alerted. Before the woman could express her further appreciation he said, 'What time would that be, Mr Underset?'

'I don't know. Around half past eleven, suppose.'

'Did you see your stepfather?'

'At that hour? Of course not. I just asked how he was and then hopped it. Roddy was waiting.'

Philip would be the second youth, Kane thought, the one who had spoken to the night sister. Odd that the identity had not occurred to him before. Philip fitted the description.

Out of curiosity he asked, 'Who is Roddy?'

'A friend,' Philip told him. 'Roddy Stone.'

Ruth shook her head. 'I wish you wouldn't see so much of him, dear. I've told you before, I don't trust him. Neither did your father.'

Philip shrugged. 'Roddy's O.K.'

'How long were you at the hospital?' asked Kane.

'Ten — fifteen minutes. It took me a while to find the right ward. Roddy said it was longer, but I'd been back at the car at least five minutes before he turned up. He'd got tired of waiting and gone to look for me.'

A knock at the door announced the arrival of more policemen. Redman went upstairs with them. When the hall was quiet again Kane said, 'Didn't this afternoon's visitor tell you your stepfather was dead?'

'No.'

'Not even indicate it in some way? By referring to him in the past tense, for instance?'

'If he did I didn't notice it.'

To Kane that seemed strange. But it was only a minor puzzle, and he said briskly, 'All right. Tell me what happened after he'd eaten.'

Nothing at first, said Philip. They had just continued to sit, with Chug staring at the telly and picking his teeth with a match. He had demanded cigarettes and beer, but they could supply neither. And then, without any warning, he had suddenly erupted into a stream of obscene oaths and had lashed out viciously at the television-set with his foot, killing the sound. When he stood up they had thought there was to be more violence, and had watched fearfully as he stumped about the room, muttering to himself and kicking at the books that still lay on the floor. But one particular book had attracted his attention, and he had picked it up and begun to thumb the pages.

'What book?' asked Kane.

Philip twisted his swollen lips into the semblance of a grin. 'An old R.A.C. handbook.'

Kane frowned. Had chummy decided to pinch a car for his get-away, and needed a route? 'You wouldn't know which map he looked at?' he asked.

'He didn't open it at the map section. That's at the back of the book. He was looking at something near the front. And after he'd found what he wanted — at least, I suppose he found it — he was suddenly in a hell of a hurry to be gone. He made Mum get her clothes-lines from the kitchen, and then he tied us up and beat it. Didn't waste a second.'

'And you've no idea what he was looking for?'

'No. He was muttering to himself all the time, but I couldn't hear what he said. Oh, yes — I did hear one thing. He mentioned some one he called H.C. Didn't like him much either, by the sound of it. Could that be a clue?'

'If it is I don't recognize it. What happened to the book?'

Philip lifted a languid foot and pointed. 'Over there.'

Kane retrieved the book and thumbed the pages slowly. 'Tolls,' he read aloud. 'Unlikely to be that.' He hesitated over Airports and Civil Aerodromes — had chummy been contemplating escape by air? — and went on through Hills and Index Marks, seeking a clue to he did not know what. 'You said he was watching television when he suddenly went berserk. What was on?'

'The news.'

There might be a lead there. 'What news?'

'I.T.V. The B.B.C. comes later.'

'Yes, yes.' Kane sounded impatient. 'But what particular item of news roused him?'

Philip shrugged. 'I didn't notice. Did you, Mum?'

Ruth had not been listening to their conversation. Now that the first shock of her recent ordeal was over she had begun once more to reflect on the money her husband had stolen. She had been so sure that the bulk of it would be in the locked drawer that, when that theory had been disproved, and in the misery that then engulfed her, she had immediately assumed that Arthur had either spent it or had never possessed it. Now she was feeling more optimistic. Arthur must have anticipated that the locked drawer would arouse her curiosity. He might even have counted on her forcing it — hoping that, if the crime were discovered in his absence and inquiries made, she would hand over that single bundle of notes and the company would assume, as she had done, that that was the sum total of what was left. They might not like it, but they would have to accept it.

Then — where was the rest? Arthur could not have spent it, and if he had had it on him his murderer would not have come to look for it. So it had to be somewhere in the house; somewhere so inaccessible or improbable that even the thorough search that the intruder had made would not disclose it. But she had more time. If it were there she would find it eventually. And the longer she took the less danger that, when she found it, some one would take it from her.

A cough from the inspector brought her back to reality. She became aware that both he and Philip were regarding her expectantly.

'I'm afraid I wasn't looking,' she said, when Philip repeated the question.

'H'm!' Kane returned to the handbook, passing hastily from Tidal Constants to Motor Sport. The search had become mechanical, there was no longer reason to it. 'Well, can either of you remember anything at all that was mentioned? Let's see if we can get at it that way.'

Ruth gaped at the screen, as though the picture still lingered. Philip's undamaged eye closed, either in the effort of concentration or in sympathy with the other.

'Somebody died. An M.P., I think; the announcer said there would have to be a by-election. There was a smash-and-grab raid which didn't come off, and the Russians have sent up another satellite. Or it might have been the Americans. I'm not sure.' He sighed. 'That's all I can remember.'

The smash-and-grab sounded the most promising. Discarding the handbook, Kane asked for details. Where, for instance, had it occurred?

'I don't know. But somewhere on the coast. The reporter was talking to this chap on the promenade.'

'What chap?'

'The chap who caught the thief. He was a professional wrestler who's appearing at some hall there to-night. The thief ran straight into him.' Philip tried a grin. 'Dead unlucky, eh, bumping into a muscle-man?'

307

Ruth said unexpectedly, 'I remember that.'

Kane smiled wryly. No doubt there had been more important items of news televised that evening than an abortive smash-and-grab in a seaside town, yet this was the only one Philip had remembered in any detail. The human interest, he thought, is always a winner.

'But neither of you remember the name of the town?'

Neither of them did.

Kane sighed. The television authorities would tell him where the incident had occurred, but what then? There was no proof that it had any bearing on the wanted youth. It might merely have instigated an unwelcome train of thought; or it could have been some other item of news which provoked him. Still more probable, his sudden outburst of undisciplined fury had had no connexion with the newsreel. The two had coincided by chance.

And H.C.? A friend? No, not a friend; not if Philip had reported correctly. More likely an accomplice with whom chummy had quarrelled. The accomplice, perhaps, who had shared in the assault on Arthur Banning. Yet why . . .

H.C. H.C.!

Even as he reached for the handbook he knew the answer. Yet some odd streak of thoroughness demanded the printed word in verification.

It was there under Index Marks; a coincidence he could not ignore. A seaside town, Philip had said. And HC was the index mark of Eastbourne County Borough Council.

14

The rain was coming down steadily now; a hard, slanting rain driven in from the sea. It pattered noisily against the windows of the police-car and transformed the surface of the puddles into circles of ever-changing dimensions. But the stocky figure in jeans and dark jersey made no move for shelter. He stood in the lee of the wall at the corner of Compton Street, his eyes fixed on the Winter Garden Theatre across the road. Occasionally he shook himself like a dog, walked a few paces, and returned to resume his vigil.

Kane said again, 'You're sure that's him? You couldn't be wrong?'

'That's him,' Philip said.

The inspector frowned, and rubbed the misted windows with the sleeve of his raincoat.

'This bloody rain won't help. When they come out they're not going to loiter.

We'll have to move fast.'

Ruth Banning had protested strongly when he had suggested that her son should accompany him. 'He's going to bed,' she had declared, her plump, round face indignant. 'After what he's been through he's in no condition to go tearing off to Eastbourne, or anywhere else. I'm surprised you should even suggest it, Inspector.' He had pointed out that only she and Philip could identify the wanted man, that without their help the police would be severely handicapped. It had made no impact on her stubbornness. Not even his brutal reminder that it was her husband's murderer they were seeking could move her. Philip was not fit to go, and she must stay to nurse him.

It was Philip who had unexpectedly resolved the impasse — unexpectedly, because Kane had regarded him as a spoilt, spineless youth who would always choose the easier way. He had listened to the argument impassively, prodding the swollen protuberances of his face with a tentative finger. It was when Kane had abandoned the struggle that he had

asked, 'Will you be going in the Healey?'
Kane had answered, sharply because of
his annoyance, that of course he would;
he had come in it, and he would return in
it. Whereupon Philip, waving aside his
mother's entreaties and objections, had
announced that in that case he was
prepared to go too.

Kane looked at his watch. Half past
ten. The traffic along Compton Street was
desultory; the rain had driven most
people indoors, and in the half-hour they
had waited pedestrians had been few. A
car passed in a shower of spray, spattering
the windscreen and side windows of the
police-car, so that the lone figure on the
street corner temporarily became a blur.

Philip said irritably, 'I can't see why
you don't arrest him. Why wait?'

Kane did not answer. He felt irritable
himself; the waiting got on one's nerves.
But Philip had been fractious ever since
they had transferred from the Healey to
the police-car at Lewes. He had suddenly
acquired a pain in his side, and he did not
let his companions forget it. Constantly
he changed his position, stretching his

legs and crowding the inspector. Kane recognized it as an act. Philip resented being no longer the central figure in the drama. He had done what they had brought him for. Now they had lost interest in him.

It was not only Philip and the long vigil that made the inspector uneasy; Philip he could ignore, and he had kept vigil many times before. Waiting was part of a policeman's life. But exactly what were they waiting for? He had assumed — and Baker had gone along with him in this — that chummy had headed for Eastbourne in search of some one or something, and that his errand was connected with the abortive smash-and-grab raid which had taken place earlier in the day. But the would-be raider was in a police cell; there could be no contact there. So, since his captor was performing at the Winter Garden, that was where they had come — to find a rain-sodden chummy waiting on the opposite side of the street.

I suppose we're waiting for whatever he is waiting for, thought Kane. Only he has the advantage of knowing what that is.

The two uniformed constables on the front seat were steadily chewing their way through a bag of toffees. They had offered them to their companions in the back; Philip had ungraciously accepted, Kane had declined. The rhythmic sucking around him began to get on his nerves, and he said, 'What time does this blasted show end?'

'It depends, sir,' the driver told him. 'If all the contests go the full distance we could be here till close on midnight. But I've never known that to happen. They should be out by eleven.' He unwrapped another toffee. 'I see they've got that Spaniard on. The one with the beard. He's good, he is. You keen on wrestling, Mr Kane?'

'Not particularly. I watch it on TV occasionally.'

'It's not the same on TV,' the driver said. He had a sad voice. 'You don't get the atmosphere.'

A man passed, walking quickly westward. He had his raincoat collar up and his chin down, and he did not even glance into the car. Maybe the rain has its advantages, reflected Kane; at least it is an aid to concealment. It had seemed to him that the waiting car must be horribly conspicuous. But chummy had not taken fright. If he had noticed it — and he must have noticed it — then apparently he had not connected it with his own business there.

They were not the only ones on watch. There were cars stationed in Carlisle Road and Wilmington Square, another down towards the western end of Compton Street. Kane could see its side-lights. 'We'll cork up all the exits,' the Eastbourne superintendent had said. 'This is one hoodlum who won't get away.' And he's right, thought Kane. Four cars and a dozen coppers. We can't miss.

But he still managed to feel uneasy. The few clues that Medwin and his boys had been able to garner from Chailey Common suggested that two men had been concerned in the assault on Arthur Banning. That dark figure skulking against the wall at the street corner had undoubtedly been one; was he hoping to contact the other? If so, would it be as friend or enemy? Was he there to get help, or to settle a grudge? Kane wished he knew the answer, it would give some indication of what was likely to happen when the audience inside the Winter Garden started to leave. If chummy were waiting for a friend, then presumably he would accost him at sight. That would simplify the job of the police. But if it were an enemy . . .

'They're coming out, sir,' the driver said.

A little knot of people was clustered at the entrance to the theatre, struggling into raincoats, adjusting collars and scarves, opening umbrellas. A man and a woman ran across the street towards Wilmington Square. Two men came hurrying along the pavement, rubber soles squelching, their heads bare.

A quick glance across the street assured Kane that the waiting figure had not moved.

'Right.' He reached for the door handle. 'Let headquarters know what's happening. After that — well, you know what to do.'

He stepped from the car and strolled leisurely towards the theatre entrance.

★　★　★

As they moved slowly up the gangway, bundled together by the jostling crowd, Vince said, 'Well? What do you think of wrestling now? Like it?'

Doris did not answer at once. Her cheeks were flushed, her body felt damp with sweat. She wanted to be alone — away from Vince, from the hot, pressing crowd — to analyse the emotions which had so recently possessed her. Least of all did she want to talk, to discuss what had happened.

She said, trying to sound apathetic, 'It's exciting as a spectacle, I suppose. But terribly primitive, wouldn't you say?'

That was what she said. But it was not what she felt. She had thrilled to every minute of it. No, not every minute; not, perhaps, the first few. After that it had gripped and held her, so that at the end of

317

each bout she had felt exhausted; it was as though every lock and hold, every vicious forearm jab, every jolt and throw, had been inflicted on her own soft body. The sweating, struggling men in the ring had looked to her like savage leviathans, ten feet tall from her ringside seat. Their skill had made little impact on her senses. It was the massive strength of their bodies, their straining muscles, the barbaric, brutal beauty of their movements which had at first horrified, then fascinated, and finally enraptured — so that it had taken all her self-control to refrain from becoming one of the vociferous crowd that shrieked and jeered and shouted encouragement or abuse. When one of the wrestlers had been thrown from the ring to land almost at her feet she had risen impulsively — not from pity or a desire to help, but from a primitive urge to touch. The closeness of his heaving chest, hairy and damp with sweat, the dark, bulging thighs, had excited her almost beyond endurance. She had sat down quickly, hoping that Vince had not noticed. For the rest of the evening she had kept a tight hold on her emotions, discussing the entertainment objectively and with apparent dispassion. Vince must not know how the spectacle affected her, he would think it unfeminine. And she could not risk that. Not until the problem posed by the photograph had been finally resolved.

As they deployed into the foyer Vince said, 'Never seen so much beef on the hoof before, eh? Hell! Look at that rain!'

It had been overcast but dry when they left the hotel; neither had brought a raincoat. But the sight of the rain did not disturb her; temporarily she was lost to external happenings. The touch of Vince's hand on hers caused her to think fleetingly of his body, slender and white and supple, and to wonder why the feel of it next to her own the previous night had awakened her not at all. Was she as unnatural in that as in the sensations she had so recently experienced?

'Let's make a dash for it,' she said. 'It's not far.'

It was not easy to run. Too many people were heading in the same direction, and as they crossed the road their hurrying feet sent water splashing on to her legs. A puddle soaked her feet, the rain beat into her face so that she had to screw up her eyes. But somehow it did not matter. It would matter later. But not now.

The Zephyr was parked in Wilmington Square, facing the sea. Vince flung open the nearside door, glad that he had forgotten to lock it, that he did not have to fumble for the key, and helped her in. He ran round the bonnet and slid into the seat beside her.

'Sorry about that,' he said cheerfully, reaching for a handkerchief with one hand and the ignition key with the other. 'I'll give you a rub down when we get back, and that's a promise.' He mopped his face. 'Phew! Talk about damp!'

A rear door opened and shut, the car sagged to one side. Behind him Vince heard the sound of heavy breathing. As he turned to look . . .

'Don't ask no questions, mate,' a harsh voice said. 'Just get moving. Quick!'

Kane stood apart from the hurrying stream of people, watching them emerge from the foyer and filter right, left, and centre. Across their heads he could see the tall figure of Ted Glossop, a C.I.D. man from Eastbourne. Glossop had been in the car parked down Carlisle Road, and somewhere in the vicinity would be men from the other cars. Kane's spirits rose. As the superintendent had said, this was one hoodlum who would not get away.

Chummy was still on the opposite corner. He had moved from the wall to the kerb, but had made no attempt to cross the street, to close with the crowd. That puzzled Kane. From where the youth stood he would be able to watch the people turning left into Compton Street or crossing to the square; but the latter group would hide from his view those who went right down Carlisle Road or towards the eastern end of Compton Street. Did that mean that he knew which way his man would go?

Kane tried to spot the quarry. A bearded youth in a leather jacket elbowed his way unceremoniously through the crowd, and Kane followed him hopefully with his eyes. But the watcher on the corner made no move, and Kane looked for another prospect. A pretty blond girl in a blue dress hurried across the pavement, stepping into a puddle as she started to cross the road; neither she nor the tall youth with her wore hat or coat, and Kane felt sorry for them. Even in the rain they made a handsome couple. A party of drunks, arguing vociferously, came out of the foyer in a solid phalanx; tough, ungainly men, who moved leisurely, apparently impervious to the pelting rain. Watching them, Kane wondered why the blond girl's face had looked familiar. Then he forgot her. A small group had been standing by the kerb, shoulders hunched, collars up, waiting for a car to pass. Now they surged forward in a body. And as they did so chummy moved into the roadway to join them.

A quick signal to Glossop, and Kane

went after him, pushing his way through the moving bodies until only a few paces separated him from the dark-jerseyed figure. The latter was immediately behind the drunks, and Kane wondered if one of them were his quarry. Ahead of the drunks the young couple ran to their car, a white Zephyr saloon parked against the railings. Other cars were drawing away from the park, and Kane looked behind him to see that his own was following. He could see it nosing through the crowd, with the tall figure of Glossop striding a few paces in front.

It was then that chummy acted. He burst through the drunks, sending one of them staggering off the pavement. Kane's first thought was that this must be his man; but as the drunk collapsed in the roadway chummy shot across to the white saloon and clambered into the back. With a shout to Glossop, Kane went after him. But he had reckoned without the drunks. Incensed at the attack on their comrade, and assuming this to be yet another assailant, they barred his way. A burly figure, voluminous in oilskins, caught his arm and jerked him back. To Kane it felt as though his arm had been wrenched from his shoulder.

'You looking for trouble, mate?' the man said, his breath redolent of hops.

Kane struggled to free himself. But the man's grip was vice-like, and his companions were encouraging his aggression.

'Let me go, you fool! I'm a police officer.'

The man stared at him, narrowing his eyes. Kane saw Glossop race past, saw the Zephyr pull away from the park. Then the police-car drew alongside, rear door opening, a peak-capped constable shouting angrily. The hand dropped from his arm, the drunks backed hastily to the kerb.

As he leapt for the open door Kane saw the white saloon swing right on to the Grand Parade. Behind it, clear in the beam from the car's headlamps, Detective Constable Ted Glossop lay huddled in the road.

★ ★ ★

Vince could feel the point of the knife pricking the back of his neck, and he kept his body stiffly erect as he changed into top gear. At the wheel he felt reasonably safe, but he was risking no sudden move. One could not take chances with Chug. Not when he was angry. And Chug, as Vince well knew, had good cause to be angry.

The traffic was light, and as he drove westward down the wide road he fought to subdue the terror that sickened his stomach and chilled his body. The foreknowledge that this moment must come, that he was living on borrowed time, had not lessened its impact. And this time there would be no turning of the tables, no lucky break. Chug might not intend to kill him, although in his savagery he might do even that. But he would maul him and maim him and break him so thoroughly that what was left would be a slobbering wreck who might well prefer to be dead.

Vince shuddered, and glanced sideways at the girl. Was there hope there? She sat erect, hands clenched tightly together across her breasts. Her face was in shadow, and he wondered what she was thinking. She had screamed once, when Chug had erupted into the car and she had turned to see his face close behind her. Chug had silenced the scream with a backward blow of the hand. Since then she had made no sound.

'No hurry,' Chug said. 'We got plenty of time. Just you find a nice, quiet spot where nobody ain't going to interfere, and then you'n me'll have a little chat. Eh, Vince boy?' He twisted the knife, breaking the skin so that a bubble of blood showed. Vince cut off the cry that involuntarily escaped him, knowing that it would incite Chug to further savagery. Chug laughed, an unpleasant, dry laugh that had no humour to it. 'And after that — ' He looked sideways at Doris, put his left hand on her shoulder, and slid it down into the V of her frock. 'How about you'n me having a bit of fun together, eh? I mean — well, like I said, we got plenty of time. And don't you worry about Vince here. Vince won't be no trouble.'

Doris held herself rigid, her teeth

clenched lest a scream should provoke him further. The emotions which had held her in thrall a short while ago had vanished; the touch of his coarse hand on her skin, the tickling hairs at his wrist, filled her with disgust. She did not wonder at this — she was too frightened to analyse her emotions — but she was vaguely aware of a difference. Those men in the ring had been outside her life; she was not physically involved, they had made no demands on her. Vince had. And so would this beast in the back.

When the exploratory hand was removed she sank a little lower in the seat, closed her eyes, and prayed to no particular god that the 'little bit of fun' might never materialize.

Vince said, his voice shaky, 'How did you find us?'

'I used me loaf, mate. Thursday night I seen you and the bird drive off in this here car, and I remembers the letters on the number-plate. HC. And HC means Eastbourne, don't it? So when I seen on the telly that there's wrestling here to-night I says to meself, 'That's where he'll be, Chug boy. If there's a spot of maul-and-muscle around young Vince'll be there. He wouldn't miss that.' Again he twisted the knife, and chuckled as he felt the car swerve. 'And I was dead right, eh? Soon as I seen HC here in the park I knew where you was. I only had to wait.'

They were in King Edward's Parade now, where the cliff ran close to the road and climbed eventually to Beachy Head. The wet tarmac glistened under the street lighting, the headlamps of an approaching car were misty blurs on the windscreen. Chug followed the car with his eyes as it passed. It illuminated the front of a black saloon coming up fast behind them, and with relief Vince felt the knife leave his skin as Chug turned and moved to the rear seat.

But relief was short-lived. Suddenly his enemy was back, breathing down his neck. He could smell the rank odour of him.

Chug said fiercely, 'Step on it, you bastard! It's the bloody cops!'

Instinctively Vince obeyed. He could see the lights of the overtaking car dancing on the road ahead, and as he felt the Zephyr surge forward he tried to calculate the odds. Where did least danger lie? With the police — or Chug? If it were a coincidence that the police were following — if he should slow, only to see their car sweep past and vanish into the murk ahead — he would have added fuel to Chug's anger with no profit to himself. Revenge would merely be the more thorough. But if they were in fact the quarry — if the police were after him or Chug or both — that meant a stretch. A long stretch — five, ten, maybe fifteen years. And it made no difference if it were Chug alone they wanted. If they took Chug, then Chug would see that they took him also. It would be the only means of revenge left to him — and Chug would never forego that.

Yet even a stretch might be preferable to what Chug was planning for him.

The thoughts whirled confusedly through his mind as, out of the corner of his eye, he saw the bonnet of the police-car draw level. Without consciously arriving at a decision he started to lift his foot from the accelerator. Chug felt the change in speed. His hands at Vince's throat, he yelled furiously, 'Put your foot down, you bloody nit! That bloke we done has snuffed it. We'll be topped if they get us.'

Vince believed him. Chug was too dim-witted to have invented such a spur. The hands at his throat felt like a tightening noose, and in a panic he threw himself forward, stamping the pedal to the boards. The Zephyr seemed to hesitate, unable to cope with the sudden urgent demand. Then it leapt ahead.

They were near the end of the parade now, with the Zephyr just keeping its nose in front. Hunched over the wheel, Vince saw the sharp right-hand bend with the ground banked high above it, and realized with a sudden qualm what lay ahead. He had been this way with Doris on Thursday, when he had taken her to Beachy Head; recalling the steep climb with its succession of acute bends, he knew that it was skill rather than speed that was needed now. The knowledge increased his panic. He was too inexperienced to have confidence in his driving.

Desperately he swung the Zephyr into the turn, cutting the corner recklessly, expecting to hear and feel the impact as the bonnet of the police-car crashed into them. But there was no impact. Anticipating the danger, the police driver had braked and veered farther to the right. Now, as the Zephyr shot ahead, he tucked in behind it. It was no part of his task to ram the car ahead. Stay with him, the inspector had said. Keep on his tail so that he'll know we're there. But let him take the risks.

Nose to tail, the two cars raced up the hill, tyres screaming on the tight bends and skidding into the straight. Vince had changed down for more rapid acceleration, but he knew that he lacked full control; his sweating hands were too tight on the steering-wheel, the rain blurred his vision. It was a left-hand bend that showed his inexperience. He went into it hugging the near side, so that it took all his strength to bring the car round. As it scraped along the far bank Doris was thrown heavily against him. He thrust her roughly away, felt the steering begin to judder, and with a panic-stricken jerk of the wheel lifted the Zephyr back to the crown of the road.

But he did not slacken speed. In imagination the rope was still around his neck. Fear of his pursuers was greater than fear of the road; their lights were bright in his mirror, and he went roaring up the hill in third gear, the revs mounting. Doris wanted to scream, to tell him to slow, to batter him with her fists until he did. But she knew it would be useless. Even if he wished to Chug would not let him. Teeth clenched, her face drained of colour, she grasped the door handle and huddled into the corner and prayed that when the crash came it would not be fatal.

They careened round another corner, the car listing so acutely that Doris shut her eyes, certain that they were going over. But somehow the Zephyr righted itself, and she opened her eyes — to utter a shrill cry as a new danger threatened. In front of them, chugging up the hill with thick smoke belching from its exhaust, was a vintage Morris Cowley. And ahead of it, clear in the Zephyr's headlights, loomed another right-hand bend.

Mesmerized by speed, by fear, by his fading ability to make judgments, Vince wavered. But not for long. Chug's fist came down heavily on his shoulder, his voice bellowing in his ear.

'Pass it, you bloody nit, pass it! It's our only chance.'

Vaguely Vince realized what he meant. To put the slow-moving Morris between themselves and their pursuers might enable them to draw away, to reach a turning down which they might vanish before the police-car had closed the gap sufficiently to see them go. And a small corner of his brain dimly registered the fact that he who had prided himself on his wits was now relying on the despised Chug for decision.

But even as he swung out to overtake he knew they would not make it. As he drew alongside the Morris he was fractionally aware of a bewhiskered face gaping at them in horrified amazement from under the flapping hood. Then the two cars went into the bend together. The Morris driver, not expecting such suicidal tactics, had left him only the minimum of room, and he felt the Zephyr brush the bank as he pushed her through the gap and swung her round. The bull nose of the Morris vanished from sight, and for a moment Vince thought they were clear. But as he depressed the pedal the impact came. The Zephyr's tail hit the other car amidships, to send it burrowing into the banked verge; the steering-wheel spun in his hands, and he jerked at it in a desperate effort to straighten her out. But now the car was completely out of control. It slewed across the wet road, skidding crazily and heading for the opposite bank. He heard Doris scream, heard himself shouting involuntarily. There was a brief moment while he braced himself for the shock. Then it came — a rending crash that jerked him forward, the sudden cessation of light, an end to Doris's scream. He did not feel the steering-wheel as it came in violent contact with his chest, did not feel the windscreen shatter against his head. He had only the sensation of pain, of falling into a dark abyss stabbed with white-hot, searing streaks of lightning. Then the lightning ceased, and he was aware of nothing.

15

They watched the ungainly figure of Chug Wallis, a constable on either side of him, go down the hospital steps and cross the wide pavement to the waiting car. When he had been bundled none too ceremoniously into the back and the car had driven off, Superintendent Baker heaved a sigh.

'Nice chap,' he said, turning away. 'One of Nature's gentlemen.'

Kane grinned. But he too felt relief. The job was done. Now only the tidying up remained.

'The girl came off worst,' he said, the stone corridor echoing their footsteps as they walked. 'Internal injuries as well as facial. They've sent for her father, but I understand she has a fair chance.'

Baker was not sympathetic. 'They're dead lucky, the lot of them,' he growled. 'Bloody young fools. With mess they made of that Zephyr they should all be in the morgue.'

'Is Glossop all right?'

'Yes, thank goodness. And that's another slice of luck — for them as well as for him.' Baker looked at his watch and yawned. 'Nine o'clock! And I promised Edna I'd take her to Matins this morning.' He yawned again. 'Oh, well! Let's go see what our star witness has to tell us. Thank Heavens there's one of 'em willing to talk. The girl can't, and that hairy ape won't.'

They had moved Vince to a room on his own. Not because of his injuries — he had a broken collar-bone and a bruised chest, and lacerations of the face and hands — but because the police had wished it. A night's rest had helped him to recover some of his former buoyancy. He even managed a sickly smile for the police when they came in.

Baker did not return the smile. He said, 'I understand you wish to make a statement.'

Vince nodded. 'I might as well. Nothing to lose, have I?'

He had decided it might be safer to

make it himself than to let Chug make it for him. That was what he meant. Chug, he had assumed, would attempt to pin most of the blame on his accomplice. That was what Vince would have done in Chug's place, what he intended to do now. In the spot he was in a chap had to look after Number One.

He did not know that Chug had refused to say anything. It would have made no difference if he did.

Baker pulled forward a chair and sat down. It was a fine morning after the rain, and the sun gleamed on his mop of white hair. It also stressed the lines in his face. He said, 'Detective Inspector Kane here will caution you, and from then on anything you say will be taken down by Constable White. It can be in the form of question and answer, or you can give us the facts in your own words. Whichever you prefer. The statement will then be typed, and later you will be asked to read and sign it. Is that clear?'

'Clear as daylight.' Kane suspected that the youth's cockiness was a front to hide his nervousness. He blinked continuously, and sounded short of breath. 'Let's get on with it, shall we, before I change my mind?'

'You do that,' Baker said.

★ ★ ★

They stopped the Morris as it was leaving the filling-station in East Grinstead. They needed a lift, they said; Brighton, Eastbourne — anywhere on the coast, it didn't matter. They had a week's holiday and were short of money, and they wanted to make the most of both. The driver asked them where they came from, and Vince told him St Albans; it wasn't true, but it sounded classier than Brixton. It had taken them several lifts and a bus journey, he said, to get them where they were.

'I'm only going as far as Lewes,' the driver said. 'Any good?'

It would suit them fine, they said. Chug got into the back, but Vince paused as he slid into the seat beside the driver, and produced a postcard.

'I suppose you couldn't sell me a

stamp, sir?' he asked. 'I'd like to post this to my mother before I forget. She worries if she doesn't hear from me when I'm away.'

The man pulled out his wallet, extracted a stamp, and waved away the proffered payment. Noting the thick wad of notes, Vince smiled to himself as he crossed to the pillar-box. They had chosen the Morris because the driver was alone, and there was a suitcase on the back seat. A suitcase usually indicated a journey, and a journey called for money. The business with the stamp had been merely an extra precaution, enabling Vince to get a look at the proposed victim's wallet. It was as well to make doubly sure that they had chosen wisely.

As he got into the car he nodded casually to Chug.

The driver seemed in cheerful mood. As they drove south through Ashdown Forest and took the Lewes road he told them his name was Banning, and that he was off for a short holiday in Paris. He and Vince did most of the talking. But Chug's heavy breathing seemed to worry him. He said eventually, 'Sounds like your friend's got a nasty cold.'

Vince laughed. 'His death rattle, you mean. He's always like that. There's something wrong with his nose. We call him 'Chug' because he sounds like a ruddy steam-engine, but his real name is Basil.'

Long before they reached Chailey crossroads conversation had grown thin. As they went down the hill the headlights lit up the common to their right, and to Vince it looked as good a place as any. There had been others equally suitable, but he had wanted to get as far as possible from East Grinstead. Now they were nearing Lewes. They could not delay much longer.

He turned and winked at Chug.

There was a movement in the back of the car. Vince was watching Banning. He saw him flinch as Chug jabbed a piece of iron piping into the back of his neck, felt the instinctive pressure of his foot on the brake pedal.

Chug said harshly, 'Take it easy, mister. This is a stick-up.' He pressed a little harder. 'And this here's a gun, see, so don't try nothink.'

Banning shivered, and eased his foot from the throttle. He gave a quick sidelong glance at Vince — half fearful, half appealing.

Vince smiled. 'You'd better take that turning to the right,' he said. 'We'll be more private there. And drive slowly, please. We don't want any trouble, do we? My friend in the back is inclined to be hasty. If he thought you were trying to play tricks — *phut!*'

The *phut!* was accompanied by an expressive snap of the fingers. To Banning it must have sounded like the report of a gun; he gave a shrill cry, and the car veered suddenly. Then, trembling with fright, he drove slowly down the hill and turned right as directed.

Now they were crossing the common. As they rounded the first bend Vince said, 'Drive off the road on to that clearing on the left.' His voice was quietly conversational. 'Take her in among the bushes.'

Banning did as he was told. The clearing was criss-crossed with ruts, shadowed in the headlights, and the car bounced over them, flinging its occupants about. With the supposed gun barrel still at his neck, Banning was careful not to brake too suddenly.

Vince switched off the lights. Gulping to ease his throat, Banning said, 'You — you can have what money I've got. And please put that gun away. I won't make any trouble.'

Chug removed the piping. Banning sighed and stretched, started to raise a hand to the back of his neck, then let it drop. For a moment there was silence. Then Chug hit him hard across the skull with the piping, and he slumped forward on to the steering-wheel.

Vince frowned. He lifted the lolling head, studied it for a moment, and slowly lowered it again.

'Was that really necessary?' he asked.

'Makes it easier.' Chug grinned evilly, showing black, misshapen teeth. 'Let's get him out and have a look at that wallet.'

They dragged Banning from his seat, bundling him unceremoniously on to the ground. Chug wasted no time. He went through his victim's pockets briskly, transferring their contents to his own. As he opened the wallet an envelope fell out. Vince picked it up and pocketed it. Then he took a quick look round. The bushes gave some cover from the road, but there was the possibility that the headlights of a passing car might pick them out.

Chug was laboriously counting the notes in the wallet. Vince said, 'Put that away, you fool. We'll split it later. Let's have a look at the suitcase, and then blow.'

The suitcase was heavy. Chug unlocked it with the stolen keys, and in the light of Vince's torch started throwing out articles of clothing. Suddenly he stopped, staring in disbelief. Vince stared too, whistling softly between his teeth.

The bottom of the case was lined with neatly stacked bundles of treasury notes.

' 'Struth!' Chug's voice was hoarse with excitement. 'What you think he done? Robbed a bleeding bank? There must be thousands of nicker there.'

'Hundreds, anyway.' Vince picked up a

bundle and riffled the notes, gloating over the unusual sensation; letting them slide slowly past his thumb, his mind trying to grapple with the possibilities that this accession to wealth presented. Then caution took possession. He pushed the bundle into his knapsack and began to collect the others.

'Let's get moving,' he said. 'We'll take the car part of the way and then ditch it.' He turned to stare down at the still figure of Banning. 'Lug him farther into the bushes, Chug, while I put his stuff back in the case.'

'I could do with some of the clobber,' Chug said. 'He's about my size. A bit fatter, maybe, but the same height.'

'And have the coppers nick you? Don't be a ruddy fool. You're rich, man. With lolly like that you can buy all the new clothes you want. You don't need his.'

Chug bent reluctantly to Banning's feet and hauled him away into the darkness. Carefully Vince collected the scattered clothing, searching the ground to make certain he had missed nothing. Chug had hit the man hard, he could be out for hours. No one had passed down the road; but it was not much after nine, and a spot like that could be a favourite with necking couples. It would be a pity if some stray article of apparel should attract their attention to the unconscious man.

He snapped the case shut and threw it into the back of the car. There was no sign of Chug. Impatient of delay, he shone his torch in the direction his companion had taken. But either Chug was beyond the reach of the beam, or he was screened by the bushes. Not wishing to call out, Vince went to find him.

He did not have far to go. As he rounded a bush Chug seemed to rise from the ground. Each was startled by the sudden appearance of the other.

'What the hell kept you?' Vince demanded.

'He started to come round.' Chug's voice was hoarse. 'I put him out again.'

He aimed a vicious kick at the recumbent body, grunting exultantly as the point of his shoe impinged against the yielding flesh. Vince heard the thud, and shuddered. Before he could pull his companion away Chug kicked again. This time the impact was louder, sharper. Leather against bone.

'You bloody fool!' Vince caught him by hand and arm and yanked him away. The hand was clammy with sweat. 'Do you want to kill him?'

Chug said nothing. He was breathing heavily, the air roaring out from between parted lips. Vince released him and stooped to the twisted body, switching on his torch. Blood was seeping from ear and nose and mouth, the bruised face was grey. Jacket and shirt had rucked up around his shoulders, drawn there in transit over the rough ground and exposing the reddened flesh at his middle. It seemed to Vince that he could see the indentations where Chug's toecap had landed.

He bent to listen at heart and mouth. Then slowly he sat back on his haunches and looked up.

'He's dead.'

Chug laughed. It was an unpleasant sound. 'That puts us on easy street, don't it?' He sounded excited, catching his breath as he spoke. 'Ain't no one to put the finger on us now.'

Vince stood up and turned away, switching off the torch, trying to obliterate the man from his mind as easily as he could from his sight. His stomach was sick, a pulse throbbed angrily at his temple. But it was not remorse that moved him, nor pity for their victim. Murder in the execution of a robbery was a capital offence.

Chug said, scowling, 'Didn't think you was chicken.'

Vince longed to hit him. But although he considered himself mentally the superior, he knew that physically he was no match for the other. Chug would eat him.

He said coldly, steadying his voice, 'I told you before, you're a fool. No one carries that amount of honest cash on holiday; a hundred to one it was stolen. So what did we have to fear? We were sitting pretty; he would never have reported it to the police.' In their two previous jobs he had been the leader. He meant to remain the leader, to keep Chug in his place. He could not subdue him with his fists, but he could lash him with his tongue. 'But you, you great nit — you have to go and croak him. So now every copper in the whole bloody country will be out to get us.' He drew a deep breath. 'We're not on easy street, mate, we're on the run — with a ruddy great noose ready for when they catch us. That's where you and your damned boot have put us. Right in the dirt.'

'They won't catch us,' Chug said. He spoke loudly, but he sounded less assured. The exultation was missing from his voice. 'Who's to know it was us what done it?' He stirred the body with his foot, and laughed. 'Not him, anyways.'

Vince pushed angrily past him. 'You make me sick. Come on, let's blow.'

They drove on down the Lewes road, with Vince at the wheel. He drove carefully; an accident now would nail them. Chug sat beside him, breathing noisily. His hands were still clammy, there were beads of sweat on his brow. Vince knew how he felt; that his throat was dry and his stomach empty — as though it had been purged, leaving a void that cried out to be filled. It was always like that with Chug after violence. And to-night he had achieved the ultimate in violence.

Chug said, 'I'm bloody hungry. And I could do with a beer.'

Vince glared at him. 'A fine time you pick for an appetite! Here! Where did you get that watch?'

Chug looked down at his wrist. 'Off his nibs. It seemed a pity to leave it. Weren't no use to him.'

Vince swore. 'Some mothers sure do have them. Take it off, you nit. A thing like that could hang you. Watches can be traced.'

Reluctantly Chug removed it and placed it in the glove pocket. His stomach rumbled noisily as he bent forward, and he broke wind, emphasizing its emptiness. Vince frowned. He had no intention of pandering to his companion's appetite, he wasn't stopping until they had put a safe distance behind them. But as they rounded a bend and the lights of a pub showed ahead, he changed his mind. He steered the car on to the parking lot and stopped.

Chug looked at him in surprise. 'We going in there?'

'You are. You're the gutsy one. Get a couple of bottles of beer and any eats that are handy. And make it snappy.' Chug was almost out of the car when he added, 'And don't flash that wallet around. You don't look right with it.'

Vince watched his companion walk across the park and disappear inside the pub. He did not like Chug; he had teamed up with him only because he had needed him. But he did not need him now. Chug was no longer an asset, he had become a liability. An expensive liability. There was something like a thousand quid stuffed in the rucksack. Split two ways it was still a tidy sum, more than he had ever dreamed of possessing at one time. But without the split . . .

He grinned happily, put the car into gear, and let in the clutch.

★   ★   ★

Baker said coldly, 'You were wrong. Banning wasn't dead. He died later in hospital. Murdered.'

Vince Harding flinched at the word. For the first time he displayed, if not remorse, at least concern. He said earnestly, 'I thought he was dead, or I'd never have left him. I'm not that callous, Superintendent. It wasn't till I read the paper next evening that I learned he was in hospital.'

'And when did you learn he was dead?'

'Chug told me last night.' Painfully he raised himself in the bed and looked appealing from one to the other of the two detectives. 'But I had nothing to do with it. That was Chug. I never meant anyone to get hurt.'

'You were there,' Kane said.

'But I wasn't! I was nowhere near.' His voice cracked a little in his anxiety to impress this fact on them. 'I told you, I stayed by the car when Chug took him into the bushes. How was I to know the fool would do a crazy thing like that? It never even occurred to me. I'm no murderer.'

'That's for a jury to decide,' Kane said. 'Where did you ditch the car?'

'In Lewes.' He was eager to help, to enlist their sympathy. He could not believe he might be indicted for murder; but there would be other charges, and co-operation now could stand him in good stead. 'Just left it in the street with the keys in. Then I took a bus to Eastbourne and found a room for the night. Next morning I got myself tarted up and hired the Zephyr, and then went back to Lewes.'

So Dick Smith had finally told the truth; he had picked up the Morris where Harding had abandoned it, he could have had no direct contact with the dead man. Kane was secretly rather pleased; he had a sneaking regard for the young Cockney. Not that Smith was completely out of the wood. He had other charges to face.

'Why return to Lewes?' he asked. 'What was the attraction there?'

'The girl. It was her letter Chug dropped when he took the wallet; she was fixing to meet Banning at the hotel. I could see the sort she was — high-class,

353

but willing if the money was right.' His voice sounded tired, but he managed a smile. 'There was a photo with the letter, showing what she'd got to offer. It looked pretty good to me.'

He reached gingerly for a glass of water, and sipped. Kane said, 'Do you want to go on with this, or do you need a rest? It's up to you.'

'I may as well finish now I've started.'

The rest was comparatively easy to tell. He was over the hump now, there was nothing in what had happened later that the cops could knock him for. And when he had finished, and before they could start again on the inevitable questions, he said, 'How's Doris?'

'Bad,' Kane told him.

'I'm sorry. And Chug?'

'Unmarked.'

He would be, thought Vince. Chug was indestructible.

Baker said, 'Where's the rest of the money?'

'Back at the hotel. But there's not much left. We did ourselves pretty well.'

Cocky, thought Kane. Maybe the

hospital bed makes him feel temporarily secure; he knows that while he's in it we can't touch him, no matter what he's done. But he won't feel so secure when he leaves.

'How much was there originally?' he asked, wondering why the superintendent had ignored that question for the other.

'Close on a thousand, I should say. I didn't actually count it.'

Kane frowned. It didn't add up. Banning might have spent a hundred or two on the girl, and there would be the cost of the tickets and the two hundred he'd left in the locked drawer. But add that to a thousand, and it still amounted to a very small part of the six thousand he was reputed to have stolen. Where was the rest? Vince Harding would have no reason to lie about the amount. One thousand or six, it could make no difference to the seriousness of his crimes.

He looked at Baker, wondering if the same problem was troubling him. But Baker was on his feet, anxious to be gone. If he hurried he could still make it back to

Lewes and pick Edna up in time for Matins.

As they walked down the corridor Kane said, 'A smooth young man. Too smooth. But he didn't kill Banning. I've checked with the hotel. As he said, he was dancing with the girl until after midnight.'

'It was never suggested that he did,' Baker said.

'No. So we're left with Wallis, as we thought.'

'As you thought,' Baker reminded him. 'Don't spread the glory.'

George Wilson was waiting for them at the entrance. He looked even thinner and older and more haggard than when Kane had seen him the previous afternoon. Despite the warmth of the sun he wore a heavy overcoat that draped like sacking from his shoulders.

'I'm sorry about your daughter, sir,' Kane said. Knowing the man's devotion to the girl, he felt a great sympathy for him. 'How is she?'

'Bad, Inspector.' Wilson raised a weary hand to his forehead, held it there for a moment, then took it back over his head and let it fall. To Kane it seemed a gesture indicative of utter defeat. 'They tell me she's got a good chance. But then doctors are always optimistic, aren't they? They were about my wife. And even if she recovers — ' Tears filled his eyes, and he rubbed at them with his long fingers. 'You saw her, Inspector. You know what a lovely girl she was. How is she going to feel when she looks in the mirror and sees what has happened to her face? She won't *want* to live. Not Doris.'

Kane said gently. 'They can do wonderful things with plastic surgery nowadays, Mr Wilson. Don't let it get you down.'

Baker added his sympathy to Kane's. But his tone was more matter-of-fact. Too much sympathy, he thought, could break a man quicker than a lack of it, and Wilson looked near to breaking now. He said briskly, 'Too bad you missed your daughter in Lewes Thursday night, sir. She was there, you know. It wasn't until the next day she moved to Eastbourne.'

'I know. She told me.' Wilson blinked at them wetly. 'She's been conscious on and off, although they won't let her talk much. But Thursday — well, I was looking for Banning's name, you see. I thought — '

He broke off. Baker knew what he'd thought — that the couple would be registered as man and wife.

'Why did she use the name of Williamson?' he asked. 'Why not her own? Did she say?'

'She thought the man who sold her the ticket might tell me where she'd gone.' He sighed. 'And he did. But it didn't help, did it? Not the way things turned out.' Momentarily the smooth voice hardened, his body straightened. 'Those two young thugs! I hope they hang, both of them.'

They left Wilson standing at the top of the steps and went down to the waiting car. As they drove away Kane said, 'I guess I know how he feels, poor chap. And he's right when he says his daughter was a lovely girl. She certainly was.'

'She was also a very foolish one,' Baker said. 'If nothing worse.'

16

As the car stopped outside No. 27 Kane said, 'That's Mark Banning's Jaguar. What would he be doing here, I wonder?'

Baker grunted. 'He'll have his reasons.' He turned to Redman. 'Your inspector doesn't seem to have made it. Do we carry on without him?'

Redman thought they did. The inspector, he said, was no stickler for formality.

Neither Ruth nor Mark was pleased to see them. Mark uncoiled his long body from the armchair, shook hands half-heartedly, and explained in his clipped nasal voice that he was there to look through his brother's papers and to make arrangements for the funeral. The only measure of his discomposure was that he should explain where no explanation was needed. He made no mention of the missing money, which Kane suspected to be the real motive for his visit.

Ruth did not attempt to hide her

displeasure. She had not forgiven Kane for whisking her son off to Eastbourne. That he had then proceeded to endanger Philip's life in the reckless pursuit of a dangerous criminal (Philip had not minimized the risks involved) had so incensed her that her customary diffidence had deserted her.

'You had no right to do it, Inspector,' she snapped at him. 'No right at all.'

The Monday-morning feeling, thought Kane. The blond hair was even more rampant than usual, the shapeless bosom had assumed an aggressive thrust; she looked like an old hen with feathers ruffled, defending her precious chick. But he managed to deflate her by agreeing with her and apologizing.

'I'm glad to see him looking so much better,' he said cheerfully. 'And he does, doesn't he?'

No thanks to him for that, she retorted. But the acrimony had gone, and after a moment of uncertain gaping she shuffled from the room to prepare coffee. He could hear her muttering to herself as she went down the hall.

Philip's bruised eye was badly discoloured, but the swollen mouth had returned almost to normal shape. He alone seemed pleased to see the police; they had been part of his big adventure, and their presence revived it. Although bored and irritable during the long wait outside the Winter Garden, once action started he had perked up. The chase, involving as it did an illusion of speed and a threat of danger that never actually materialized, had thrilled him. He had shuddered delightedly at the crash; Kane had not allowed him to leave the car, so that he had seen only the spectacle and none of the horror. The evening had discounted the pain and humiliation of the afternoon, had given him a gratifying sense of victory over his tormentor. He had been in at the kill. His scars had become the scars of battle, not of defeat.

Baker took advantage of Ruth's absence to relate what Vince had told them of the hold-up on Chailey Common. He told it briefly, anxious to be done before she should return. It would make unpleasant hearing for the widow; her son or her brother-in-law could give her the facts later if they wished. When he went on to describe Vince's subsequent adventures Philip grew impatient. Vince was a shadowy figure he had not met and in whom he had little interest. It was Chug Wallis he wanted to hear about.

'He tried to bolt after the crash,' he informed Mark, anxious to recapture the centre of the stage from which the superintendent seemed to be ousting him. 'He nearly made it, too. It took three policemen to hold him.'

Kane suspected that the latter fact gave him satisfaction. It excused his own inadequacy in dealing with the redoubtable Chug.

'He's tough all right,' he agreed, playing along. He owed Philip that, he thought. 'A real ugly customer.'

'Did he confess to killing the old man?' Philip asked eagerly, hopeful that evil might be piled on evil.

'He confessed to nothing.' Baker's tone was curt. Jimmy might feel like one of the family, but he did not. He had a job to do, and the sooner it was done the better. 'He's acting dumb, is our Mr Wallis. But he'll talk in time. They always do.' He turned to Mark. 'I'm glad you're here, sir. You've saved me a journey.'

'You wanted to see me? Why?'

Before the superintendent could explain Ruth returned with the coffee. Her brief outburst of truculence over, she was again the harassed housewife. The apron had been removed, but she still wore the unsightly woollen slippers. Both blouse and skirt looked as though they had been donned in a hurry and never properly adjusted.

Baker drank his coffee black. For most of the previous night he had lain awake, listening to Edna's heavy breathing and trying to clarify in his mind the facts relating to Arthur Banning's death. Jimmy's assumption that Chug Wallis had killed Banning to avoid possible identification was entirely plausible. But was it correct? Wallis had been at the hospital that night, but his presence did not necessarily make him a murderer. More proof than that was needed to turn theory into fact, and without a confession it seemed unlikely to be forthcoming.

Dawn had broken before he thought he had the answer. But because he was not sure he said nothing of it to Jimmy; events might prove him wrong, and it would have hurt his pride to admit it. To avoid discussion in the car he had closed his eyes and pretended to sleep. Pretence had soon become reality. They were in Croydon when Jimmy woke him.

He said, grateful for the new alertness which the coffee gave him, 'You and the two ladies arrived at the hospital at six-thirty that evening, Mr Banning. Did you notice a constable on duty outside your brother's room?'

'Yes. Young fellow. Why?'

Kane wondered if it were disapproval of this new and unexpected interrogation which caused Mark to clip his words. It could not be nervousness. He must know he had nothing to fear from the police.

Baker did not say why. 'What happened next?'

Mark frowned. 'How do you mean, what happened? Nothing happened.'

'No one entered or left the room?'

'Oh, that!' The frown was directed at Ruth. 'You went to phone Philip, didn't you?'

Ruth had been gazing at them vacantly, a lump of sugar balanced in her spoon so that the coffee might soak into it. She liked the contrast of coffee and sugar savoured independently. The direct question startled her, and the sugar fell into the cup.

'Yes,' she said, searching for the lump. 'At ten minutes to eight. I saw the clock in the main ward.'

Gradually he got times and sequence of events from them. Ruth had returned soon after eight, and had spoken to the constable near the entrance to the wing. He had told her that he was shortly to be relieved; and it was while she was talking to him that she had seen Chug. The blond nurse, and later the surgeon, had followed her into the room. Westwood had arrived some ten minutes after the surgeon.

'About eight-thirty, would that be?'

'Something like that.' Mark was growing impatient. 'We weren't clocking in, you know. And frankly, Superintendent, I can't see what this has to do with my brother's death. The four of us left together at about a quarter past nine, and Arthur was alive then.'

'I'm aware of that, sir,' Baker said stolidly. 'Would you happen to know if there was a constable on duty when Mr Westwood arrived?'

'No, I wouldn't. Why not ask him?'

'I intend to. Was there one there when you left?'

Somewhat ashamed of his irritation, Mark knit his brows in an effort to remember.

'I don't think so. There were several people wandering around, but no policeman.'

Ruth had not seen a policeman either. Philip, who had listened to the conversation with marked boredom, suddenly showed interest. But his suggestion that this apparent dereliction of duty by the police might have been responsible for his stepfather's murder earned him a sharp rebuke from the superintendent, and he relapsed into sullen silence.

Ruth, unhappy at the incident, started to collect the coffee cups. Baker said, 'I understand the surgeon was optimistic about your brother's chance of recovery, Mr Banning?'

'Reasonably so. The next twenty-four hours would decide, he said.' Mark lifted one leg and settled it comfortably across the thigh of the other. He did it so easily that Kane decided his joints must be unusually supple. 'And how right he was!'

Baker ignored this, and asked about the window. Yes, Mark said, Westwood had opened it — at his request. Why Westwood? Because he happened to be standing next to it. 'With the three of us ranged along the other side of the bed it was about the only place he *could* stand without being trampled on by the medicos.'

Baker removed his spectacles and thoughtfully chewed one end. He said, 'And the window remained open while you discussed the missing money and its probable whereabouts, eh?'

'Yes.' Mark scratched his elegant

moustache with a well-manicured thumb-nail. 'I gather we dropped a clanger there. That's how Philip's friend got his information, isn't it? I'm sorry about that. Very careless of us.'

Baker suspected he regretted the indiscretion rather than its unhappy sequel. Mark Banning would probably regard indiscretion as a major sin.

'None of you heard him, I suppose?' he asked.

'Outside the window, you mean? No. Although Westwood was right by it, you'd think he — ' The frown that had settled on his face brightened. 'No, he wasn't. When the medicos left he moved to the foot of the bed. None of us was near the window.'

Kane had grown tired of being a spectator, of listening to the superintendent steal the thunder he had worked so hard to prepare. But Baker was officially in charge of the case; all he could do was dip an occasional oar to remind him he was still in the boat. He said, 'Was the window left sufficiently wide to allow some one to climb in from outside without opening it farther?'

'Not unless he were a mere shadow — which I'm told our friend Wallis is not.' The brown eyes narrowed. 'Is that what happened, do you think?'

Before Kane could answer, Baker interposed. He knew how Jimmy felt, and this was like handing a meaty bone to a starving dog. Jimmy would leap at it.

'Probably. But not necessarily Wallis, Mr Banning.' Kane's lips were parted, he was leaning forward eagerly. Determined to forestall him, Baker said deliberately, trying to sound casually impersonal, 'I believe your brother's death has come at an opportune moment for you — hasn't it, sir? I'm referring to the insurance, of course.'

Kane's lips stayed parted; not in preface to speech, but in astonishment. Mark sat up with a jerk, releasing the foot he had been nursing and letting it slide to the floor. But his pale face reflected embarrassment rather than the anger Baker had expected. The look he gave Ruth was almost furtive.

'No, Superintendent, it has not. I hold

a policy on his life, certainly; I considered it a sensible investment, since Arthur was the elder by twelve years. As I told him, it would enable me to take care of his dependents in the event of his death. In any case, no matter how straitened my finances — and in my business they fluctuate considerably — I would never have considered my brother's death to be opportune.' His tone hardened. 'I presume you are not suggesting I was privy to it in any way.'

'No, sir. Although I suppose you could have come under suspicion. People have a habit of jumping to premature conclusions.' He gave Kane a sly smile. 'A very dangerous practice, that.'

Mark might not have been privy to it, thought Ruth, but he had wanted Arthur to die. She had no doubt of that, just as she had no doubt that none of the insurance money would ever come to her or Philip. In a dark corner of her mind was the conviction that he would even have been prepared to effect Arthur's death personally had not the savage Chug done it for him. But she said nothing. All she wanted was to be rid of them, to continue the search that had gone on intermittently throughout the previous day, and which Mark's arrival that morning had interrupted. Philip would be at home for the next few days, and that would hinder her; even though he knew of the money, its discovery must be her secret alone. But she would find it eventually. She had to.

With relief she saw that the three policemen were on their feet.

Baker thanked her for the coffee. He said sincerely, 'Believe me, Mrs Banning, you have our sympathy. I only hope the future will be kinder to you. No sign of the missing money, I suppose?'

'None,' she said, flushing.

'Well, don't waste too much time looking for it,' he told her. 'I doubt if it's here, you know.'

Ruth did not share his doubt, but she was glad that he had one. It made the money feel more securely hers.

They moved out to the hall. Kane found himself in the rear with Philip, and he said, 'Many thanks for your help on

Saturday. How's the face? Sore?'

'Yes.' But for once Philip lacked interest in himself. 'Inspector — you remember I told you I'd seen my stepfather haring about in shorts the week before last? What do you think he was up to?'

'Trying to lose weight, I imagine,' Kane said. 'Most men of his age get the urge at one time or another. You will yourself, I dare say.'

He did not add that it was Doris Wilson, with her expressed dislike of fat men, who had given Banning that belated urge.

Much of his irritation at Baker's monopoly of the interrogation slipped from him as the door of No. 27 shut behind them. This was probably the old man's last chance to make a splash before his retirement. He could not grudge him his swan song. Even if they had got nowhere that morning, at least no harm had been done.

Except, perhaps, in one instance.

'A trifle premature, sir, weren't you, in telling Mrs Banning the money was not in the house?' he said, trying to blend respect with reproof. 'I mean — well, you can't be sure.'

Baker sighed; partly from satisfaction, partly out of sympathy for his companion, partly because he was tired. Now he was 99 per cent sure. Westwood, he hoped, would confirm the missing 1 per cent.

'I can, you know, Jimmy,' he said. 'And I'll tell you for why.'

★　★　★

Hugh Westwood had much on his mind that Monday morning, but he knew he could not be too busy to see the police. They made an impressive group as they trooped into his office. Now, with the addition of the Croydon inspector, there were four of them.

'Rather an invasion, I'm afraid, sir,' the inspector said, his tone a nice blend of apology and officialdom. Unlike Redman, he had not met the manager before. 'These gentlemen are from the East Sussex police. They wish to ask you a few questions.'

Westwood nodded. He had risen at their entrance, but he did not come forward to shake hands, or invite them to be seated. He stood behind the massive desk, tapping the blotter impatiently with his pen.

'Inspector Kane and I have met,' he said, in his deep, precise voice. 'I had hoped that with the arrest of those two young thugs the questions would be over. Apparently I was too optimistic. I don't see how I can help you further, Inspector, but you'll have to ask your questions, I suppose. I'm glad to hear they are few. I have a lot to do this morning.'

Kane could believe that. He's a pompous, aloof creature, he thought; must be depressing to live with. Well, maybe he won't be so pompous after the old man has cut him down to size.

The superintendent stepped forward, introducing himself.

'A nice place you have here, Mr Westwood.' He gazed round the large room. 'And well stocked with chairs, I see. It might be as well if we all sat down. The questions may be more numerous than Inspector Tracey here led you to expect.'

Westwood shrugged, waved a slim hand at the chairs in reluctant invitation, and sat down himself.

'Don't let's waste time, then. As I told you, I'm a busy man.'

Baker took him through the same series of questions as he had put to the Bannings. Westwood's answers confirmed most of what they had said, and supplied the additional information that he had seen no policeman on duty at the ward, either when he arrived or when he left.

'Should there have been one?' he asked, surprised. 'Don't tell me you were actually expecting an attempt on Banning's life.'

'No, sir, we weren't expecting that.' Baker ignored the query. 'But about this money that was stolen. Any fresh developments? I presume you've informed the company.'

'Of course.' He pulled thoughtfully at his long nose. 'Phelps, the area manager, is dealing with it. As for developments — ' He ceased pulling, and shrugged. 'None that I'm aware of. I understand from Mrs Banning that, apart from a couple of hundred found in a drawer, there is no trace of the money at the house. And frankly, Superintendent, that doesn't surprise me. I never expected it to be there. I imagine it is safely stowed away in a bank, either at home or abroad.'

'My own opinion entirely, sir.' Baker leaned forward, so that the light glinted on his spectacles to give him an oddly menacing look. 'I suppose you wouldn't care to tell me which bank? It might save a lot of trouble.'

'Eh?' Westwood stared at him, brown eyes almost popping from his head. 'What the devil are you getting at? How should I know which bank?'

'Because I think you put it there,' Baker told him.

Westwood's gaze shifted to Kane, and then to the others. All four were watching him intently. His eyelids drooped, and after a pause he picked up his spectacles, polished the lenses carefully with his silk handkerchief, and returned the handkerchief to his breast pocket. But he did not place the spectacles on his nose. Still holding them, he leaned forward to rest his arms on the desk.

'I see,' he said eventually. His voice was steady if not quite so deep. 'I wonder if you realize what you are saying, Superintendent? It practically amounts to the accusation that it was I, not Banning, who was the thief.'

'That was what I meant it to amount to, sir. Do you deny it?'

'Of course I deny it. But I'd be interested to hear you substantiate it.'

'I'll do my best.' Kane smiled to himself. The old man in a courteous mood was at his most deadly. 'Now, let me see. Let's start with that holiday of yours, shall we, when you met with that unfortunate accident and had to delay your return? I don't doubt your lapse of memory, Mr Westwood; I just think it didn't happen quite the way you said. I believe you were so preoccupied with your holiday arrangements that you forgot to tell anyone, Banning included, about the new properties. But something jogged your memory on your return

— perhaps you came across the documents Phelps had handed over at the interview — and you were puzzled by the fact that no query had come from head office. Knowing Phelps, you made a few inquiries — and arrived at the startling conclusion that Phelps had omitted to inform his office of the transfer, and that no one but you had any record of it. Are you with me, sir?'

'I understand what you're saying.' Westwood's voice was tart. 'Don't expect me to agree with it. It's altogether too far-fetched for credulity.'

'Is it?' Baker sat up, straightening his heavy shoulders. 'Not as far-fetched as your assertion that both you and area headquarters had forgotten the transfer for all these months. One or the other might possibly be so incompetent, but not both. And it was that conclusion among others which made me give your story some very serious thought.'

Westwood lit a cigarette, his fingers steady as he flicked the lighter.

'Well, that's something, anyway.' He inhaled deeply, letting the smoke dribble out from nose and mouth. 'I was beginning to think it was just a wild guess or a madman's flight of fancy. Tell me — what were these other conclusions of yours? Or shouldn't I ask?'

Baker ignored the taunt.

'Your description of Arthur Banning — dull, unimaginative, lacking initiative — didn't seem to fit a man who could plan and carry out the scheme you outlined. Yet other people substantiated that description. So there was a discrepancy somewhere.' He paused, expecting the other to comment. But Westwood said nothing, and he went on, 'The police have been looking into your affairs over the week-end, Mr Westwood. It seems that your tastes are considerably more expensive than your salary warrants. So the rents from those new properties must have come in very handy. There were risks, of course; but then there always are, aren't there? No doubt you minimized some of them. For instance, I imagine that when you collected the back rents for the month you were away you satisfied yourself that none of the tenants had contacted the company about them. Then you were free to go ahead. You knew there was a limit to how long your luck could hold — discovery would certainly come with the next audit, if not before — but two hundred pounds salted safely away each week for several months amounts to quite a tidy sum. Perhaps you set yourself a target, intending to disappear when it was reached — with alternative arrangements, no doubt, for the sudden crisis.' He shook his head. 'Forging your own signature on the rent-books was a nice touch, ensuring as it did that a tenant would come direct to you with any query. There must have been a strong temptation to use Banning's or Wilson's or some other collector's name. And yet, you know, that was something else that made me suspicious. You see, for the same reason, Banning would have signed his name had he been the thief. Or that's how it seemed to me. You might argue differently, of course.'

'At this stage, Superintendent, I'm not arguing at all. I am lost in admiration of your genius for invention.' The sardonic gloom of his expression, intensified by the dark chin, was momentarily lightened by a grim smile. 'There is, however, one small point that occurs to me. I hate to crab your lovely theory, but how does it account for the large sum of money (close on a thousand, wasn't it?) those two young men found in Banning's suitcase? Not to mention the two hundred in the drawer, or what Banning may have spent on Miss Wilson. Are you saying it never happened? Or are you suggesting he saved it from his salary?'

'Neither, sir. I'm saying you gave it to him.'

'Really? And why should I do that? Pure altruism?'

Baker shook his head. 'I fancy he discovered your racket and blackmailed you. Threatened to expose you unless you cut him in on the deal. That, I should say, is the logical conclusion. It is certainly more in keeping with Mark Banning's description of his brother as a small man.'

The smile faded. His nerve is beginning to show signs of wear, thought Kane, noting how the man's fingers shook as he lit another cigarette from the stub of the first.

'I see.' Westwood sounded as though he were having difficulty in breathing. 'And have you arrived at any other logical conclusions, Superintendent?'

'I have, sir.' Baker stood up, and his voice was taut. For some reason he did not try to analyse Kane stood up also. So did the two Croydon men. 'I am going to arrest you for the murder of Arthur Banning while he was a patient in Chawtry Memorial Hospital. I should warn you that you are not obliged to say anything further at this stage unless you wish to do so, but whatever you say will be taken down in writing and may be given in evidence.' He took a deep breath. 'And now I must ask you to accompany us to Lewes police-station, where you will be formally charged.'

'Spoken like a good policeman.' With the finale that he must have known was coming, Westwood's mood seemed to lighten. 'May I ask on what evidence you base this arrest, Superintendent? If you have any, that is. So far we have only had theory.'

Baker hesitated. He knew that judges were inclined to frown on statements obtained from a prisoner by questioning after he had been warned, maintaining that the police officer was thus usurping the function of the trial court. Some judges would shut out such evidence altogether, and he could not afford to weaken his case. On the other hand, were he to lay some of his cards on the table, make his hand appear stronger than in fact it was, the man might be handled the easier. He might even break down and confess — although that, thought Baker, was unlikely in so cool a customer.

Yet the unlikely sometimes happened.

'I'm prepared to be more explicit, if that's what you wish.'

'It would be something, anyway.'

'Very well. As I see it, the knowledge that Banning was in hospital and likely to die without regaining consciousness seemed to provide you with a miraculous way out from your difficulties. And you were in difficulties, weren't you? Even if you could trust Banning to keep his mouth shut you must continue to pay him. The bonanza was over. But now, provided you were not sacked for incompetence, you could have your cake and eat it; keep both the money and the job. For who would disbelieve you if you accused Banning of the theft? Even if his assailants were never traced nor the money you had given him found, his behaviour, the obviously forged name in the rent-books, the fact that he was in charge at the time of the transfer, would substantiate the accusation. Only Banning and the tenants concerned could prove it false. But Banning was as good as dead; and why should the tenants be consulted unless your story were suspect? If it were — well, at least you would be given breathing-space.' He shook his head. 'The surgeon's reference to Banning's possible recovery must have given your optimism a nasty jolt. For there was no going back; you had already accused Banning to his wife and brother. He *had* to die — and quickly. And since you could not afford to gamble on a natural death, it had to be murder.'

'Very interesting, Superintendent. But still only theory.' Westwood lit another cigarette. It was nearing midday, and already the large cut-glass ashtray was full. 'You have yet to answer my query. Where's the evidence?'

'I'm coming to that, sir. Let's take it in order, shall we?' Baker's voice was growing hoarse. He had used it a lot that morning. 'You may not have liked the prospect of murder; I imagine few do. But this one was easier than most, for the assumption would be that Banning's death was the direct result of his injuries. Or that was what you thought. So, having fortified yourself with four large whiskies at the hotel, you returned to the hospital shortly before midnight, entered the room through the window, and smothered the unconscious Banning with his pillow.'

Westwood shivered, and a shadow seemed to cross his lean face. But his voice was light enough as he said, 'How you do go on, Superintendent! I'm perfectly prepared to agree that that is how Banning died, but nothing you have said puts the finger on me. It could have been one of his earlier assailants, come to finish the job. Or George Wilson; he was really gunning for Banning. Or even a member of his family. Every one of them had a reasonable motive for murder. You know that.'

'Do I? The brother, yes. The wife — ' Baker shrugged. 'Well, maybe. Though I can't see a woman of Mrs Banning's build climbing through a window. But the stepson, no. He disliked Banning, but Banning lodged and fed him. One doesn't destroy one's bread and butter without a very strong motive. Besides, he didn't know which room Banning was in. Harding is also out; he was in Eastbourne at the time.' This, he thought, is taking too long. Yet he decided to go on, if only to speak aloud the thoughts that had occupied his mind over the week-end. It helped to give them purpose and meaning. Abruptly he said, 'Would you go into a room to commit a murder knowing that just outside the door was a policeman who

386

was likely to enter at any moment?'

'Of course not.'

'No. And that is why none of the others would have killed Banning, even had they wished to.'

Westwood stared at him. 'But that's not true. There was no policeman there, either when I arrived or when I left.'

'There was, you know. You didn't recognize him as such because he was in plain clothes; shortly before you arrived at the hospital he had relieved the uniformed man the others had seen. What is more, when your party left he and the nurse moved into the room with Banning. Unfortunately both of them left it again for a few minutes prior to your arrival outside the window.' He shook his head. 'A pity. If you'd appreciated the risk there might have been no murder.'

For a few seconds Westwood continued to stare at him. Then he reached for the drawer at his side. Impulsively Kane started forward — to stop abruptly when he saw what the man held in his hand.

It was a packet of cigarettes.

'I see. You got to me by the process of

elimination.' Slowly Westwood unwound the red strip from the packet and slid away the two pieces of cellophane. 'But you need something more positive than that, Superintendent; something that points directly at me. So far you haven't produced it.'

'I will, sir. At the right time.'

'And this isn't it?'

'No.' Baker hesitated. 'But I'll remind you that your fingerprints were found on the window.'

'Oh, come off it, man!' Westwood gave a short, dry laugh that ended in a fit of coughing as smoke temporarily choked him. 'Of course they were. It was I who opened it. Mark Banning will vouch for that.'

'He has already done so. Very exactly, too. You lifted the arm by the knob and pushed it out one hole. Right?' Westwood gave no sign. 'But whoever came in later through the window had to open it farther. Again the arm had to be lifted. But the knob was out of reach, so he grasped it near the hinge — which is where we found your second set of prints.'

'All right, so I touched it twice. What of it?'

'Simply that, from inside the room, only a contortionist could have planted those prints the way they were.'

'I see. Proof at last, eh?' Again Westwood reached into the drawer. But not for cigarettes. This time it was a revolver, an old four-five, that he held in his hand as he leaned back in the swivel chair and smiled across the room at the four policemen. 'I wouldn't call it particularly strong, Superintendent, but I'm taking no chances. You may be holding something in reserve.' The smile faded. The revolver was steady in his hand as he sat up purposefully. 'Get over there, all of you.' He jerked his head at the far corner of the room. 'And no heroics, please. I don't want to use this thing, but I will if you push me. I've nothing to lose.'

None of the four moved. They stared back at him with set faces. Kane felt his eyelid quiver; he had never considered himself a coward, but he was scared now. This was a situation he had never thought to experience. He knew that if Baker gave him a lead he would follow. But — a heavy gun like that! It could make an awful mess of a man.

He wondered if the others shared his fear.

Baker said grimly, 'Put that down, man. Shooting can solve nothing. You may get one of us, but after that you're finished. Stop fooling, and put it down.'

'I'm not fooling, Superintendent. I'll shoot if I have to. You've been bang on the target so far; don't miss out now. Not if you want to stay alive.' His voice was shriller. 'I was ready for this, you see. I didn't think it would happen, but I was ready for it. Everything's laid on, right down to the last detail. All I need is a few minutes' start. So either I kill you, or you get over there and I lock you in. But you choose. It makes no odds to me.'

Baker took a step forward. The others followed as though jerked by invisible strings. They would have gone past him had he not put out an arm to stop them. He had seen Westwood's finger twitch as it curled round the trigger.

'One more step, and you've had it.' Westwood snapped out the words. There were white flecks of saliva at the corners of his mouth.

He means it, Kane thought, and felt his stomach heave. He prayed fervently that he would not be sick, that he could see this through like a man. For he knew that they had no choice. At any moment now Baker would give the signal and they would rush him and the revolver would spit lead — and one of them at least would feel a searing pain in his body and know that the future was not for him.

That was how it would be, he thought unhappily.

The sickness passed, and he felt better. Baker was slightly ahead of him, the two Croydon men behind. He wanted desperately to see their faces, to strengthen himself in their comradeship. But he could not turn his head. He had to keep watching, to recognize the moment when it came.

Baker was judging the odds. With that massive desk as a barrier it would not be easy to rush Westwood from where they stood. Yet to pretend to submit, to move to the far wall and wait for him to come out from behind the desk and cross to the door — that would be to increase the distance between them, to give him more time in which to shoot.

They could lose out either way. But at least where they now stood they were between him and the door.

The telephone on the desk rang shrilly, startling them all. For a while Westwood let it ring, frowning in indecision; then his free hand moved to the receiver. Baker wondered if this was the moment. But the revolver did not waver, and he saw that the man was watching him expectantly.

He made no move.

'Yes?' Westwood almost shouted the word. But the disembodied voice at the far end of the line seemed to calm him, and he said quietly, 'No, sir, I hadn't forgotten. Yes, at half past four. Yes, I'll bring them with me.'

'Phelps getting nosy,' he said, as he hung up. 'Well, I've had Phelps and all his works. Come on — move!'

Baker shook his head. 'We're taking

you in, Westwood. Put that gun down.'

'No.' There were beads of sweat on Westwood's brow, but no hint of indecision in his voice. 'And you're fools, the lot of you, if you think I won't shoot. I will. But it's so damned unnecessary.'

'Murder is always unnecesary,' Baker told him. Keep him talking, hope for a moment of less acute watchfulness to shorten the odds. 'Banning's certainly was. The post mortem showed that he would have died without your assistance, and almost certainly without regaining consciousness.'

'Ironic, eh?' Westwood seemed unmoved by the information. 'But the fool would still be dead. Whereas if he hadn't got talking to one of my new tenants in his poky little snooker club he might never have discovered what was going on, never have got involved. He'd still be alive. Or what he called alive. It's not my idea of life, but — '

There was a slight movement of Baker's left arm, a faint sound that might have been the flick of a finger against a thumb. Kane, his nerves stretched almost to breaking-point, accepted it as a signal. Accepted it almost with relief. Anything, even the firm knowledge that he might stop a bullet, was preferable to the interminable waiting, to staring wide-eyed at that finger twitching on the trigger.

He and Baker moved together, the others a fraction of a second later. As he leapt towards the desk Kane saw Westwood step back, heard the click as he squeezed the trigger. But there was no explosion, no thudding bullet. He did not stop to wonder. Urgency restored the agility of youth, and he spread-eagled himself across the desk, heard the crash as telephone and trays, clock and ashtray, were swept to the floor with him. He was scrambling to his feet when something hit him hard on the back of the head, and he blacked out.

He was not out for long. He regained consciousness to see Baker crouched beside him, gun in hand.

'Phew!' With Baker's help he stood up and leaned against the desk, ruefully rubbing the fast swelling bump on his head. 'What hit me?'

'This,' Baker said, breaking the revolver. 'He dropped it when we collared him. Your head just happened to get in the way.'

Westwood stood a few feet away, the two uniformed men beside him. His dark hair was tousled, his tie and collar awry; his breast pocket was torn where one of the men had grabbed at him. But his face was unmarked. He looked dejected but resigned.

'Why didn't the gun go off?' asked Kane.

'No firing-pin,' Baker said. 'Here, see for yourself.'

Westwood laughed. It was a dry, brittle laugh that suited the lean, sardonic face.

'I might have known,' he said, and grunted. 'I damned well should have known.'

They stared at him. 'Known what?' Baker asked.

'That the gun would misfire. It wasn't mine, it was Wilson's. And everything connected with that miserable clot misfires.'

They took him away then. The clerks in

the main office followed them with curious eyes, voices and typewriters suddenly silent. Out in the street a cool breeze was blowing, and Baker paused in the wide entrance to fasten his jacket.

''Ironic' was the word he used, wasn't it?' He watched Westwood go down the steps between the two policemen. 'He was dead right there. Apart from the fact that Banning would have died without his help, he has unwittingly saved those two young thugs from the gallows. For that's what it amounts to, Jimmy; if he'd stayed his hand they would have swung for murder. As it is — ' He settled his hat more firmly on his head. 'Well, all he achieved was to transfer the noose from their necks to his.'

THE END

Jimmy Ellis believes his parents have died in a car crash when as a young boy he is taken to live with relatives in Australia. The years pass happily, then the nightmare comes. Terrifying images flit through his mind in the dark — all through the eyes of a child, a witness to grisly events seventeen years before. He begins to delve into the past, and soon he finds himself on the trail of a double murderer — a murderer who is prepared to kill again.

THE DEAD TALE-TELLERS

John Newton Chance

Jonathan Blake always kept appointments. He had kept many, in all sorts of places, at all sorts of times, but never one like that one he kept in the house in the woods in the fading light of an October day. It seemed a perfect, peaceful place to visit and perhaps take tea and muffins round the fire. But at this appointment his footsteps dragged, for he knew that inside the house the men with whom he had that date were already dead . . .

THE CALIGARI COMPLEX

Basil Copper

Mike Faraday, the laconic L.A. private investigator, is called in when macabre happenings threaten the Martin-Hannaway Corporation. Fires, accidents and sudden death are involved; one of the partners, James Hannaway, inexplicably fell off a monster crane. Mike is soon entangled in a web of murder, treachery and deceit and through it all a sinister figure flits; something out of a nightmare. Who is hiding beneath the mask of Cesare, the somnambulist? Mike has a tough time finding out.

MIX ME A MURDER

Leo Grex

A drugged girl, a crook with a secret, a doctor with a dubious past, and murder during a shooting affray — described as a 'duel' by the Press — become part of a developing mystery in which a concealed denouement is unravelled only when the last danger threatens. Even then, the drama becomes a race against time and death when Detective Chief Superintendent Gary Bull insists on playing his key role of hostage to danger.

DEAD END IN MAYFAIR

Leonard Gribble

In another Yard case for Commander
Anthony Slade, there is blackmail at
London's latest night spot. Ruth
Graham, a journalist, and Stephen
Blaine, a blackmail victim, pit their
wits against unusual odds when
sudden violence erupts. Then Slade
has to direct the 'Met' in a gruelling
bout of police work, which involves a
drugs gang and a titled mastermind
who has developed blackmail into a
lucrative practice. The climax to the
case is both startling and brutal.